IN DAN
FOOTSTEPS

My Journey to Hell

A Modern Divine Comedy

CHARLES PATTERSON

ISBN 978-1-64299-261-8 (paperback)
ISBN 978-1-64299-354-7 (hardcover)
ISBN 978-1-64299-262-5 (digital)

Christian Faith Publishing, Inc.
832 Park Avenue
Meadville, PA 16335
www.christianfaithpublishing.com

Printed in the United States of America

In memory of Dante Alighieri (1265–1321)

who paved the way

PART 1

LAST RITES

1

It began the morning an e-mail with "Invitation" in the subject line was waiting for me on my computer. "Ready to have me as your Virgil again?" it said. "More later. Edward."

Huh? Edward had been dead for seven years! I stared at the screen in disbelief trying to make sense of what I was seeing. Having imaginary conversations with him from time to time was one thing, but now there he was on my computer. Or was he? Was this some kind of a sick joke?

I thought about the inscription he wrote on the flyleaf of the *Commedia* (Dante's *Divine Comedy* in Italian) he presented me with at Commencement. I hadn't looked at it in a long time, so I went to my bookcase, took it out, and read what he wrote: "Thomas, it was an honor and pleasure to be your Virgil. You were a wonderful travel companion. Dante would be proud. Perhaps we can do it again sometime. Blessings to you always, Edward."

That's what it said all right. *Perhaps we can do it again sometime.* I went back to the e-mail, clicked Return, and typed, "Is it really you?" Moments later, it bounced back with a message saying the address was not valid.

I thought of my seminary friend John as the possible culprit. He used to kid me about my church family and predicted half-jokingly that I would be the Presiding Bishop of the Episcopal Church by the time I was 40. But he knew what Edward meant to me, so I couldn't imagine him making fun of it. Still, I was curious to find out what his take on it might be, so I forwarded the e-mail to him and wrote at the top: "John, what do you make of this? Love to Wendy and the kids. Tom."

That night he wrote back. "Messiah! It's great to hear from you. If anybody deserves to go to Hell, you do. Maybe your Father Edward really does want you to join him. With your Dante background, I can't think of a better candidate. Go for it, my friend. Give my regards to Satan. John."

Three weeks later something much more unnerving happened. I was in bed starting to fall asleep after watching the eleven o'clock news when I saw a blurry light across the room that reminded me of the ghost of Hamlet's father I had recently seen in a black and white film on late night television. I sat up for a better look as the blur got closer and came into better focus. Oh my God, I can't believe it. Can it be? It looks like . . . yes, I think it is. It's Edward!

I closed my eyes hard and opened them to make sure I was seeing what I thought I was seeing.

"Thomas, it's wonderful to see you again under these unusual circumstances."

It was Edward's voice all right. I would know it anywhere. Was he a ghost? He certainly looked like one.

"You're not going to believe this, but I'm here to invite you to join me in the Underworld."

"Underworld?"

"That's what they call it."

I was in total shock. Seeing Edward and having him talk to me was more than I could handle. He looked and sounded like Edward, but was it really him? When I had imaginary conversations with him, I always pictured him in my mind's eye, but this was different.

"I can't believe it's you. I mean, I know it's you, but I can't believe you're really here because . . . well, because you're dead."

Edward smiled impishly. "Rumors of my death are greatly exaggerated."

"Mark Twain."

"Very good, Thomas."

The Mark Twain quote proved he really was Edward. He loved quotations, and by the time I graduated, I knew many of his favorites.

"Thomas, my resurrection, so to speak, was a big surprise as you can imagine. To suddenly wake up and be conscious again. And now to be up here talking to you. I can't believe it."

"I can't believe it either. Let me make sure I have this right. You want me to go down to the Underworld? There really is such a thing?"

"There are more things in Heaven and earth than are dreamt of in your philosophy." The quote from *Hamlet* was another one of his favorites. "To answer your question, yes, there really is an Underworld, but it's very different from what Dante had in mind."

"So then you're not talking about the Inferno, or are you?"

"Yes and no. Hell is down there, but it has its own separate area. I can't answer the many questions I'm sure you'll have because I'm very new at this. They told me it's all going to be explained later. They're starting a visitors program, and they sent me to invite you to be part of it. That's why I'm here."

I heard what he was saying, but I was having trouble making sense of it. "Will there be other visitors?"

"That's their plan. They want the visitors to come back up here and spread the word. They don't think people up here are getting the right message about what happens after they die and what's expected of them while they're alive. They think the visitors program will help change that. You'll be one of the first visitors . . . that is, if you agree."

I couldn't believe I was having this surreal conversation. I was glad I was on the bed because I was beginning to feel dizzy.

"Can you believe this, Thomas? It looks like we'll be able to go on another Dante adventure together. But this time it will be for real."

"Do you remember what you wrote on the flyleaf of the *Divine Comedy* you gave me at Commencement?"

"Refresh my memory."

"You wrote, 'Maybe we can do it again sometime.'"

"Is that what I said?" He smiled. "How prescient of me."

"This may sound like a strange question, but did you send me an e-mail?"

"Ah, so they sent it after all. I told them I didn't think it was a good idea, but they thought it would help break the ice."

"It broke the ice all right and drove me crazy trying to figure out what was going on."

"Sorry about that."

"How long is this visit you want me to make supposed to last?"

"Just a weekend. Friday to Sunday. In and out like Dante."

By now I was thinking this must be some kind of waking dream. What else could it be?

"Thomas, there's something else you should know. It's something they think may help you make up your mind. It's about your father."

"What about my father?"

"He's down there."

"My father's in Hell?"

"He's not in the Hell part. Some areas down there are for good people, and he's apparently in one of them."

"I don't understand."

"I'm just telling you what they told me."

"Does that mean I'll be able to visit him?"

"I don't know, but I don't think they would have me tell you he was down there if that wasn't a possibility. But I can't promise anything. There's something else I should mention. On the weekend they want you down there, there's going to be a 'great thinkers' conference with lots of famous people from history. And there's something else too, but I'm not sure I should tell you."

"What?"

"It has to do with them wanting us down there together as a teacher-student pair. I probably shouldn't say anything, but you have a right to know what's going on." He stopped as if he wasn't sure if he should tell me.

"What do I have a right to know?"

"If you decide not to go, I won't go either."

"What do you mean you won't go either? What will happen to you?"

"They'll send me back."

"Back to what?"

"Back to where I came from. The Big Nap."

"Big Nap?"

"That's what they call it."

"Back to being dead?"

He nodded.

"So if I don't agree to go down there, I'll in effect be killing you. That's what it sounds like."

"Thomas, I shouldn't have said anything. It's not fair to put you on the spot like this. But I want to be honest about what's happening."

I didn't know what to make of this bizarre conversation. The whole premise was wrong. Everybody knows that the so-called Underworld or Hell or the Inferno or whatever you want to call it doesn't exist except in ancient myths and in Dante's fertile imagination. And now in modern times in the rantings and ravings of demented imams and preachers. Yet here I am talking to Edward's ghost as if Hell really exists and he wants me to go there.

"Is it safe to assume you don't want to go back to being dead?"

"That's a fair assumption, but listen, Thomas, I feel bad about barging in on you like this. I can imagine how unsettling it must be. Don't worry about me. I shouldn't have mentioned it. Do what's best for you. 'If I am not for myself, who will be?'"

"If I am only for myself, what am I?"

"If not now, when?" we said together and laughed. It was his favorite Talmud quote and mine too.

"Good memory, Thomas."

"Are you living down there?"

"For the time being, I am, but as I told you, I'll only get to stay if I can get you to join me. Thomas, my time's up. I have to go. It's been wonderful talking to you. I hope you accept my invitation, but if you decide you can't or don't want to, I'll understand. I won't hold it against you. I'll be back soon to find out how you're doing with this."

Before I could ask him any more questions or even say good-bye, he disappeared like a light suddenly turned off.

2

My getting hooked on Dante began my junior year at St. George's when I was in Edward's office in the chapel after I finished my Sunday chores following the school Eucharist. He was the acting school chaplain on loan from the Church of England who was my Latin teacher and soon-to-be advisor.

"Well, Thomas, have you decided what you want to do for your project?"

He had suggested writing a paper on one or more of the classics and had mentioned Homer, Sophocles, Dante, and Shakespeare as possibilities. Not Virgil because I was reading the *Aeneid* in Latin Honors. I was fascinated by the Sophocles play about Oedipus, the Greek prince who killed his father and married his mother, but Dante's

Inferno sounded much more interesting, especially after Edward told me Dante put clergy and even popes in Hell. That got my attention right away since my father and both my grandfathers were clergymen.

"I've been thinking about that Hell poem you told me about. Can I do that one?"

"You certainly can. I had a feeling you were going to choose that one. You already know enough Latin that you can read him in the original. With the help of a dictionary, of course."

"Really? Won't that be too hard?"

"Not at all. The vernacular Dante wrote in flows right out of Latin. Here, let me show what you'll need." He went to the bookcase and brought back a big black book that looked and smelled like the old books in my father's study. He put it down on his desk and opened it.

"This is an Italian dictionary of the Middle Ages that has all Dante's words in it. I'll also give you an English trot so you don't have to worry about getting stuck. And I'll be here every step of the way to answer your questions. How does that sound?"

"Sounds good." I moved my fingers over the black letters. "Yes, this is what I want to do."

"*Eccellente*, Thomas. It's all set then. In the fall, you'll follow in Dante's footsteps, and I'll be your Virgil. We'll go to Hell together." We both laughed.

The day before Commencement, Edward invited me to his office to say good-bye. He was going back to England to teach at Sussex University, so in a way we were graduating together.

"So tell me, Thomas," he said over tea, "what do you think you'll be doing farther down the road?"

"I don't know. I guess I'll probably do what my father does." I heard the note of resignation in my voice.

"You don't have to do that, but if that's what you decide, I'm sure you'll make a fine priest. Just don't do it because you think you should, or because others think you should. Whatever you're meant to be—writer, teacher, lawyer, priest—your calling will keep after you and won't let you go."

I liked what he was saying. It gave me more breathing room. I thought it was interesting that when he listed the possibilities, he put writer first and priest last.

"My guess is you won't find your true vocation right away. I think you'll be more like Dante, who had to take a long detour through the Inferno and Purgatory to get to Paradise. Don't misunderstand me. There's nothing wrong with detours. More often than not, they're the way we get to where we're meant to go. Just don't make up your mind too quickly. What you end up doing may surprise you."

Commencement took place on the lawn in front of the chapel with my parents in the front row (my mother's favorite place to sit). When it came time for the academic awards and it was Edward's turn, he went to the podium and announced that I was the recipient of the Latin Prize, which he had already told me, so it wasn't a surprise when he announced I won the prize. When I went up to the podium, he handed me Dante's *Divine Comedy* in Italian. I recognized it immediately as his not so subtle hint that he wanted me to read *Purgatorio* and *Paradiso* as well, which I did in college. When I got back to my seat, I read his inscription about our doing it again sometime. He had already invited me to study more Dante with him in the United Kingdom, so I assumed that's what he was talking about. At the end of our last class, he had told me he would love to be my Virgil again. "And who knows? If you keep going at this rate, maybe someday you'll be the new Dante."

Huh? I had no idea what he meant by that, but I never forgot it. How could I?

3

In the meantime, the atmosphere at home changed after my bishop grandfather called for the election of his successor, an announcement that sent my mother into high gear to make my father the next bishop. After being the bishop's daughter for seventeen years, she thought it only right that she should continue her preeminence as the first lady of the diocese.

By the time I came home for Thanksgiving, the battle lines were set. My first night back, I was in the kitchen getting a snack when I heard them talking in the sitting room.

"God will decide who the next bishop is going to be," my father was saying. "It's not for us to try to arrange the outcome. His will be done."

My mother had always found my father's professed submission to divine will annoying, but now that the special convention to elect the new bishop was set for the spring, she found his passivity especially irritating.

By the time I came home for Christmas, their positions had hardened even more as I found out the night I was in the kitchen getting a snack and heard my mother tell him, "Thomas, at least pretend you want to be the bishop. The delegates aren't going to vote for somebody who's not interested in being the next bishop. People need to know you want the job. Otherwise, they're going to turn to somebody else."

That was the problem. My father liked being the rector of his parish and had always seen himself as more of a pastor than an administrator. Early in his career, he wanted to teach New Testament at one of the church seminaries, but he got so caught up in parish work he never got around to writing his doctoral dissertation. He had long since accepted that he wasn't going to be a seminary professor, much less a seminary dean like his father.

Still, as the son of a nationally respected church leader and the son-in-law of the bishop, he was thought to be one of the favorites to be the next bishop. His Lincolnesque features—long face, bushy eyebrows, and soulful, brown eyes—made him look even more like a bishop than my grandfather. But his heart just wasn't in it, much to my mother's consternation.

By the time I came home for summer vacation, they were at odds about a fund-raising event my mother was planning for the fall. She was chair of the diocesan committee to raise funds for the restoration of historic churches, which was my grandfather's pet project. She wanted to hold the event in my father's church, knowing that many of those in attendance would also be convention delegates electing the new bishop in the fall.

One night when I was in the kitchen getting something to eat, I heard them in the sitting room talking about it.

"This is not the time to wrap yourself in false humility," my mother was saying. "You have the right credentials and background, and you're very well thought of in the diocese. And being married to the bishop's daughter certainly doesn't hurt either."

My father mumbled something I couldn't make out.

"You underestimate yourself, Thomas. I know you'll make a wonderful bishop."

"I have nothing against being nominated, and if I win fair and square, I'll accept it as God's will. But it's unseemly for you to promote me as if I'm a politician running for office and you're my campaign manager. That's not the way it should be done."

"Don't be naïve. Ask Father to tell you what he had to do to win his election. There's nothing wrong with going after what you want. As Father always says, 'God helps those who help themselves.'"

During the silence that followed, I pictured my father sipping his martini.

"I don't know," he finally said. "I just don't feel right about it, that's all."

"Well, there are plenty of others who want to be the next bishop. Clark Howard is preaching all over the state. Do you know who he had breakfast with last week?"

"How am I supposed to know who he had breakfast with?"

"The vestry of St. Peter's, Waterbury, that's who. Barbara told me this morning."

"What's wrong with that?"

"St. Peter's is choosing its convention delegates this week. You don't think that's just a coincidence, do you?"

"Oh, nonsense. Clark Howard isn't running for bishop or anything else. He's just doing what he likes to do."

"Clark Howard would give his right arm to be the next bishop, and you know it. If you don't let people know you want the job, the delegates are going to turn to him or somebody else. You need to stand up and be counted. That's always been your problem."

I closed the cupboard loudly to let them know I was back and went into the sitting room.

"Oh, hello dear," my mother said. "Sit down and tell us about the movie. Your father and I were just talking church business."

"That's all we seem to talk about these days," he said. "It's time we talked about something else." He got up and walked over to the table to refill his glass.

My mother prevailed, as usual. The church restoration fund-raising reception was held in our parish hall. Although that brought a temporary truce, I knew there wouldn't be lasting peace until the question of the next bishop was settled once and for all.

At the convention to elect the new bishop, my father got more votes on the first ballot than anybody else, but he fell short of the majority needed to win. On the second ballot, he only received a few more votes, even though two of the candidates dropped out. Clark Howard got enough new votes to move up from third to a virtual three-way tie with my father and Harvey Morgan, the popular young dean of the cathedral.

My father then did something my mother never forgave him for. He went to the podium and not only withdrew his name but told the convention either one of the other two candidates would do honor to the episcopate. Not only did my mother have to witness my father's capitulation, but she had to see Clark Howard go over the top on the third ballot. Later she would complain that my father made the speech for his rivals that he was never able to make for himself.

When my father called me at school with the result, he sounded relieved. "It was God's will, Tommy. His will be done."

I could only guess what my mother's reaction was because I never got to talk to her. My father told me she wouldn't be coming to the phone as she usually did because she "wasn't feeling well."

That spring Clark Howard was consecrated in the cathedral as my grandfather's successor. In the letter my mother wrote to me about the consecration, she described it more as a farewell tribute to her father than as the consecration of a new bishop. She included a copy of my grandfather's sermon. Toward the end of the letter, she wrote that during the service she imagined me one day being consecrated bishop in the same cathedral. "Just think," she wrote, "I would be twice blessed. I would have been both the daughter and the mother of a bishop. Just imagine!"

Was she now going to focus her ambition on me? When I was growing up, she loved it when my father's parishioners called me "our little bishop" and said things like "Just look at Little Tommy. He even walks like a bishop." I remember how mother's face lit up when her best friend told her, "Tommy looks just like his grandfather. He's going to grow up to be a bishop too. I just know it."

My mother sent me a picture of the four of them in front of the cathedral after the consecration. Flanked by the two bishops in their purple cassocks, she's in the center of the picture smiling like a debutante while my father in his black cassock is standing off to the side looking like he's not sure he should even be in the picture.

4

Before Edward left and went back to England, he told me he was going to send me a graduation present, but he didn't say what it was. Several weeks later, I received a new edition of the Italian Dictionary of the Middle Ages he had me use for my senior project. That summer before I went off to York College, I started reading *Purgatorio* in Italian on my own. However, without Edward there to guide me, I didn't get very far.

"Two down, one to go," I wrote to let him know I started reading *Purgatorio* and intended to read *Paradiso* as well.

"That's very good news," he wrote back. "Now you get to meet Beatrice, who makes her first appearance at the end of *Purgatorio*."

What good timing that turned out to be because at York not only did I meet Dante's Beatrice in the final cantos of *Purgatorio*, but I met Beatrice Stern at the conference on student activism I went to at Vassar College (I wasn't an activist but thought maybe I should be). She was an English major at Sarah Lawrence College and a real activist as I found out when we were assigned to the same discussion group. That summer she had worked with a Quaker group in Costa Rica, and the summer before that she taught children in Ethiopia. She was also vegan, not just vegetarian like Edward and me. I was impressed by the way she kept taking on new challenges. She wasn't just coasting along on the momentum of the way she was brought up like me.

Between sessions, we took walks around the campus and talked about what we were reading. She was into Camus, Weber, and Fanon while I was reading Kierkegaard, Buber, and, of course, Dante. When I told her about my family and that I was thinking about going to seminary, she seemed a little disappointed.

When she found out how hooked I was on Dante, she asked me about her namesake. I told her what little I knew about Dante's Beatrice—that she was apparently somebody he saw at mass or in the market in Florence. Most scholars think he may not ever have met or talked to her since she was older and may have been betrothed or even married. After she died when Dante was in his late twenties, he wrote love poems to her that he included in his *La Vita Nuova*, the long essay he wrote about courtly love published in 1295. He remained devoted to her memory for the rest of his life. When he wrote *Paradiso*, he made her the symbol of eternal love who leads him through the Spheres of Heaven.

After the conference, we talked on the phone a few times, but that's as far as it went. When she told me she was going to another conference, I signed up for it only to find out she changed her mind without saying why. When she wrote to tell me what "a good friend" I was, I had to accept the fact that she didn't feel as strongly about me as I did about her.

When I told Edward I met my Beatrice ("Dante had his Beatrice to inspire him, so why shouldn't I have mine?"), he wrote back, "Very good, Thomas. See what good things come from reading Dante? It sounds like you're now ready for *Paradiso*. No cameo appearances for Beatrice in that one. She's front and center the whole way. And remember, Thomas, if things don't work out with your new friend, that doesn't mean she won't inspire you and be an abiding influence. Even though Dante's Beatrice was married to somebody else, she was the light of his life and the inspiration for the greatest poem ever written."

Whatever hopes I had of continuing my quixotic quest were dashed when she signed up for the Peace Corps and after graduation went off to Kenya. The fascinating letters she sent me only inflamed my unrequited love. I kept her picture that she inscribed "To my beloved infidel" on my bureau and revered it like an icon even after she came back from Africa, moved to Washington, and married a lawyer.

At York, I majored in philosophy and religion and studied advanced Hebrew and Aramaic on the side with Rabbi Moskowitz at the local synagogue. He was impressed by how much Hebrew I already knew, thanks to my father's tutoring, and by how quickly I picked up Aramaic when he started me reading the Talmud. "If you ever change your mind about going into the ministry," he said, "you might think about studying for the rabbinate." I think he was joking.

I also got involved in theater. My appetite had been whetted at St. George's where I played Bishop Cauchon in Bernard Shaw's *Saint Joan*. He was the judge who condemned Joan of Arc to death and had her burned at the stake. Not my kind of guy obviously, but that's what acting is all about—pretending you're somebody else. At York, I took the drama course and was in several plays, mostly minor parts except for the lead as Prince Hal *in Henry IV, Part I*. Being a prince came naturally to me.

5

The possibility I might not go to seminary never would have occurred to anyone, except maybe Beatrice, but that was what was most on my mind senior year, especially walking back from play rehearsals or up in my study nook in the attic late at night.

"Do something else before you tie yourself down to the church," Beatrice wrote from Kenya. "See the world. Live! This is the time to do it because once you head down that road, there will be no turning back."

Although I thought about other possibilities— graduate school, taking time off to travel or study abroad, going off to a writing colony somewhere, and even studying acting in New York—I wasn't ready yet to get off the path fate assigned me.

Against Beatrice's better judgment (and mine too), I sent Bishop Howard my statement of intent to become a "Postulant for Holy Orders" and wrote to the Cambridge Theological Seminary for an application. Since all my clerical forebears went to CTS and my grandfather had been its dean for thirty years, my application would only be a formality.

When I got the application, I filled out the first part right away, but when it came to the essay about why I wanted to study for the ministry, I put it aside. A couple of weeks later, my father called to tell me Dean Parkington told him CTS had not received my application and wondered if anything was wrong. I told my father I was very busy with schoolwork, but now that I handed in my big paper, I was going to finish the application and send it in. The big paper was my *Paradiso* term paper for my Classics of World Literature class.

When I wrote to Edward and told him I was finally reading *Paradiso*, he congratulated me for doing something that very few people do—read all three parts of the *Commedia*. When he again invited me to study more Dante with him at Sussex, I was tempted to accept his offer since that would have been a good excuse not to rush off to seminary. However, I knew that would only be postponing the inevitable.

So now it was crunch time. Either I had to finish the application and send it in, or I had to make up my mind once and for all to do something else. That night alone in the attic, I took out a quarter out of my pocket. My roommate at St. George's told me his father taught him that the best way to make a difficult decision was to flip a coin and let your reaction to it decide. So that's what I decided to do. If the quarter comes up *heads*, I'll send in the application, and if it comes up *tails*, I won't. The coin will decide (Divine Providence?).

I took a deep breath and flipped the quarter up in the air but out too far for me to catch it before it hit the desk and bounced on the floor. I picked it up without looking to see how it landed and flipped it again. This time I caught it with my right hand and slapped it on the back of my left. I hesitated for a moment, then raised my hand.

Tails!

As soon as the meaning of the toss sank in—I was *not* going to seminary—I shuddered at thought of having to tell my father, mother, grandfathers, Bishop Howard, my father's parishioners, and everybody else. That made me realize *I had to go to seminary*. There was no other way. Was it for me to try to change what had been ordained for me from the beginning? Besides, the first flip, the one that fell on the floor, was the one that counted, and that could very well have been *heads*.

That was the point of the coin toss, of course—to force a decision. As I put the quarter back in my pocket, I wondered what my father would think if he knew his son was deciding whether or not to go to seminary by flipping a coin.

I finished the application that night and mailed it the next morning. A few days later, I received a personal letter from Dean Parkington in which he invoked the memory of my grandfather and made it clear that CTS was doing more than accepting me. It was welcoming me home.

6

How could I feel anything but welcome at CTS being the grandson of Dean Reed, a fixed star in the firmament of seminary history whose portrait in the dining hall stared down at me at mealtime. Surrounded by seminarians with similar interests from different parts of the country and the world, I felt much more at home at CTS than I did at York. The qualms I had been having about the direction my life was taking began to fade, at least for a while.

However, in October of my second year, I got a jolt when my mother called to tell me my father had a stroke and had been taken to the hospital.

"But the good news is," she quickly assured me, "he's out of danger and back home."

"Why didn't you tell me sooner?"

"Dear, I didn't want to upset you at school. Besides, I wanted to wait until the situation was clearer. He's doing much better now. His speech is back, but he slurs his words. There's a nurse with him around the clock."

I wanted to go home, but I was scheduled to give my practice sermon in Homiletics class the next day.

"There's no need to rush home," she told me. "Everything's under control."

"OK, then I'll come home tomorrow after my class."

"Tomorrow will better. He'll be glad to see you."

As soon as I hung up, I realized I was too upset to think about my sermon or anything else for that matter, so I told my Homiletics professor about my father and got a postponement. I put together a few things and set out for home without telling my mother I was coming.

I drove straight through to Dalton, stopping only for gas and a snack. When I arrived at the rectory a little after eight o'clock, all the downstairs lights were on, including the sitting room. The only light on upstairs was from my father's bedroom. I put my bag down in the front hall and walked back toward the sitting room. Feeling apprehensive about seeing my father, I paused at the door and took a deep breath. Then I went in.

My mother was in her usual chair, but when I looked at my father's chair, it wasn't my father sitting there. It was Bishop Howard!

Dressed in dark gray slacks, a blue sports shirt, and shiny brown loafers, he looked relaxed with his legs crossed and a drink in his hand.

"Why hello, dear," my mother said. "I didn't expect you back tonight. This is quite a surprise." She glanced at the bishop. "But certainly a pleasant one." She held out her arm in that regal way she had as if everybody was supposed to kiss her hand. I went over and gave her a peck on the cheek.

The bishop stood up. "Hello, Tom. I'm very sorry about your father. How was the drive down from Cambridge?"

"Fine." I turned to my mother. "Where's Dad?"

"He's resting upstairs. He may be sleeping, but you can go up and see him. The nurse is with him. Introduce yourself."

There was something disconcertingly different about my mother. She was wearing lipstick and eye shadow that she hardly ever did, and a strong scent of perfume was in the air. There was a vivaciousness about her I never saw before.

When I excused myself and left, she followed me to the foot of the stairs. "Clark's been wonderful. He's been a real source of strength and comfort, even though he has his own burden to bear." She was talking about his wife's cancer.

"How is Mrs. Howard?"

"No better, no worse." My mother shook her head. "Poor man."

When I put my hand on the railing to go upstairs, my mother put her hand on mine. "Dear, I don't want you to be too upset, but I think you should know. Your father isn't the same. He's different, very different. I want you to be prepared."

I climbed up the carpeted stairs I had walked up and down my whole life. At the top, I turned and went down the hall toward the room my parents had once shared. My stomach was upset, and I was beginning to get a headache.

A nurse dressed in white introduced herself and took me into the dimly lit bedroom. My father was sitting in a wheelchair on the other side of the bed with his back to me. He was wearing his navy-blue bathrobe. When the nurse excused herself and left, I circled slowly over to him not sure what I might find.

"Dad?"

No reaction.

"Dad?" His head turned slightly. "It's me, Tommy."

I went over to his wheelchair and knelt in front of it on one knee. I was shocked to see that the left side of his face was immobile. I held his hand that was limp and cold. When his eyes finally showed that he recognized me, I embraced him as best I could.

"Tommy, Tommy," he said in a voice barely audible. His eyes were watery, and it was hard for him to talk. He slurred his words, so I did most of the talking, not sure how much of it he was taking in. When the nurse came in to tell me my father tired easily, I patted his hand and said it was time for him to get some rest. I kissed him on his forehead and told him I would see him in the morning.

When I went back downstairs, my mother came out of the sitting room.

"Come in and join us, dear. We're discussing diocesan business, but we would love to hear how you're doing at the seminary."

"I'm quite tired, Mother, so I'm going to have to turn in."

"Whatever you want, dear. I'm sure this is very upsetting for you. I won't see you in the morning because I'm going back to Hartford with Clark. I have an important meeting early." She kissed me good night on the cheek and suggested we have lunch in Hartford.

It wasn't until I heard my mother and the bishop leave that I realized how upset I was. It was one thing for my mother to forgive the man who beat my father out of the episcopate, but it was quite another for her to take up with him so publicly.

7

I wrote my senior honors thesis on Dante—who else? It combined the work I did on the *Inferno* with Edward at St. George's and the *Purgatorio* and *Paradiso* papers I wrote in college, plus I had Edward's transatlantic coaching, which I footnoted with lots of *Ibid*s. I dedicated the thesis to him, but I didn't tell him because I wanted it to be a surprise.

When I told him that I was having reservations about getting ordained, he wrote back. "Doubts are definitely in order, Thomas, but you're going forward doesn't mean you have to stop and go back if and when you decide you didn't make the right choice. My crystal ball tells me you're not so much going into the church as *through* it. Through it to something so big you can't even begin to imagine what it will be."

I wrote back and asked him if he remembered what he said to me at St. George's when he invited me to study with him in England. "I would love to be your Virgil again and who knows?" he had said. "If you keep going at this rate, maybe someday you'll be the new Dante."

He wrote back that he didn't remember saying that, "but if I did, I said it because it's true. I don't know what form it will take, but I believe in you and have the feeling that the future has something very big in store for you. Don't ask me what that means because I don't know."

I knew the thesis I turned in to Professor Ross was good, very good, but there was no way my 90-page paper was going to make me the new Dante. When I sent Edward his copy, I thanked him for his help and encouragement and told him to be sure to read the dedication page. He always answered my letters right away, so when I didn't hear from him, I hoped nothing was wrong.

As I moved toward my clerical fate by officially becoming a "Candidate for Holy Orders," my qualms about the treadmill I was on got stronger. It wasn't just my qualms about getting ordained; it was also about the church I was going to give my life to. My church history courses and access to one of the best theological libraries in the country had gotten me to look more objectively and more critically at the church my father raised me to respect and believe in. How did that small, persecuted band of Christians who met in catacombs and sang hymns as they waited to be fed to the lions grow up to become such a bully? How did the early church grow up to be the church of the Inquisition and Crusades that burned witches and heretics, persecuted Jews, condemned Galileo, and made life Hell for anyone who disagreed with it? How did the David of the early church turn into the Goliath of Christendom?

The more church history I studied, the more I identified with the rebels and reformers even though the ones

I admired most, like Jan Hus, were convicted of heresy and burned at the stake, hardly a comforting prospect for somebody about to get ordained.

The day before Commencement, I received a letter from the Headmaster of St. George's that he sent to all the alumni, telling us that Edward died. I was stunned, and then when it sank in, I was devastated. Now I understood why I hadn't heard from him. I hoped he got my thesis and read the dedication. I had planned to write him a long letter after graduation.

That night, I thought back to St. George's and the journey through the *Inferno* I took with Edward as my Virgil and our correspondence after he went back to England. I read some of his letters and let myself have a good cry. As it turned out, that wasn't the end of the Edward story, but I didn't know it at the time.

At the Commencement in the chapel the next day, I received my Master of Divinity degree (M. Div.) and my thesis—*The Gospel According to Dante Alighieri*

(Edward loved the title)—won the prize for being the best senior thesis. My father didn't attend, but my mother did with Bishop Howard, no less. They rode up together from Hartford in the bishop's chauffeur-driven limousine. The bishop had business he had to take care of in Boston, or so he said.

After the ceremony when the three of us had lunch at the Hawthorne Inn, I was taken aback to learn that my mother was now on the diocesan payroll as "Assistant to the Bishop for Policy and Planning." I was even more aghast to learn that she also had her own apartment in the diocesan Synod House near the bishop and was moving her things out of the rectory into her new living quarters. She looked radiant with happiness.

My father's name didn't come up until dessert when my mother informed me she was looking for a nursing home for him. "The vestry has been wonderful about it. They let him stay on in the rectory longer than we had any right to expect, but now he has to leave. Wayne, who has been filling in so wonderfully, accepted the call from All Souls in West Hartford. The vestry is beginning their search for a new permanent rector."

It was disgusting. There they were the happy couple—Bishop Howard with his wife dying of cancer and my mother with her husband confined to a wheelchair. The sight of the two of them smiling, touching each other's hands, and tasting each other's food made me want to vomit. What should have been a happy day was anything but. I hoped to God my father didn't know what was going on.

8

Putting my father in the nursing home in Farmington was the hardest thing I ever had to do. My mother made the arrangements, but when it came time to move him out of the rectory and take him there, I had to do it by myself because she was busy as usual working on a project for the diocese. The home seemed clean and well managed enough, but having to leave my father there with strangers felt like death, his penultimate death before the final one.

By then I was Keith Harper's curate at Christ Church in Darien. He had been my father's assistant in Dalton when I was growing up, so it seemed only right that I should start off working for him. Every Tuesday on my day off, I drove up to the nursing home and visited my father. We usually sat in the parlor or enclosed porch, but when it was nice outside and my father was up to it, I would wheel him out to his favorite spot under the oak tree that overlooked the pond.

During my curacy, my interest in Dante got put on hold. With a busy schedule of meetings, services, home visits, and the youth work that took up much of my time, I barely had time for myself, much less for Dante. I never forgot what Edward told me about being the new Dante someday. Whatever he meant by that felt more remote than ever.

Feeling trapped in Darien, I began thinking about leaving and going off and doing something else although I had no idea what that might be. "See the world," Beatrice wrote from Kenya. "This is the time to do it because once you head down that road, there will be no turning back."

In the meantime, my mother called to tell me "Clark" would be contacting me about an opening he thought I might be interested in, and sure enough the next day he called to tell me about a vacancy at St. Luke's in Pineville, a small town near the Massachusetts border.

"It's a quiet parish," he said. "The congregation is mostly elderly. It should be an interesting challenge."

I flinched at prospect of sinking deeper into church life, but I knew how much my father wanted me to have my own church, and I didn't know how much longer he was going to be around to see that happen. I told my mother to let the bishop know I would be interested in finding out more about the opening.

Later that week, Ken Talbot, chairman of St. Luke's vestry, called and invited me to visit the church, so on my next day off, instead of visiting my father, I drove up to Pineville where Talbot showed me around the church, and I had lunch with him and another member of the vestry. They knew my father by reputation and were impressed that Bishop Howard recommended me. Although the visit and interview seemed to go OK, I had the feeling they thought I was probably too young and inexperienced. That apparently wasn't the case because a few days later, Ken Talbot called and offered me the job.

9

St. Luke's Episcopal Church was a forlorn, gray stone building on Main Street next to the Post Office that was all past and no future. It had no Sunday school, no youth group, and no young couple's club. There was a vestry, of course, and a rump choir that could be rounded up for special occasions. And there was an altar guild, but it only had three members, the youngest of whom was 71. Bishop Howard had used the word "challenge" to describe the job, but that was clearly a case of episcopal understatement. Raising Lazarus would have been easy compared to what it would have taken to pump new life into that corpse of a parish.

The formal service of installation took place on the second Sunday in October after I had been on the job for five weeks. Bishop Howard's office sent out printed invitations that read: "The Bishop of Connecticut will institute and induct the Reverend Thomas Aaron Reed III as Tenth Rector of St. Luke's Church in the Town of Pineville" etc.

Most of the out-of-towners who showed up were my father's parishioners, plus a few clergy, including Keith, who showed up with their vestments to join the procession and be part of the service. Jim Tucker, the minister of the town's Congregational church, was also there. I would have liked to send Beatrice an invitation to let her know what I was up to, but I lost track of her.

I wished my father could have been there since my getting my own church was more his dream for me than my dream for myself. But at least he knew it was happening, and he wasn't forgotten because I had a special prayer for him inserted into the service.

Bishop Howard delivered the sermon, but I had trouble concentrating on what he was saying with my mother in the front pew lapping up her lover boy's every word. He preached on his favorite topic—Christian Servitude—using images and examples having to do with imprisonment, slavery, and sacrifice. Was that how I was going to end up if I stayed in the church? Always preaching about bondage and sacrifice?

When it came time for the installation, I went up into the chancel in my white vestments, knelt down in front of Bishop Howard, and said aloud the prayer that asked God "to be always with me in carrying out the duties of my ministry." As I found out later, the installation made me at age 26 the youngest rector in the Diocese of Connecticut. After growing up as the prince of my father's parish, it seemed only natural that I should now be the boy wonder of the diocese.

What St. Luke's lacked in parish activities and social services it made up for in sacraments and lots of them. I said mass every morning, except Saturday, and on Sunday, I said three of them back-to-back. Since I had no assistant to help me, I had to say all eight masses every week and more during Lent, plus the private masses I said when I brought communion to parish shut-ins. I made so many home visits to shut-ins I kept a box of wafers in the glove compartment of my car.

Even Saturday—my Eucharistic day of rest—wasn't free of sacraments. The sign in front of the church read:

CONFESSION

Saturday 10 AM—12 Noon

or by Appointment

That meant that every Saturday morning, I had to hang around the church in case somebody showed up. Almost all parishioners who made confessions arranged for theirs "by appointment." When somebody showed up on Saturday morning, it was usually an out-of-towner looking for an anonymous confession.

One Saturday a man I never saw before came in and went straight into the confessional. I took my place on the other side of the curtain, made the sign of the cross, and said, "Let us begin in the name of the Father and the Son and the Holy Ghost. Amen."

"Amen. I have sinned in thought, word, and deed," he said, and off he went into his confession, which mostly had to do with an extramarital affair he was having and felt guilty about. I quickly realized he was under the impression I was a Catholic priest, but since the adultery he was confessing had lots of juicy details, I didn't interrupt him or try to hurry him along. When he finished, I broke the news to him that I wasn't a Catholic priest but offered him an Episcopalian absolution for whatever it was worth. He shouted an obscenity at me, bolted out of the confessional, and hurried out the back door. He scurried across the lawn, jumped into his car, and drove off. I never saw him again.

After that, I always made sure that before visiting penitents entered the confessional, they understood that despite the cross on top of the church, the dark confessional, and the smell of incense, St. Luke's was a *Protestant* Episcopal Church.

What kept it afloat was its large endowment—money bequeathed tax-free through the years by departed benefactors conspicuously memorialized with stained-glass windows, altar flowers, memorial masses, prayers, plaques, dedications, and inscriptions in loving memory of. It was a case of subsidized atrophy. I was the manager of a mausoleum.

But as I soon found out, I wasn't even the manager. The real power, legal and political, lay in the hands of the vestry, the lay trustees who controlled the expenditure of funds, set church policy, and paid my salary. As far as they were concerned, St. Luke's was fine just the way it was. What it did, it had done as long as anyone could remember. They defended the status quo like a sacred flame.

Except for Thanksgiving when the congregation brought in cans of food for the needy, St. Luke's did nothing in the way of outreach. It didn't even seek new members, not that Pineville was fertile ground for missionary work. It made no apologies for what it was—a church of, by, and for itself. That was the way the vestry wanted it, and that was the way it was. I was ecclesiastical window dressing, rector of the parish in name only.

10

With a big rectory to wander around in and lots of time to myself, I finally got back to reading Dante both in English and in Italian using the dictionary Edward sent me. It wasn't the same as having him there in person or getting his transatlantic feedback, but it felt good to be connected to him again even though he was dead, or so I thought. When I had conversations with him, his voice inside my head was so real it sometimes felt that he was right there in the room with me.

Not only did I get back to reading Dante, but I started putting him in my sermons. At first, it was just bits and pieces, but when Advent arrived, I devoted an entire sermon just to him. That spring I wrote a series of four Dante sermons that became a permanent part of my repertoire for the rest of my time at St. Luke's.

The series treated my flock to a deluxe tour of the Dante afterlife, complete with a descent through the circles of the Inferno, an ascent up through the terraces of the Mount of Purgatory, and a journey through the Heavenly Spheres of Paradise with Beatrice as our guide. In the *Inferno* part of the series, I got to explain Dante's principle of symbolic retribution (as they sinned, so they are punished), and the *Paradiso* part allowed me to conclude the series with Dante's message of light, hope, and joy. It also allowed me to talk about his Beatrice, which helped me feel more connected to my own Beatrice wherever she was.

It wasn't all death and maintenance of the status quo at St. Luke's. I managed to plant some seeds, two of which grew into trees that bore fruit. The first began with 12-year-old Elijah Boone, who lived with his mother and younger brothers down the street from the church (they were the only black family in town). When he started coming around the church, I told him Bible stories that he passed on to his brothers and classmates with missionary zeal. He was especially enthralled by the stories about his prophet namesake.

Since there was free time on Sunday between the nine and eleven o'clock masses, I told him to bring his friends and brothers to the church the next Sunday at ten o'clock, and I would tell them more Bible stories. When they came and kept coming back, there it was—voilà, the Sunday school!

My other success was the youth group that started when Sarah Richardson began meeting with her friends in the church basement on Sunday nights to talk and play music. When more kids came and brought their friends, St. Luke's quickly became the most popular meeting place for the town's teenagers on Sunday nights.

Sarah would start off with a meeting, but most of the kids came just for the social part afterward. There was nothing especially Episcopalian or religious about it, but it served a social need in Pineville and beyond since kids from other towns started showing up as well. Unused most of the week, the church basement came alive on Sunday nights when it filled with voices and music and dancing and laughter.

One day Sarah came into my office bursting with excitement to tell me she and her friends wanted to start a "social club" after school and wanted to know if they could use the church basement. I liked the idea, but I told her it I would have to take it up with the vestry.

At the next vestry meeting, as soon as I brought her idea up, it was quickly shot down. Sam Waller spoke for the others when he said that letting the youth group use the basement after school "would ruin the quiet atmosphere we've built up over the years."

The next day when Sarah came to my office, I told her what happened.

"Oh, damn!" she said slapping her side. "I mean darn."

"I'm sorry, Sarah." I felt bad that I let her down and wondered if she would hold it against me.

"It's not your fault, Father Tom. You did your best."

Did I do my best? Was I doing my best? Her remark with its hint of well-meaning ineffectiveness stayed with me for the rest of the day.

That night I rattled around upstairs in the rectory feeling sorry for myself. Except for Emily Stone, a grandmother who often had me over for supper, I didn't really have anybody to talk to. I loved Emily because she rescued cats and dogs and found homes for them. I helped her out by keeping some of her strays in the rectory until she could place them. The only other person around close to my age was Gladys, the church secretary, who was married to a plumber and had two children.

I would have liked to talk to my father about my plight, but he was in no shape to talk things over with. Besides, he would only recommend infinite patience. Keith wasn't in the diocese anymore although I knew I could always call him in a pinch. Bishop Howard might have taken more of an interest in me if for no other reason than that I was my mother's son, but he was busy and remote, and besides, I was in no mood to warm up to him.

So there I was trapped in a parish that was my father's dream for me—saying mass, conducting funerals, delivering sermons, hearing confessions, taking communion to parish shut-ins, telling Bible stories to Elijah and his friends, and conducting more funerals and saying more masses. Sometimes at the end of the day, I would look at Beatrice's picture on my bureau and sigh about what might have been. I felt like I was drying up inside, as if my collar was squeezing all the vital fluids out of me.

Nonetheless, I soldiered on dutifully as St. Luke's "Father Reed"—priest of the church, dispenser of sacraments, keeper of the sacred flame, and parish mascot, complete with collar and invisible leash. If Edward was right that my sojourn in the church was going to be a detour like Dante's, where was I now? The Inferno? Purgatory? Maybe both. I certainly wasn't in Paradise.

11

When the nursing home called and told me my father died, the first thought that popped into my head was *I killed him*! I obviously knew I wasn't responsible for his death, but cause and effect did seem to be at work. As soon as I started thinking seriously about leaving St. Luke's and working outside the church, at least for a while, my father took a turn for the worse and died. According to oedipal theory, I grew up wanting to replace him, so I could have my mother to myself, but that never made much sense to me. Marrying my mother and sleeping with her? Ugh! Just the thought of it made me sick to my stomach.

I didn't remember what Dante said, if anything, about patricide, so I got the *Inferno* down from the shelf and turned to the first round of the ninth and final circle of Hell, called the Circle of Treachery. That's where those who betray family ties spend eternity frozen in ice with only their heads sticking out. The circle included two brothers from Dante's day, Alessandro and Napoleon Degli Alberti, who killed each other over their father's inheritance, and Focaccia, who murdered his cousin. However, I didn't find anybody who killed his father or mother.

Was there something oedipal about being angry at my mother? Was I mad at her for choosing Bishop Howard over me as my father's replacement? I obviously didn't kill my father, but I guess on some unconscious level, that's what it felt like.

That night I had a dream that my father was trapped in quicksand and I was holding onto him to keep him from getting pulled under. I held onto his hand for as long as I could before I let go to keep from getting pulled under myself. The dream ended with me watching in horror as my father disappeared into the sand. Should I have held onto his hand longer? Held it tighter? Did my letting go make me an accomplice to his death in some way? Whatever the meaning of the dream, it was very upsetting. Just when my father needed me the most, I let him down *literally.*

I always knew I would be the one to bury him when the time came because that was the Reed tradition. Grandfather Reed buried his father, and my father buried Grandfather Reed, so now it was my turn. Having to conduct yet another funeral, my father's no less, was the last thing I wanted to do, but I had no choice. It was my duty.

The funeral took place in my father's church on a cold, rainy morning in March. Despite the rain, the church was so full that folding chairs had to be set up in the aisles and in back. I shared the service—The Order for the Burial of the Dead and Eucharist in Loving Memory of The Reverend Doctor Thomas Aaron Reed Jr.—with Bishop Howard and Keith. Keith read the lessons, Bishop Howard gave the eulogy, and I conducted the funeral mass.

When it came time for the eulogy, it was painful to have to watch the man who cuckolded my father climb up into his pulpit and see my mother in the front pew looking up at him adoringly with an inappropriately radiant smile. I didn't like it when he called my father "a foot soldier in the army of the Lord" as if to remind everybody my father never made it out of the infantry while he was a member of the ecclesiastical Joint Chiefs of Staff.

As if that wasn't bad enough, toward the end of his eulogy, he suddenly pointed at me and told the packed church that I was my father's "living legacy." I wanted to charge up into the pulpit and knee him in the balls, but I didn't, of course. Saying the funeral mass, which helped calm me down, provided me with some small comfort knowing my father was finally going to find peace.

I drove to the cemetery in the hearse with my father's body and conducted the burial in a steady drizzle with my father's friends and parishioners huddled around the grave. After I finished the burial prayer, I picked up a handful of dirt, as was the custom, and threw it on my father's casket as it was lowered into the ground. I said the final prayer that I knew by heart that asked God to grant my father "an entrance into the land of light and joy in the fellowship of thy saints." By then, I was so choked up I barely finished the prayer.

I remained at graveside as my father's friends and parishioners expressed their condolences to my mother and me before making their way back down to the gate. My mother looked properly mournful, while Bishop Howard remained discreetly in the background.

After the last mourners left, she suggested I join them for lunch, but the last thing I wanted to do was go to lunch and listen to them coo at each other so soon after burying my father. I told her I had to get back to St. Luke's.

"I'm sorry you won't be able to join us," she said and kissed me on the cheek. "You were a wonderful son. You were good to your father to the very end."

I felt like saying, "I'm sorry I can't say the same about you," but I held my tongue.

Bishop Howard shook my hand. "Congratulations, Tom, you did a top-notch job. You handled yourself splendidly. God bless."

I winced when he raised his hand and made the sign of the cross. "The Lord be with you." I wanted his blessing about as much as I wanted an appendectomy.

My mother suggested we leave together, but I told her to go ahead because I wanted to stay there longer.

I watched her take the bishop's arm as they made their way down the hill. I didn't like the way they leaned together, nor did I like the little bounce in my mother's walk. It was a step not of mourning, but of barely contained jubilation.

When they reached the bishop's limousine, the driver got out and opened the back door for them. Bishop Howard must have said something to my mother as she got in because she looked up at him and laughed. Her short, sharp laugh shot up the hill and hit me like a sniper's bullet. After the limousine backed around and drove down out of sight, my mother's laugh lingered in the air like the smell of gunpowder.

12

That night, I had another father dream. I was in a tunnel and up ahead of me was an open casket on a stand. When I got closer to it, my father suddenly sat up and reached out to me. That jolted me awake and made me wonder if my father had some kind of other life like Edward sometimes seemed to have. Why was he reaching out to me again so soon after sinking into the quicksand? In both dreams, the message was clear: he was in trouble and needed my help.

I spent the next day in a funk until irrepressible Sarah came to my rescue without knowing she was doing it.

"Father Tom!" she said bursting into my office. She was wearing faded jeans and a green T-shirt that said

"Just Do It" on the front. "What do you think of this idea?" She stopped to catch her breath. "We want to find a storefront or someplace else where we can have our afterschool club. What do you think of that idea?"

"Good for you for not giving up. But if you decide to rent a storefront or whatever, how are you going to pay for it?"

"That's why I'm here, Father Tom. We thought you might have some ideas."

I sat her down next to my desk, and we talked about ways to raise money—raffle, bake sale, babysitting, dog-walking, lawn-mowing, etc. The idea she liked best—and it was her idea—was to have a concert in the church and charge admission. I knew right away that would be asking for trouble, but I would be on firmer ground this time since scheduling events in the church was my responsibility. After we talked some more about it, I gave her a tentative green light but decided not to tell the vestry, at least not yet.

At the next vestry meeting in the church basement, we were sitting around the oval table. I was doodling on my yellow pad as the "Old Business" part of the meeting droned on. I had taken two aspirin before the meeting since the headaches I used to get in Darien were coming back.

When the meeting turned to "New Business," Sam Waller, who was sitting across from me, was the first to speak.

"What's this we hear about a rock concert?" His protruding forehead made him look like a Neanderthal.

The room was so quiet I could hear the scratching of my pen on the pad. I pretended I didn't hear him and kept doodling.

"Father Reed," he said.

I looked up. "Yes?"

"What's this about those kids planning a rock party in the church?"

"First of all, they aren't those kids. They're *our* kids."

"Our kids? Except for Sarah Richardson, they aren't even members of the parish. They certainly don't come to church on Sunday."

"Secondly, it's not a rock party. It's a fund-raising concert."

"I don't care what you call it. It sounds like a rock party to me."

Ken Talbot, chair of the vestry and the one the others respected the most, stared at me. He was wearing a dark-gray blazer with a white handkerchief sticking out of the pocket.

"Father Reed, did you tell the youth group they can use the church?"

"As a matter of fact, I did." Knowing there would be no turning back now, it felt exhilarating but also scary. "Our youth group is part of the parish. They have as much right to use the church as any other parish group."

"But . . . but . . . " sputtered Waller.

"Furthermore, the concert will have a religious theme, and the youth group plans to give part of the proceeds to the church as their offering."

I felt a surge of energy like a prophet speaking up at long last. "If we had let them use the basement in the first place, they wouldn't need to raise money now to meet someplace else. The fact they want to donate part of the money they raise to the church speaks well for them. Letting them use the church is the least we can do."

They all looked at me in disbelief, amazed their mascot was off his leash.

"And besides," I said, "it's wrong to discriminate against the young."

Dead silence. Was I winning them over, or was this just a lull before the counteroffensive?

"Father Reed," said Talbot. "I for one appreciate the good work you're doing with the young people."

"Amen," said Ed Denton, who came the closest to being my ally.

"But in questions about how church property is used, the vestry has the final say. If we decide that we want the church to be used for this purpose, so be it. But if we decide we don't, that will be the end of the matter. If there was a question in your mind about this, you should have discussed it with us first."

"Here, here," somebody said.

While part of me was willing to be accommodating the way my father would have been, another part of me—the part that had been silenced for too long—refused to back down. Remembering what Martin Luther said to his accusers at the Diet of Worms, I thought, "Here I stand. I cannot do otherwise."

I looked around the table. "This is not something that needs to be discussed here because it's a matter of scheduling a service in the church, which is my responsibility."

"Church service?" Waller's face was crimson. "Who are you trying to kid? If we let those kids loose in the church, it will be a mob scene. Who knows what might happen?"

"You're overly complimentary about the size of our youth group."

"I don't think so. I hear it's quite a circus down here on Sunday nights. Every hippie in Connecticut knows about it."

Talbot looked at me. "We can't just turn the church over to these youngsters, no matter how well-intentioned they may be. We have no idea what kind of people this sort of thing could attract."

Waller said, "It would take a month just to get the smell of pot out of the sanctuary. I never liked the idea of those kids hanging around here or anywhere else for that matter. It's not something we should encourage. Who knows what they might do with a place of their own and no supervision. It could turn into a den for sex orgies."

"What are they going to do with the money?" asked Wayne Keen, a wimpy sort of guy always a step or two behind everybody else.

"I told you. They want to rent space to have a place where they can meet after school. As I already said, part of what they take in will go to the church. It's their way of contributing.

"Well, they're going to have to find some other way to contribute," said Talbot. "We can't let St. Luke's be used in this way."

"I second that," said Waller.

There were nods and murmurs of agreement around the table. When I looked at Ed Denton and he didn't look at me, I knew all was lost.

"I say we vote," said Waller.

"I agree," Talbot said. "It's time to settle the matter unless somebody has something more he wants to say. Father Reed, is there anything you want to add?"

I shook my head.

"I move the question," said Waller.

"Second."

Ken Talbot looked at me one last time, but I had nothing more to say.

"All in favor of voting on this issue signify by saying 'aye.'"

"Aye."

"All right then, it's time to vote on the issue before us. How many of you are in favor of letting the church be used for a young people's concert? Raise your hands."

Not a single hand went up.

"Opposed?"

All the hands shot up, even Ed Denton's. Waller grinned at me triumphantly.

"There's no need for you to vote on this," I said. "A request to use the church has been made by a parish group, a group not represented at this meeting I might add. So that's the way I'm going to treat it."

"Father Reed," Talbot said in a tone of voice meant to remind me he was thirty years my senior. "In all my years here, we've never let the church be used for any purpose that wasn't strictly religious. I'm sure you will understand that we don't want to break that tradition now."

I banged my fist on the table. "That's not true! Before I came here, the VFW used to parade around the church in all their getup."

It was true. Emily Stowe told me Father Thompson let the local chapter of the Veterans of Foreign Wars use St. Luke's for their annual service. So every year VFW veterans marched around the church—with rifles no less—until they finally moved over to the Methodists in the next town.

"And now every morning, we fly the American flag in front of the church."

"What's wrong with that?" said Waller. He was wearing his American flag pin as usual.

"Since when is patriotism wrong?" chipped in Wayne Keen, a stray mutt joining the pack.

"The flag has nothing to do with politics," Waller said.

"Just flying the flag out there every day is a political statement, and you know it."

"That's ridiculous," said Waller. "It's our Christian duty to support our country. It's in the Bible."

"Yeah," I said, "right next to the passage that says God is an American."

I stood up and fixed them with my fiercest stare. "All right then, if you're not going to let our young people do their thing on church property, we're going to be totally consistent."

I stormed out of the room and slammed the door behind me.

13

That night I sulked in my tent. I would have liked to go over to Emily Stowe's, but she was in Pennsylvania visiting her daughter. I was feeding her cats and keeping two of her rescued dogs in the rectory.

I tried to read some Dante to settle myself down, but I was too upset to concentrate. I kept hearing my father's voice counseling compromise, which was his special talent. He was a master of deflection, retreat, and smoothing things over unlike my mother who was more direct. There was something to be said for his approach in many situations, but this wasn't one of them.

Besides, the part of me that didn't want to be a chip off the old block was getting stronger. It felt good finally to speak up at the vestry meeting. Now that I was out from under the rock, I was in no mood to crawl back under it again. Why do I always have to give into the vestry just because they pay my salary? Why should I let them settle back into their self-satisfied complacency? Wasn't I called to rouse them to new life? To put new wine in old wineskins? To comfort the afflicted and afflict the comfortable? Wasn't that why I was ordained?

The next morning I woke up to a familiar voice outside my window.

"Father Tom! Father Tom!"

It was Elijah, faithful acolyte and star of the Sunday School, on the lawn under my window. He had already raised the flag.

I opened the window and called down to him, "Come on in, Elijah. I'll be right down." He was the acolyte for the morning mass.

I splashed water on my face, brushed my teeth, and put on my black shirt and gray suit. Then I clamped on my collar and went downstairs where the gangly 12-year-old was waiting.

"Morning, Elijah. Good thing you woke me up. I forgot to set the alarm."

I went into the kitchen and took a container of orange juice and box of doughnuts out of the refrigerator.

"It's *cooooooold*," he said, blowing on his hands.

"Sure is. Want some orange juice or a doughnut?"

"Nope."

I poured myself a glass of juice and drank it as I ate a doughnut. I decided to break the news to Elijah then rather than wait.

"You know the flag you put up every morning?"

"I didn't forget."

"Oh, I know you would never do that. It's just that . . . well, maybe we shouldn't put it up anymore.

Elijah stopped shifting. "How come?"

"Let's just say that maybe we shouldn't fly the flag anymore because the church doesn't worship what it stands for, at least it shouldn't. Respect is one thing, but worship is another.

I picked up another doughnut. "Sure you don't want one?"

"No, thanks."

"Not hungry?"

"I always fast before mass."

"Oh, yeah, I forgot." I ate the doughnut.

There were only three people in the chapel, but that was average for a weekday mass, except during Lent when there were more. Back in the sacristy after it was over, Elijah was unusually quiet.

"Father Tom?"

"Hm?"

"What you said about the flag. Is it like how those old prophets said it's wrong to worship idols?"

"That's right. A lot of people treat the American flag like it's an idol."

Elijah's eyes got wide. "Is it like when the first Elijah was with all them bad prophets on the mountain? He was for God, but they worshipped the Ball gods."

"Baal gods. Yes, exactly."

"Then Elijah caused the fire and chased the bad prophets down to the brook and . . . " He drew his finger across his throat and made a loud sucking noise.

I was amused he remembered the end of the story so well. "That won't be possible here, of course, but you have the right idea."

I felt bad that one of Elijah's proudest church duties was now being taken away from him.

Suddenly his face lit up. "Can we fly the other flag instead?"

"Other flag?"

"You know, the church flag with the red cross and blue square. It's in the closet."

He was talking about the Episcopal Church flag that used to get paraded up the aisle with the American flag during the Offertory at the high mass before the vestry voted to fly the American flag out front.

"That's a very good idea. That makes more sense than having no flag at all. And it is, after all, our flag. It's red, white, and blue, but it's *our* red, white, and blue. Elijah, you're a genius!" I gave him a hug.

"I'll do it every day like I do now. Should I change it now?"

"No, no, not now. We'll start tomorrow morning."

When we went to the closet to find the church flag, there it was folded up on the bottom shelf. Dusty but ready to go.

"What should I do with the American flag when I take it down after school? Put it in the closet?"

"No, no, don't do that." I didn't want it anywhere in the church where they might find it and put it back up. What I really would have liked to do was wrap Sam

Waller up in it and send him to the Pentagon. "For now, I just want you to take it home and keep it there. Will you do that?"

"Anything you say, Father Tom. I'll take good care of it."

"I'm sure you will. But do me a favor and don't tell anybody, OK? You can show it to your brothers, but don't tell anybody here at the church. It will be our little secret."

"Whatever you say."

We shook hands.

"Now, young man, it's time for you to go to school."

14

Early the next morning I watched the scene from my window. Elijah raised the church flag to the top of the pole, but instead of saluting it like he used to do with the American flag, he genuflected, crossed himself, and ran across the lawn toward school all in one motion.

It didn't take long for the news to spread that the rector was off his leash, if not his rocker. At 10:17 Sam Waller called, followed a few minutes later by Ken Talbot, who was calmer but no less upset. I quickly found out how determined they were when Father Thompson, who was living in retirement in New Hampshire and had never contacted me before, called to find out what was going on. I explained the issue to him as best I could.

Toward the end of the conversation, he said he was curious to know why I preached about Dante so much. The parishioners who stayed in touch with him were obviously keeping him informed about what was going on. I told him that I thought Dante was an important voice and offered to send him my seminary thesis. When he not only accepted my offer, but read it and sent me a long, thoughtful letter about it, my respect for him shot way up.

When Gladys told me the vestry was having a special meeting that night at Ken Talbot's house, I decided not to hang around (Emily was still in Pennsylvania). So, I got in my car and drove across the state line into Massachusetts where I had an early supper at a vegetarian restaurant in Springfield and treated myself to a science fiction movie about war on a distant planet that was so bad it was entertaining.

Shortly after I got back to the rectory, the phone rang. I was tempted to ignore it, but I decided I better answer it.

"Tom? It's me, Clark."

Just the person I didn't want to talk to. "Hello, Bishop Howard."

"Tell me, Tom. What in the world is going on up there?"

"There was a little misunderstanding."

"Little?"

"Well, it started out little, but it got bigger."

"I should say so. What's the problem? Do you mind telling me? Is it something I can help you with?"

"No, the problem is basically solved, or at least it will be soon."

Hearing my father's voice as I drove around Massachusetts, I decided it didn't make sense to do battle with the vestry over a flag, even though it was an important issue. What would be the point of fanning the flames and alienating everybody even more? Besides, I made my point.

"Are you sure everything's under control? One would never know it from the call I got from Ken Babbitt."

"Ken Talbot?"

"Yes, Ken Talbot."

"It's all over as far as I'm concerned. There are still some troubled waters to calm, and I'll do that tomorrow. Don't worry. Everything will soon be back to normal."

"That's good to hear, Tom. I believe you, and I believe in you. What happened? Do you mind telling me?"

"Well, there was a difference of opinion about the use of church property, and it got out of hand." I didn't like the way I was sounding. Was I was going to spend the rest of my life being like my father? Always accommodating, always apologizing, always turning the other cheek? "I'm sorry," I heard myself say.

"No need to apologize, Tom. It's all part of the growing pains of being a shepherd. Didn't I tell you it would be a challenge?"

"I can't say you didn't warn me."

"Take my word for it, Tom. These problems that loom so large at the time soon fade and become part of the larger fabric of your ministry."

Why do I have to listen to this crap? The question surprised me just popping into my head like that.

"I appreciate your interest, Bishop Howard, but this is something I have to work out myself."

"Of course. You know, Tom, sometimes it's hard to relate to certain parishioners because of differences in background and education. And then there will always be those with difficult personalities. But just remember that as annoying as they can be sometimes, they're the people the Lord has called us to minister to. I always remember what your grandfather used to tell us at clergy conferences. We're called to meet people where they are, not where we want them to be. I think that's very good advice, don't you?"

Is this why he called? To patronize me like this, quoting my grandfather no less?

"Many of your people have been loyal and generous through the years, not just to St. Luke's but also to the diocese. Mrs. Dexter's family has been a godsend."

Oh no, not this again. He told me about the wealthy Dexter family when he called me about the job opening. He's obviously fixated on the money they've given to the diocese over the years.

"But money isn't the issue," he said.

"Of course not." I tried not to sound sarcastic. I was in enough trouble already.

"Tom, as long as you're faithful to the Gospel and to your ordination vow, you won't go wrong. Remember your grandfather in his first parish? Your mother told me the story."

Now she's telling him family stories? The bishop must have sensed my irritation because he never got around to the story.

"Tom, I want to be helpful. Is there anything I can do?"

"Nothing I can think of, sir. As I told you, the problem is basically solved, or will be very soon."

"Something about hiding a flag."

"I didn't hide the flag!" I pressed my forehead with the palm of my hand because I felt a whopper of a headache coming on. "It's a long story. It has to do with more than just a flag."

"I'm sure there's more to it. In fact, Tom, that's the real reason I'm calling. We definitely need to talk. I sense something isn't quite right up there. I'm concerned about you, and so is your mother."

Leave my mother out of this, I wanted to say.

"As you know, I had great respect for your father, and I'm very fond of your mother. I ordained you twice now—to the deaconate and to the priesthood. And I encouraged you to go to St. Luke's. So I feel responsible. I *am* your bishop after all. I think I have the right to know what's going on, don't you?

My mind was racing off in a thousand different directions. When I finally spoke, my voice was so muted I almost didn't hear it. "I need time to think things through."

"Maybe you need some time off."

"Maybe." I thought how my father never needed time off.

"Tom, I don't think we should let things slide any longer. Maybe they've slid too far already."

I didn't say anything.

"So then, we'll definitely meet soon, OK?"

"OK."

"Good. Call Lydia and set up an appointment. Tom, I'm going to let you go now. Good for you for deciding to settle things down up there. I knew you would."

"Thank you."

"Your mother sends her love. She would love to hear from you."

"Say hello to her for me."

"Will do. Good-bye, Tom. God bless."

The next morning, Ken Talbot called to tell me the vestry voted unanimously that it was now official church policy to fly the American flag on the front lawn. He read me the part of the by-laws that stated the vestry's authority to do so. When I told him I would abide by the will of the vestry, he sounded surprised and relieved I was suddenly being so accommodating.

That afternoon after Elijah took down the church flag, I asked him to come into my office.

"There's been a change about the flags," I told him. "The vestry wants us to fly the American flag, not the church flag. So that's what we have to do."

He looked puzzled. "You want me to go back to putting up the American flag?"

"That's right."

"OK, Father Tom . . . if you say so." He obviously didn't think I was living up to the uncompromising standards of his namesake.

The next morning, I watched the ritual from my window. Elijah raised the American flag, but when it reached the top of the pole, instead of saluting it like he used to, he just squinted up at it, shrugged his shoulders, and trotted off to school. I looked at my watch. It was 8:19. The insurrection lasted 47 hours and 57 minutes.

15

That Sunday after the High Mass and coffee hour, I barricaded myself in the rectory and plotted my escape. My plan was to resign from the parish and apply for a leave of absence from the diocese for a study sabbatical of some kind, preferably in New York. But first I needed to resign from St. Luke's and present Bishop Howard with a *fait accompli*. That way he won't try to talk me out of it.

I thought about what would be the best way to break the news. I planned to tell Emily, Elijah, Sarah, and a few others personally, but I needed a way to make it official to the parish as a whole. A dramatic announcement from the pulpit at the Sunday eleven o'clock mass would certainly get their attention, but I finally decided the best thing to do would be to write a letter to the vestry and let them decide how to inform the parish.

As I sat down at the desk in the rectory and began to write the letter, the enormity of what I was doing sank in. No one in my family had ever done such a thing. I hesitated about going through with it until I finally decided to take the plunge. In the words of the Talmud, *If I am not for myself, who will be? If I am only for myself, what am I? If not now, when?* I finished the letter, and that night I drove over to Ken Talbot's house and put it in his mailbox.

To the Vestry of St. Luke's Church:

In the words of Ecclesiastes, there is a season for all things. After three and a half years as your rector, I've decided it's time for me to move on. My plan, the details of which I will work out with the bishop, is to spend a semester in a suitable study program. For that reason, the second Sunday in January will be the last time I'll be available to perform my clerical duties. Please accept this as my official letter of resignation. I'm grateful to you and to the parish as a whole for letting me serve St. Luke's and for giving me the chance to grow as a priest and as a person. It was an honor and privilege. Although I made my share of mistakes, I like to think I made a positive contribution. Please accept my heartfelt thanks for your patience and understanding.

Sincerely,

The Rev. Thomas A. Reed III

cc: The Right Reverend Clark S. Howard

I hoped that the copy of the letter I sent to the bishop would be enough to keep me from having to discuss my decision with him, but that hope evaporated a couple of nights later when the phone rang.

"Tom, are you free to talk?"

I was reading *Paradiso*, savoring one of my favorite passages about Beatrice.

"Yes, sir."

Rain was hitting the windowpanes.

"Good. Just a minute."

There was a click, then silence. Was he recording the call? Or arranging for my mother to listen in?

After another click, he was back on the line. "Tom, I had no idea things had gone this far. The last time we talked I had the impression things had settled down up there. What's going on?"

"Things *have* settled down. It's just that I decided I need a break from parish work for a while, so I wrote to Union Seminary about a possible study program."

"Tom, this is definitely something we need to talk about. Your letter was the first I heard about this. It's also the first your mother heard about it. I wish you had talked it over with me first."

That was exactly what I didn't want to do. "I appreciate your interest, but this is something I have to work out on my own."

"Of course. It's your decision. I respect that. Only you can make it. But I *am* your pastor, and this is something we need to discuss. So I'm going to insist you come and see me so we can talk."

But I don't want to talk to you, I thought to myself.

"Don't misunderstand me, Tom. I'm not necessarily opposed to what you're proposing. Maybe you do need a study sabbatical. You always had a strong academic bent."

There was silence that made me wonder if he was still on the line.

"I must confess I feel guilty about this," he finally said. "When your letter came out of the blue, I realized how out of touch I've been with you. I should have been keeping better track. I want to make up for that now. I would like you to come over this Friday and have lunch with me. Are you free to do that?"

"Hm, Friday's not a good day for me," I said even though I was free.

"How about Thursday?"

"That's not good either."

"Wednesday."

Knowing he would just keep making it another day, I said, "How about a week from this Friday? I think I can maybe switch some things around. Let me see. Yes, that Friday should be OK."

"Good. Let's make that definite then. Come to my office at noon. I see here on the calendar your mother has a meeting in New Haven that day. Would you prefer to make it some other time?"

"No, no, that won't be necessary."

"Whatever you want. When I see you, we can discuss the possibility of a leave-of-absence if that's what you want."

"Yes, sir, that's definitely what I want."

"OK, Tom, I won't keep you any longer. I'm glad we talked. I already feel much better knowing I'll see you a week from Friday. Do give your mother a call.

She'd love to hear from you. I want you to know you're very much in our prayers."

Our prayers? They say their prayers together at night before they hop into bed?

After the call, I sat for a long time listening to the rain and watching it drip down the windowpanes. I felt exhilaration, anxiety, emptiness, and fear all at the same time.

16

Bishop Howard took me to lunch at the Empire Club at the top of one of the tallest buildings in Hartford. My father had eaten there often, but this was my first time. Over lunch I gave the bishop a brief, sanitized summary of my time at St. Luke's, careful not to come across as angry or disturbed. I didn't want to give him any reason to send me to the diocesan psychiatrist. He was less resistant to my taking a leave-of-absence in New York than I expected.

"I think you should definitely be enrolled at a seminary and have a defined project, perhaps culminating in a paper or report."

"Yes, sir, that's how I see it. I want to enroll in a program at Union that one of my CTS classmates was in and was very pleased with." It was an independent study program that didn't require class attendance, but I didn't tell him that.

"Sounds good, Tom. Would that we all had more time for study." He stared out the window with a far-away look. "Sometimes," he said, but he never finished his thought. "By the way, how do you plan on financing your leave? What are your thoughts about that?"

"I have some money saved. Not a lot but enough to get started. I wrote to Union about financial assistance, but I haven't heard from them."

"I might be able to help you in that department. I have money in my discretionary fund for just this sort of thing."

"That would be very helpful. Thank you."

"I imagine you'll want to do part-time work at one of the churches to exercise your ministry, at least on Sunday. I don't think all study and no ministry is a good idea, do you?"

I nodded but didn't say anything.

"I bet Keith Harper would love to have you back working for him again. He thinks the world of you. Maybe you can hook up with him in the city." The bishop leaned back in his chair and folded his hands over his pectoral cross. "Just make sure you don't follow in his footsteps. I don't want to lose you."

After Keith left Darien to be the rector of St. James in Manhattan, he transferred his affiliation to the Diocese of New York. Bishops don't like losing their clergy to other dioceses.

"You don't have to worry about that," I told him. Working at a church, Keith's or anybody else's, was the last thing I wanted to do.

My mother's name didn't come up at lunch, but on the way down in the elevator, he told me again what a wonderful woman she was and how indispensable she was to the diocese. "I don't know what we would do without her."

I bristled at the memory of how she had always been so busy with her diocesan work that she hardly ever visited my father in the nursing home.

"As you know, Tom, your mother has high hopes for you, as do we all. She's heartbroken she had to miss you today."

"Please give her my regards."

A few days later, I received a letter from his office that I opened right away and read. "This letter is to confirm in writing what we discussed at lunch. Upon the termination of your duties at St. Luke's, I'm granting you a leave-of-absence from the diocese for the purpose of pursuing a semester of theological study and reflection under my authority."

I breathed a sigh of relief. The letter went on to say that he made an appointment for me to meet with him in his office on Monday, June 8 and suggested I drop him a line from time to time to keep him informed about what I was doing.

"Finally, Tom," he wrote, "I wish you the very best in the coming months and assure you of my continuing support and affection. I have known you a long time and feel close to your parents, so please permit me to speak personally. Ever since I've known you, I've been convinced you're endowed with special gifts for living a consecrated life that only a few of us are called to live. While one can never be certain what direction such an ordained life will take, I'm sure you'll continue to walk in the way of the Lord as your beloved father and grandfathers did before you. Please know that you remain in my thoughts and prayers. The Lord bless you and keep you and may his face shine upon you and be gracious unto you now and forever more."

Attached to the letter was a check for $1,500 from the "Bishop's Discretionary Fund." Although I hoped it would be more and knew there were strings attached, I was glad to have it. If I wanted to live in an apartment rather than be cooped up in a dormitory room at Union, I was going to need all the money I could get.

17

During my last weeks at St. Luke's, I was a paragon of pastoral solicitude. Now that I was no longer locked in combat with my parish and was on my way out, I experienced a mini-repentance, a softening of the heart that made me stop looking at certain members of my flock as dolts, dullards, Philistines, and yahoos. Instead, I saw them as struggling human beings, coming together on Sundays for companionship and trying their best to make it through the week with a modicum of dignity and comfort.

With Keith's help, I got a one-bedroom sublet on the Upper West Side of Manhattan near Columbia, which meant I wouldn't have to live in a Union dorm after all. The son of one of his parishioners who was going to

California agreed to sublet it to me. During my last days at St. Luke's, I tried to temper my good mood because I didn't want to hurt anybody's feelings by coming across as being happy to be leaving.

In the Class Notes of the *York College Alumni Magazine*, I read that Harry Boland, my freshman roommate, was working on Wall Street and had gotten some kind of a promotion. I figured if I ever got hard up for company in New York, I could always look him up.

On the Sunday after Epiphany, I delivered my last sermon, appropriately titled "Quo Vadis?" It was about traveling light, something I was giving a lot of thought to. At the end of the sermon, I thanked my parishioners for their support and understanding and asked their forgiveness for my lapses in patience and charity.

At the reception in the basement, I was moved by how many parishioners came up to me, some with tears in their eyes, to say good-bye and wish me well. Ken Talbot gave a speech thanking me for my service to the parish and presented me with a silver communion chalice with my initials on it. Just what I didn't need, but I appreciated the thought.

Sam Waller showed a sense of humor I didn't know he had when in front of everybody he presented me with "a present for your car." When I took it out of the wrapping and held it up, everybody laughed, including me. It was an American flag bumper sticker. Judging from Sam's purple-faced guffaws, he got the biggest kick out of his joke. Later when he took me aside to say goodbye, he told me, "I never thought I would say this, but you're going to be missed around here. You're a strange bird all right, but at least it wasn't dull."

"Why thank you, Sam. I appreciate that." When I went to shake his hand, he grabbed me and gave me a bear hug.

Sarah Richardson, who stayed to the end, asked to speak to me privately. I followed her to the side of the room where she told me she felt bad that she and her friends had to go over to the Congregationalists to get their afterschool club.

"Good for you for doing what was best for you and your friends and for not giving up. You did the right thing. I'm proud of you. Besides, God doesn't care if people go to the Episcopal Church, Congregational Church, or any church for that matter. It's only us narrow-minded people who think those things are important."

She was beaming as only she could. "Father Tom, I want you to know you're the best priest I ever had."

"Why thank you, Sarah. That's very nice of you to say that."

"I hope your next church will be a really good one and you'll be happy there."

"I'm going to miss your wonderful enthusiasm. But I want you to promise me something."

"What?"

"I want you to promise me you'll stay as nice as you are now for the rest of your life."

She giggled.

"Promise?"

"I promise." She kissed me on the cheek, and I gave her a hug. "'Bye, Father Tom. Keep the faith."

That left Elijah. Except for the women cleaning up, he was the only one left in the basement. After he ate one of the last rolls, he went to the corner where he was now hop scotching on imaginary lines.

"Elijah, I have to go over to the rectory now. Want to give me a hand?"

He was balancing on one leg. "Sure."

We crossed the lawn to the rectory where I had left my bags in the hallway. After Elijah helped me put them in the car, we went through the rooms one last time to make sure I didn't leave anything behind. I gave him the cross I had set aside for him. It was the cross my father gave me when I was his age.

I took him into the kitchen and poured two glasses of apple juice. After he drank his down, Elijah asked me if I knew "Father Swanbird." He was talking about the supply priest who was going conduct the Sunday services while they looked for my replacement.

"Father Swanson? Yes. He's a very nice man. I think you'll like him. I'm counting on you to help break him in. Will you do that?"

"Anything you say, Father Tom. But he's only going to be here on Sunday, right?"

"That's right. That's all the more reason he'll need your help."

"Father Tom?"

"Hm?"

"Are you going to have a new church?"

"Not right away."

"What are you going to do on Sundays?"

"Oh, I don't know. Maybe I'll just go to church like a regular person."

When we said our good-byes at my car, I felt bad about leaving him. As I backed the car out and started down the street, he waved, and I blew the horn and waved back. At the end of the street, I saw in the rearview mirror that he was still in the street waving, so I blew the horn again and put my arm out the window and waved one last time.

As I headed toward the highway, I didn't know if my tears were tears of sadness or tears of joy. Probably both. When I came to the toll booth and opened the glove compartment to get out some change, there was the box of wafers I kept there for when I brought communion to parish shut-ins. I should have left them at the church, but in my haste to get away, I forgot. I certainly wasn't going to turn around and take them back, and I certainly wasn't going to put them in a trash can either. What was I going to do with a box of communion wafers in New York City?

18

The dream I had my first night in New York was disturbing but understandable under the circumstances. In it, after my parishioners found out I ran off with the wafers, they piled into their cars and came after me. They followed me to New York and caught up with me in front of my building and kept me from entering. Tucking the box of wafers in my arm like a football, I charged through my flock, breaking tackles like a halfback. Once I forced my way into the building, I raced upstairs with my parishioners in hot pursuit. I reached my apartment just in time to slam the door and lock it before they shouted, pounded on the door, and broke out into an angry chant. "Hell, Hell, send him to Hell!"

When somebody yelled, "Where do we send him?" a chorus of voices shouted, "To Hell!"

"When do we send him?"

"Now!"

Other parishioners, mostly women as it turned out, including my mother, climbed up the side of the building and banged on the windows until they broke them and forced their way in. I woke up with my heart pounding wildly. I hid under the covers until I decided it was safe to get out of bed and go out to the kitchen. When I opened the refrigerator, I was relieved to see the wafers were still there. What a way to start my sabbatical.

The next day I registered at Union and spent the rest of the week sitting in on classes that looked interesting and picking up reading lists. The program allowed me to audit classes at neighboring institutions affiliated with Union like Columbia, Barnard, and the Jewish Theological Seminary, so I had a lot to choose from.

One of the classes I stayed with was a Columbia General Studies night course on Dante taught by a visiting professor from the University of Pisa. I liked his class and often stayed and talked to him afterward. Once we went to the West End Bar and had a longer conversation over beers. In the small world department, it turned out he knew Edward and had once been on a panel with him at a Dante conference in Amsterdam.

Toward the end of the semester when he came down with the flu, he asked me to fill in for him so he wouldn't have to cancel the class. At first, I thought he was joking, but he was serious. I was naturally very flattered to be asked, but I didn't think writing a few Dante papers in school qualified me to teach his class for him.

"You don't have to prepare anything," he told me. "Just talk about your thesis and lead a discussion."

So that's what I did. I read parts of my thesis, and we talked about Dante and lots of other things too. It was great fun.

The other class I got permission to audit and stayed with was Abraham Heschel's seminar on the Prophets at the Jewish Theological Seminary, which was just across the street from Union. At the first meeting when Rabbi Heschel had us go around and introduce ourselves, he was surprised to find out I was an Episcopalian clergyman on sabbatical. He was even more surprised when he found out how much Hebrew and Aramaic I knew and that I had already read parts of the Talmud.

We had a couple of conversations in the great man's office where we talked about Israel, the prophets, anti-Semitism, and, of course, Dante. He was curious why I was so interested in him, so I told him about Edward and the Dante papers I wrote in college and seminary. When he asked me how Jews fared in Dante's writings ("Not so good I would guess"), I told him the two main non-Christian groups in the *Inferno* were Jews and so-called "virtuous pagans"—famous Greeks and Romans like Homer, Aristotle, and Ovid Dante put in the first circle called Limbo where there was no punishment.

"How about the Jews? Where did he put them?"

"They're in the last round of the ninth and final circle closest to the center of Hell, which they share with "treacherous sinners" who, like them, spend eternity frozen in ice. Satan, who's also frozen in ice, is at the exact center of Hell, and guess who's in his mouth besides Brutus and Cassius?"

"Who?"

"Judas. Judas the Jew who in the Middle Ages symbolized all Jews."

"Would you say the *Inferno* is anti-Semitic?"

"Definitely. It's anti-Semitic to the core. *Literally* to the core."

"How about Paradise? Are there any Jews in Dante's Heaven?"

"Niente. Not a single one. Paradise is an exclusive Christian country club. No Jews allowed."

19

One day at lunch in the Union cafeteria, my ears perked up when I overheard a conversation about a small employment agency, called New Beginnings, run by an ex-nun who helped church people find nonchurch jobs. Since a new beginning was just what I wanted, I called and made an appointment even though I knew my father would turn over in his grave if he knew what I was doing.

The morning of my appointment, I took the crosstown bus through Central Park to Lexington Avenue and walked up to the New Beginnings office in a brownstone on East 89th Street. After I rang the bell and was buzzed in, I walked up the stairs to the third floor where Mrs. Brogan was waiting for me at the door. Dressed in a black pants suit and with her brown hair tied in a bun behind her head, she looked as formidable as she had sounded on the phone. She gestured for me to come in and sit down in the chair next to her desk.

When I told her I wanted to work outside the church, at least for a while, she told me I came to the right place.

"Let me tell you how we operate so you'll know what you're getting into. After we find you a job, you give us one month of your annual salary that's payable in installments. That's what keeps us going. We have some private funding, but it's nowhere near enough. We're barely keeping afloat as it is. We think one month's salary is fair. How does that sound to you?"

"Sounds fine."

"Good. The first thing I want you to do is start thinking about the work you did in a new way. People who come here tend to underestimate the value of what they did. The truth is you've dealt with many different kinds of people and have had experiences most people haven't had. That's why employers will be interested in you. So, when you fill out the questionnaire I'm going to give you, you'll understand why it's so detailed. But for now, just give me a brief rundown of your church experience so I get the picture."

She took notes while I told her about my father and grandfathers—my father's father who had a long career as the Dean of the Cambridge Theological Seminary (CTS) in Massachusetts and my mother's father who was the Episcopal Bishop of Connecticut for thirty years. Then I told her about my three years at CTS, my two-year curacy in Darien, and my five and a half years as the rector of St. Luke's Church.

When I finished, she put her pen down and leaned back. "Let me make sure I have this right. You resigned from your parish, and now you're in New York with your bishop's permission. You want a new lease on life and would like to earn some money."

"That's right."

"What's your bishop's name?"

"Bishop Howard. My leave of absence is until June. That's when I have to report back to him."

"Does he know you want to work outside the church?"

"No, all he knows is that I'm here on a study sabbatical."

"Good. That's all he needs to know. Do you have any church responsibilities now? Sunday work? Anything like that?"

"No, I don't have any church duties."

"Why did you leave your parish if you don't mind my asking?"

I gave her a very brief summary of the problems I had with the vestry and left it at that.

"You left voluntarily?"

"That's right."

"No hanky-panky?"

"Excuse me?"

"They didn't catch you in bed with the bishop's wife? Or with the bishop?"

"No, no, there was no big scandal if that's what you're asking."

"Because if there was any funny business, I need to know about it. These things have a way of coming out sooner or later."

"There was no funny business, as you call it."

"What kind of work would you like to do?"

"Something to do with writing if that's possible. One of the things I liked best about the parish was writing the sermons. I have a box of them in my apartment if anybody's interested. They're not bad if I do say so myself, especially my Dante sermons."

"Dante?"

"I know that's not a usual sermon topic, but I got hooked on him in school."

"How so?"

"I read Dante's *Inferno* in high school, parts of it even in Italian with the help of a dictionary, of course. And then in college I wrote papers on *Purgatorio* and *Paradiso*.

"That's impressive."

"And in seminary I wrote my senior thesis on Dante."

"Very interesting. Why do you think you got so hooked on Dante?"

"Well, the first thing that got my attention was all the clergy he put in Hell."

She laughed.

"I was fascinated that people like my father and grandfathers could end up in Hell, and I guess I could too if I follow in their footsteps. But mostly I like Dante because he takes on big subjects like death, love, sin, Heaven, Hell, things like that. Plus, he's a great poet. The greatest ever in my opinion."

"Do you think your interest in him might have something to do with your thinking about leaving the church?"

"What do you mean?"

"Well, you're obviously going against the grain of how you were brought up, so maybe you feel guilty about it. Maybe you think that if go against your church family, you'll be punished. Go to Hell."

"I never thought about it that way. Are you a therapist or something?"

"I was, but not anymore. At least not officially. But it does come in handy when I see people doing things that undermine their progress."

She opened a drawer and took out a large envelope that put on her desk and pushed toward me.

"This is everything you need to know about us. Take it home and read it. If you have any questions, give me a call. The questionnaire I want you to fill out is in there. Get it back to me as soon as you can so I can get started on your resumé and line up some interviews."

"Sounds good."

"And there's something else that's important. On the first Monday of every month, we have what we call a 'transition workshop.' The next one is Monday night. Everybody's expected to attend. It's right here." She pointed at the room next to her office that had a long table, chairs, and a podium.

"It's a combination rap session, support group, and social hour. Sometimes we have a guest speaker, and we'll have one on Monday. You'll get to meet the others, so it's important that you be here. It starts at 7:30. Will that be a problem for you?"

"Not at all."

"Good. As I'm sure you know, the job market isn't the best these days, but don't worry about that. We haven't failed anybody yet. Every person who comes through that door gets help sooner or later. But you have to be patient and persistent because it can be a slow process and usually is. But I can promise you this—if you want to make a new life for yourself, you will."

"That's good to know. How long have you been doing this work?"

"Nine years." She turned and pointed at a chart with colored markings on the wall behind her. "That's what makes it all worthwhile. Each mark stands for somebody who made it."

"What do the different colors mean?"

"Catholic, Protestant, marital status, children, that sort of thing."

"Who gets the gold stars?"

"That's for a priest, nun, or monk who gets a secular job, gets married, and has at least one kid. That's doing pretty good as far as I'm concerned." She stood up and pointed at one of the gold stars. "That's my favorite. It's my husband, Joseph."

"Oh?"

"We have two boys, and we're in the process of adopting a little girl from Vietnam. Joseph was a Jesuit, so he likes to tell people he's starting his own Society of Jesus. The boys and I have fun calling him Father Superior."

"It looks like I won't be a candidate for a gold star since I'm not Catholic, I'm not married, and I don't have any children."

"You'll get a red circle. That's for a Protestant clergyman who gets a secular job. But we don't have to worry about that now. First things first. Fill out the questionnaire, and we'll take it from there."

She got up, and I followed her to the door.

"Thank you very much, Mrs. Brogan."

"Call me Ma."

She had told me that on the phone, but calling her Ma was going to take some getting used to.

"OK. I already feel much better."

"Good. You're on your way."

"Thank you, Ma."

We shook hands.

"See you Monday. Welcome to our little underground railroad."

20

On Monday when I went back across town to the workshop, Ma introduced me to the others—a Cuban priest with a thick accent, a Unitarian minister with a goatee trying to get into advertising, a Jesuit priest working for a foundation, a Presbyterian pastor from Westchester starting to work for the city, a hippie-looking ex-Baptist seminarian, and a young nun, who used to be Sister Mary Theresa but was now on her way back to being Patty Sullivan.

After snacks in the conference room, Ma had us take our places at the table when the speaker arrived. He was tall and lanky with shiny black hair and sparkling blue eyes that gave him a look of amiable intensity.

"This is Al Corrigan," Ma told us. "He used to be a priest in Boston, but he now has his own electronics store on Long Island. He's married and has three kids. Welcome back, Al."

"Thank you, Ma. It's always good to be back." He went to the podium and settled himself behind it.

"My friends, I'm going to start right in by guessing that by now you're probably feeling that you're a loser. It's something we all go through. I certainly did. After many years in the church, I suddenly found myself in a strange new world where I had to play by different rules and I didn't really know what those rules were. I won't bore you with all the mistakes I made when I left the priesthood or tell you how long it took me to get a job because I don't want to discourage you. For a long time, I didn't think I was going to make it." He looked at Ma. "If Ma here hadn't come to the rescue, I wouldn't be here tonight. So thank you again." He smiled at her and gave her a thumbs-up.

She smiled back, then said she had to take care of something in the office and left.

He looked at the door. "Now there's a great woman if you don't already know it by now. With her on your side you can't go wrong. She saved my life. So, let's see, where was I? Oh, yes. In those days I kept thinking, 'Corrigan, you messed up the religious life, and now you're out there making a fool of yourself in the big world where everybody else is miles ahead of you.'"

I liked the spirit of this Irish Moses leading us to the Promised Land, but as he talked, my attention kept shifting to Patty Sullivan who was sitting across the table from me. She looked about my age, maybe a little older. She had an open face, bright, alert eyes, and that pale look that comes from spending too much time indoors.

"Your biggest enemies are going to be loneliness and feeling like a failure."

I thought, I bet she has an interesting story to tell. Maybe I can get to know her. Go out for coffee or a drink. I never went out with a nun, but then she probably never went out with a minister. The possibilities boggled my mind: we could hear each other's confession, take in a novena, stroll down Fifth Avenue, and go into St. Patrick's and light candles.

"You've had experiences other people haven't had," Corrigan was saying. "You've been closer to people's problems, to what makes them tick."

When Patty Sullivan uncrossed and recrossed her legs, my imagination shot off in a new direction. I pictured us back in my apartment embracing, kissing, me taking her into the bedroom. Just as I was starting to wonder what intercourse with a nun might be like, the door opened, and Ma came in with a young monk with a shaved head wearing the brown robe of the Franciscans. He fingered the white cincture around his waist as he looked around the room.

"This is Brother Michael," Ma said, "but from now on, he's Mike. He's one of us now. Make him feel at home, will you, Al?"

"Over here, Mike." Corrigan pointed at an empty chair.

Ma looked preoccupied as she left and closed the door.

"Welcome, Mike," Corrigan said. "How long have you been out?"

"A . . . a . . . about an hour."

"An hour?"

"About."

"Where did you come from?"

"Fr . . . fr . . . from Brooklyn."

"Take it easy. We're your friends here."

I heard voices on the other side of the door, and they were getting louder.

"I don't care!" I heard Ma shout. "You have no right. Get out! Get out! Out! Out! Out!" Something slammed against the wall.

Corrigan went to the door and opened it. Ma was cursing two monks dressed like Mike as she shoved them out the door and pushed them down the hall toward the stairs.

"Get out and stay out!" She pushed one of them so hard he fell down, but he got up quickly and scurried downstairs after the other one.

Ma came back with fire in her eyes. "Filthy bastards!"

"What was that all about?" asked Corrigan.

"That's the goon squad from the monastery. They came to get Mike."

Mike looked frightened.

"That's outrageous," said Corrigan.

"They're the same two who came nosing around here last year. I guess I was too easy on them." She went to the window.

"See anything?"

"It's hard to tell. They might decide to wait down there. But don't worry, Mike. Those bullies aren't going to bother you anymore. I promise."

Corrigan said, "Maybe we should call the cops."

"No, we can handle this ourselves. But I do need a place for Mike to stay tonight. He can't stay here like I planned. Not with those vultures circling around outside. I've got him booked into the Y tomorrow, but that leaves tonight. I could try to put him up at our place, but with our two boys living on top of each other as it is, I don't think Mike would get much sleep. Any ideas?"

"I can put him up," I said.

"Can you? That would be a big help, a *very* big help. That won't put you out?"

"Not at all."

"Great. It's just for tonight. Many, many thanks. Sorry for the interruption, Al. Let's settle back down and try to use the time we have left."

The atmosphere was subdued for the rest of the workshop as Mike looked uneasy and every so often Ma went and looked out the window. When Corrigan finished, she opened the window wide and looked up and down the street.

"It looks OK, but with those bastards, you never know. I'm going to have all of us leave together just in case."

She went to the closet and took out a yellow raincoat with a hood. I thought, that's strange. There hadn't been a cloud in the sky all day. She told Mike to wear it and helped him put it on over his robe.

We all went downstairs together and walked to the corner where we said our good-byes. The Presbyterian minister was on his way to Grand Central, so he walked with Ma, Mike, and me to the bus stop on 79th Street. Every so often Ma looked around to see if anybody was following us.

"It looks like the coast is clear, but just to make sure, I'm going to wait here with you until the bus comes. Call me in morning, Tom. Not too late because I want to take Mike shopping after I check him in at the Y."

"Here comes the bus," said the Presbyterian.

"Thanks, everybody," Ma said. "And don't forget, Tom, the earlier, the better." She gave Mike a hug. "You're safe now. I'll see you tomorrow."

"Good night, Ma."

As soon as we got on the bus, everybody stared at Mike in his strange yellow outfit. Most of the seats were taken, so we stood in the aisle where everybody got a good look.

"We made it," I whispered to him. "You can take the hood off now if you want."

He did, giving the passengers something else to stare at—his shaved head.

When we got back to my apartment, Mike was immediately drawn to the aquarium. He stayed there watching the goldfish while I put clean sheets on the bed and got an extra pillow and blanket out of the closet for me to sleep on the couch. I made him a peanut butter and jelly sandwich and took it out to him with some fruit salad.

"This OK with you?"

"Yes, thanks. I'm hungry."

"I bet. Leaving the church makes you work up an appetite."

"Yeah." He smiled shyly and started eating the sandwich.

"Want a beer to go with that? I'm having one if you want to join me."

His face lit up. "Yes, please."

When I came back and handed him his beer, he took a sip and made a face.

"I've got something else if you want."

"No, no, this is what I want. I just have to get used to it." Mike rubbed his hand over the fuzz on his head as if checking to see if it was growing. "But then I'm going to have to get used to a lot of new things. Like girls and stuff like that."

"How long have you been a monk?"

"Not that long. I went to the school the order ran and was an acolyte and good in Latin. Before I knew it, I was in the minor novitiate."

"How old were you when that happened?"

"Sixteen."

"How old are you now?"

"Nineteen."

"Getting to be a real old man."

"Yeah." He smiled and took another sip of beer.

"How did you find out about Ma?"

"Through the grapevine. Everybody knows about her."

"How did you get to her office tonight? How did you know where to go?"

"She wrote and told me how to get there from our Brooklyn retreat house. She even sent a subway map."

"How did she know you'd be in Brooklyn?"

"I told her. We wrote back and forth. One of the brothers knows how to get her letters in. It's not that easy because they're on the lookout."

"She doesn't fool around."

"That's why they're scared of her. The abbot's worried she's going to drain off a lot of the young monks. I'm the third one so far, and more are thinking about it."

I pictured hordes of young monastic malcontents pouring into Manhattan.

"Who were those two tonight?"

"I didn't see them, but they were probably Brothers Timothy and Herman. I'm just glad I didn't have to find out. I was upset enough. I just thank God I'm out, but now comes the hard part."

"Don't worry, Mike. You'll make it. You've already done the hardest part. It's time for you to get some sleep."

"Yeah, I'm tired. But I'm still excited."

"Of course. You've had quite a day."

I showed him the bed and bathroom, then said good night and went to the kitchen and cleaned up.

As I put things back in the refrigerator, I spotted the box of wafers I forgot to leave at the church. There they were still in the fridge until I figured out what to do with them.

I pushed the box back behind the mayonnaise jar so Mike wouldn't discover them in the morning. That's all the poor guy would need—to open the refrigerator and be eyeball-to-eyeball with the sacrament.

When I checked the bedroom, the light was off, but I could see Mike kneeling at the side of the bed with his head in his hands. It was hard to tell if he was praying or resting or crying or what. Poor guy. When I turned off the light in the living room, the aquarium light gave the room a ghostly shimmer. Sitting on the couch and watching the goldfish, I thought about the workshop and Mike and Ma and Patty. A few minutes after I heard Mike get into bed, the sound of his breathing told me he was asleep.

21

The next day after Ma took Mike shopping, I went to meet him at the Y for supper. I left early so I could pay my respects to Dante as I liked to do when I was in that neighborhood. His statue is set in the slender triangle called Dante Park on Broadway across from Lincoln Center a half a block from the Y on 63rd Street. If there was anything to what Edward told me at the end of our last Latin class ("If you keep going at this rate," he had said, "maybe someday you'll be the new Dante"), it seemed only right that I should touch base with Dante's statue from time to time.

After I gave him a little wave and said, "Ciao, Dante," I went down 63rd Street to the Y and met Mike in the lobby. I barely recognized him in his flashy new lavender sport shirt, khaki slacks, and gym shoes. All that was left of the old Mike was the fuzz on his head. We ate in the cafeteria and afterward played ping-pong in the basement if "play" is the right word to describe my attempts to return his lightning-quick serves and bullet-like slams. Even after he switched hands and played me left-handed, he still beat me. He told me later he was the top-ranked player in his monastery. Before we parted, we agreed that whichever one of us got a job first would buy the other one a beer. We shook hands on it.

Lent lumbered on without my getting an interview, much less a job. Unless I started earning money soon, I was going to have to crawl back to Bishop Howard and take any church job he offered me. Then I finally got my first interview.

"It's with the New York Savings Bank," Ma told me on the phone. "They have an opening in their training department. They want somebody to help their employees improve their communication skills. Your background is just what they're looking for, so don't hide your light under a bushel."

"OK, if you say so."

"And for God's sake, don't apologize for having been in the church. Be proud of it."

I grunted noncommittally.

"Remember what David did to Goliath."

"Yeah, but at least he had a slingshot."

"Don't worry, you'll do just fine. Call me when it's over and tell me how it went, OK?"

"OK."

"And Tom."

"Yeah?"

"Good luck."

At the bank's main office in Lower Manhattan, it didn't take long for the interviewer to zero in on my church background. He was a dour man with thinning gray hair and rimless glasses.

"I see here that your background is in the ministry."

He was looking at the resumé Ma put together for me.

"That's right."

"And you had your own church?"

"Yes, sir."

His eyes darted from place to place on the resumé.

"You weren't there very long I see." His nostrils dilated like a hound picking up a scent. "Why did you leave? Were there problems?"

"There are problems everywhere, but the main reason I left was it was time for a change. I wanted to go in a new direction."

His left eyebrow arched ever so slightly. "Does that mean you're still in the clergy?"

"I am, but only officially."

"What does that mean?"

"It means I'm ordained, but I'm not in the active ministry anymore." I obviously wasn't getting anywhere with this guy. "I'm in the city to find a job. As soon as I do, I'm going to resign."

"I see."

I disliked the man intensely. The chemistry was all wrong. He had the personality of a safe deposit box.

"So then, if you worked for us, you would still be an ordained clergyman?"

What was he afraid of? That I was going to proselytize in the cafeteria?

"As I told you, when I get a job, I plan on leaving the ministry." I shifted in my chair. As far as I was concerned, the interview was over.

"What makes you want to go into banking?"

What was I supposed to say? That I want to be where the money is? Or I now realize Jesus was wrong to drive the money changers out of the Temple? I looked him straight in the eye and said, "I need a job, and this happens to be my first interview."

His face slammed shut as if voiding a transaction. I left the bank feeling like a bounced check.

"It was a disaster," I told Ma from the pay phone on the corner.

"What happened?"

"He kept trying to find out why I left the parish."

"They all do that. You have to get used to it."

"He thought I had some big, dark secret."

"That's just their way of probing. All you need to remember is stay positive and never knock your past. Otherwise, they'll think you're a malcontent."

"Well, I *am* a malcontent."

She laughed. "Listen, Tom, if you made waves where you were, then you're going to make waves where you're going. That's how they think. Tell them how meaningful your church experience was, but now you want to broaden your horizons even more. Make them think you're still motivated by the same idealism that made you go into the church in the first place. They'll love it."

"OK, if you say so. Hopefully I'll do better next time."

"I'm sure you will. It takes a while to get the hang of it."

My second interview was at a small advertising agency on Madison Avenue. They were looking for a copywriter, so Ma told me to bring along a sample of my writing. Since all I had were sermons and school papers, I brought three of my Dante sermons.

When the interviewer asked me what I had done in the way of writing, I told him and handed him the sermons with the best one on top.

"There're a lot more from where these came from," I said as I watched him read down the first page.

He never got to the second page. "This is very nice, Mr. Reed, but it doesn't sell toothpaste."

22

The next day I was at home in the late afternoon reading Elie Wiesel's *Souls on Fire* when the phone rang. At first, I thought it might be Bishop Howard calling to check up on what I was up to since he already did that once. Instead, it was my mother who had taken to calling me more often, ostensibly to see how I was doing, but she obviously wanted to keep an eye on me now that I was rattling around the big city unchurched and unsupervised. After all, New York is where people go to reinvent themselves. I was careful not to give her any reason to suspect I was deviating from the straight and narrow.

"I'm glad you're in," she said.

"Hello, Mother. I can't talk now. I have to meet somebody." I was going to meet Mike at the subway to go up to a choral drama at Riverside Church.

"Well, whatever it is, it can wait because I have some wonderful news. It's about Clark and me."

I sat down on the bed and braced myself for what might be coming.

"I'm sure you know by now that I'm very fond of Clark."

I felt my stomach tighten.

"Well, we're getting married. Isn't that exciting?"

Silence.

"Tom?"

"Yes, I'm listening."

"He proposed to me last night, and I accepted. We're setting the date for the first Saturday after Easter."

I had been dreading this possibility ever since my father's funeral, but I didn't expect it to happen so soon. I thought of the line from *Hamlet* about his mother's quick marriage to his uncle after his father's death: *The funeral baked meats did coldly furnish forth the marriage tables.*

"I feel like a bride all over again," she gushed. "I'm as excited as I was when your father courted me."

More silence.

"Of course, no one can ever replace your father." Was she saying this for my benefit? "Clark is a wonderful man, as you'll find out when you get to know him better. As you remember, I didn't think very much of him when he was running against your father." She laughed. "But that's all forgotten now. Clark certainly respects you. He told me how proud he is to be your bishop."

The more she prattled on, the angrier I got.

"You know, Tom, Clark never had a son. Just two daughters. So I'm glad he'll finally know what it's like to have a son."

"I'm not going to be his son!"

"Of course not. You had a father, and a very fine father he was. Stepson I meant to say. You like him, don't you, dear?"

"Mother, I don't have time to talk. I'm meeting somebody, and I'm late. Tell me again when you're getting married, and I'll write it down."

"April 13, the first Saturday after Easter. It will be a small, private ceremony in St. Stephen's Chapel in the cathedral. Just family and a few friends. We're counting on you to be there."

My mind was racing to come up with an excuse to get out of it. "April 13? That should be OK unless . . . oh, wait, that might be when I have an oral exam at Union. Yes, I think it is. I'll have to check."

"Oh, dear. I hope there's no problem. I suppose we can always change the day if we have to."

"No, don't do that. The 13th should be fine. I'll double-check to make sure."

"Please do. We chose the 13th because the following week Clark will be in San Francisco for the House of Bishops meeting, and he wants me to join him. We're thinking of taking some time off in Hawaii. It will give us a chance to have a little honeymoon." She giggled. "Or maybe at our age, we should call it a wedding trip."

What made all of this hard to take was having to listen to her sounding like a giddy schoolgirl.

"Mother, I can't talk anymore. I have to meet somebody."

"A young lady perhaps?" she asked coyly.

"No, as a matter of fact, it's a young man."

Pause. "Oh, that's nice."

As soon as I got off the phone, I dashed over to the subway and apologized to Mike for being late. I told him my mother called to tell me she was going to marry my bishop. Mike said they don't do things like that in his church, and he sounded glad about it.

We took the subway to 116th Street and walked up to Riverside Church. Mike was excited because he had never been inside a Protestant church. We arrived just as the choral drama was starting. It was based on the Book of Job.

At the reception afterward, we had wine, cheese, and crackers, then walked back down Broadway and stopped and had a beer. When I got back, I watched a little bit of a late movie, then turned in.

23

The next morning I was sitting on the couch with my morning coffee, staring at the goldfish and brooding about my jobless, moneyless plight. When the phone rang, I hoped it was Ma with an interview.

"Reverend Reed?"

Any call that began like that meant trouble.

"Yes?"

"Hello, Reverend Reed, you don't know me. My name is Lucy Amory. I'm calling because I have a problem I hope you can help me with."

"What's the problem, Mrs. Amory?"

"A terrible thing has happened." Pause. "Winston passed away."

"I'm sorry to hear that." Right away I guessed what she wanted. In Pineville, the tilt of my priesthood had been toward death and funerals. I felt like a marked man.

"I would like to know if you would be willing to do the service."

"I'm sorry, Mrs. Amory. I'm not in the active ministry anymore. I suggest you call one of the churches."

"I tried that, but I'm afraid they haven't been helpful. Besides, I'm not much of a churchgoer these days."

"Then a funeral home will be your best bet."

"But I want something special right here in our home. I've made the arrangements for the burial, but I'm having a terrible time . . . " Her voice started to crack.

"I'm sorry I can't help you, Mrs. Amory. I've retired from parish work. In fact, I'm in the process of switching careers."

"I know. That's what Mrs. Brogan said."

"Mrs. Brogan?"

"That's right. She gave me your name. She told me what a fine young man you are. I'm sorry to bother you like this, but with the burial scheduled for Thursday I'm getting desperate."

"How long ago did Mr. Amory pass away?"

"Mr. Amory?" Silence. "He passed away last month."

My God! She has a reeking, rotting corpse in her apartment, and she wants me to bury it?

"I do so much wish Russell could have been here. He loved Winston as much as I did. For both of us, he was much more than just a dog."

Dog? She wants me to bury her dog? I had read about these things in the newspaper. What was I supposed to say? That I'm only ordained to bury people? That the church in its wisdom has decreed that dogs don't have souls? That dogs are not sufficiently high up on the evolutionary ladder to rate sacraments?

"I'm sorry, Mrs. Amory. I'm sure Winston meant a great deal to you, and I'm sorry he's no longer with you, but . . . "

"I'll pay you an honorarium, of course."

"That's not the point."

"Five hundred dollars."

"Five hundred dollars?"

"That's right, but if you don't think that's enough."

"No, no, that's plenty. I mean, it's just that . . . are you sure Mrs. Brogan recommended me for this?"

"That's why I'm calling. She gave me your number and told me to call you. She thought you might be willing to help."

"Listen, Mrs. Amory, I'm going to have to call you back about this. I need a few minutes." I wrote down her number and promised I would call her right back.

"Thank you, Reverend Reed. Thank you very much."

I hung up and was starting to call Ma when the phone rang.

"Hello, Tom. It's me. I'm calling to let you know that a Mrs. Amory is going to call you."

"She just did."

"Ah, she beat me to it. Poor dear, she's very upset."

"She caught me by surprise."

"I bet. I'm sorry I didn't get to you first to explain the situation. I know it's a little off the beaten path."

"Little?"

"Let me fill you in on the background, so you don't think I've lost my mind. Her husband was one of our biggest supporters. Not just giving us money but getting jobs for our people. In fact, Russell gave Joseph his first job. We owe them a lot. So when she called me at her wit's end, I thought of you. I hope you don't mind."

"I don't mind. It's just that it was unexpected to say the least."

"I know, I'm sorry. But you should have heard some of the abuse she had to take, especially from your people because she mostly tried your churches. When she called St. Bartholomew's, the secretary laughed and hung up."

"Really?"

"I figured you might be in just enough of an anti-establishment mood to help her out. She's a little eccentric, I know, but she's a dear. Besides, I didn't think you would be against picking up a little extra pocket money. I knew you could always say no."

"What kind of dog was he?"

"Black Labrador. They used to show him. As you can tell, he meant everything to them. His death really hit her hard coming so soon after Russell passed away." Ma was quiet. "So what did you tell her?"

"Nothing yet. I told her I'll call her back. I just wanted to check with you first to make sure this is for real."

"Oh, it's for real all right. Are you going to do it?"

I thought about Mrs. Amory. I thought about those bastards laughing at her. And I thought about the money. "Sure. I'll do it."

"Thanks, Tom. I knew you would."

24

Thursday morning, I took the box of my church equipment out of the bedroom closet, never dreaming I would ever have to wear my clericals again. As I put on my dark gray suit, black shirt, and collar, I thought about wearing my raincoat and a scarf to hide my identity, but it was a bright, sunny day without a cloud in the sky. I left the building quickly and was glad not to run into anybody I knew. I went to the corner, took the crosstown bus through the Park to the East Side, and got off and walked down to 810 Park Avenue.

"Good morning, Father," said the doorman. "Mrs. Amory is expecting you. Go all the way back and take the elevator to the ninth floor."

I walked through the lobby with its mirrors and tropical plants past a marble fountain to the private elevator that took me up to Mrs. Amory's apartment. A maid in a black and white uniform met me and took me down a carpeted hallway past a library and a room filled with trophies, ribbons, and photos.

A strong scent of flowers greeted me when I entered the living room, now emptied of all furniture except for a stand covered by a white satin spread with gold tassels. The flowers were everywhere—surrounding the stand, on tables, under windows, and in every corner.

"Reverend Reed?" said a voice behind me. "I'm Lucy Amory."

A petite woman with immaculately coiffured gray hair and soft blue eyes, she was dressed in black and was wearing a corsage of white roses.

"I'm so glad you could come early. You don't know how much better I feel having you here." She took my hand and gave it a squeeze. "As you can see, this is where we'll have the service. Do you think it looks all right?"

"It looks very nice. I'm going to do the service from this." I held up the prayer book I used for funerals in Pineville.

The maid reappeared. "Excuse me, Ma'am. Mr. Dolan is here."

"Oh, good." Mrs. Amory touched my arm. "Excuse me for a moment."

She left and came back with a short, balding man with a ruddy complexion. "Reverend Reed, this is Mr. Dolan."

"Glad to meet you, Reverend." We shook hands.

Mrs. Amory sighed. "I don't know what I would have done without the both of you."

"Pets are my business, Ma'am."

I heard grunting, then voices.

"Chrissake, Tony, don't hit the wall."

Around the corner came two men, one pulling, the other pushing a large maple casket set on wheels. They were wearing green uniforms with "Dolan Animals" scrolled on their shirts.

"Over here," Dolan said.

They rolled the casket over to the stand, then lifted it up and set it in place. The shorter man wiped his nose with his sleeve while the other one looked around the room.

Dolan checked to make sure the casket was secure. "OK, that should do it."

Mrs. Amory followed them out but soon came back and stared at the casket with sorrowful eyes. She took me to a small room off the living room where she said I would be more comfortable.

"You can't imagine what a lifesaver you are." She gave my hand another squeeze. "I'm so glad it will be done right." She told me she would come back and let me know when it was time to begin.

Waiting in the side room, I thought back to the time in Dalton when my friend Bobbie and I found a dead sparrow behind the parish house and dug a hole and had a funeral for the bird with me doing the officiating naturally. I was an animal lover from the beginning. When my parents taught me to say my prayers before getting into bed, I always prayed for animals as well as for family, friends, clergy, Congress, the President, etc. After I got through the list of the people I was supposed to pray for, I would pray for our cat, Constantine, and for the other dogs and cats in the neighborhood, and for birds, squirrels, horses, cows, sheep, goats, ducks, crows, chickens, raccoons, elephants, hippopotamuses, and any other animals I read about or saw on television. I even prayed for rats, lizards, snakes, and the cockroaches my mother and the housekeeper used to kill in the laundry room. If I didn't grow up to be a clergyman like my father and grandfathers, I wanted to be a vet since I thought of them as ministers to the animal kingdom.

Sitting in the side room waiting for the funeral to begin, I felt more at peace with myself than I had in a long time. It was good to be needed again the way I used to be needed at St. Luke's, especially at funeral time.

When Mrs. Amory came back and whispered it was time to begin, I put the stole over my shoulders and went out into the living room that was now brimming with dogs and people. As if on cue, all the dogs suddenly stopped sniffing and scratching and looked at me with ears perked, heads cocked, and nostrils taut. Realizing I was challenging some sort of canine equilibrium, I went to the casket slowly and carefully.

The dogs in front were deciding what to make of me—an Afghan hound with flowing, hippie-like hair; a nervous little Chihuahua with bulging eyes; a flat-nosed, bowlegged bulldog, panting audibly with his pink tongue dangling out of the side of his mouth, and an aristocratic white poodle, attired in fur bracelets, collar, pom-pom tail, and pink and blue ribbons, who stared at me with icy contempt. My most immediate concern, however, was the German shepherd on my immediate left who was barely being restrained by a woman in a blue pants suit and dark glasses.

I opened my prayer book and began. "I am the resurrection and the life, saith the Lord. He that believeth in me, though he were dead, yet shall he live."

With the shepherd baring his teeth, growling, and straining against his leash, I felt like a missionary who had stumbled onto a tribe of cannibals.

"We brought nothing into this world, and it is certain we can carry nothing out."

While these biblical sentiments seemed to be having a calming effect on the people and most of the dogs, they weren't doing anything to pacify the shepherd. I looked out at Mrs. Amory for help, but she was in back caught up in the tribute to her beloved. I decided to skip the psalm and go straight to the gospel.

"Here beginneth the fourteenth chapter of The Gospel According to St. John."

"Grrrr."

"Theodosius! Shush!"

"Jesus said, 'Let not your heart be troubled . . . '"

"Grrrrrrrr."

"Theodosius! Be nice to the minister."

"Grrrrrrrrrrrrrr."

The sound of a distant noon whistle set the dogs off. The shepherd jumped up on his hind legs and barked ferociously while the other dogs yelped, howled, and did nervous little dances. In the back, a fight broke out between a Skye terrier and a Pomeranian. A basset hound broke loose and rushed forward to the casket while a Doberman pinscher showed his teeth and rolled around erratically on the rug. To quell the pandemonium, Mrs. Amory went around the room admonishing the dogs by name, scolding the worst offenders until order was restored.

When it was quiet again, I finished reading the Gospel and moved closer to the casket to give the blessing. I saw Winston for the first time through the flowers. He was lying there black, beautiful, and serene with his eyes closed as if sleeping. The room was absolutely still. Even Theodosius looked woeful.

"Unto God's gracious mercy and protection, we commit you. The Lord lift up his countenance upon you and give you peace, both now and ever more."

As I made the sign of the cross over Winston, I remembered a line from *Hamlet* that seemed appropriate, so I said it out loud: "Good night, sweet prince, and flights of angels sing thee to thy rest."

In the elevator on the way down, Theodosius looked up at me with his head cocked to one side and his ears perked. When I made a smacking sound with my lips, he answered with a bark, but not an unfriendly bark. He sniffed my hand and licked it.

"See, he really likes you," said the woman. She bent down and hugged his neck. "Theo's my love. Theo, Theo, Theo, you're my love."

The door opened, and the dogs on leashes pulled their human companions through the lobby past the dribbling fountain out onto the sidewalk.

25

I finished my duties at the animal cemetery in Wantagh on Long Island. The burial was a small, private affair—just Mrs. Amory, Mr. Dolan, two cemetery workers, and a friend of Mrs. Amory with a beautiful black poodle who watched the proceeding with incredibly sad eyes.

"Man, that is born of woman, hath but a short time to live."

The poodle was whimpering. Probably Winston's girlfriend, I figured.

"He cometh up and is cut down like a flower." I picked up a handful of dirt. "Unto Almighty God we commend the soul of our loved one, Winston, departed, and we commit his body to the ground, earth to earth, ashes to ashes, dust to dust." I threw the dirt on the casket and gave the final blessing.

As the workers started lowering the casket down into the hole, the poodle broke free and rushed to the grave. I have no doubt that if she had not been quickly restrained, she would have jumped in on top of the casket. She whined and pawed the ground as she looked down at the casket in its final resting place.

I rode back to the city with Mrs. Amory in the back of her limo. I had accompanied the deceased to the cemetery in Dolan's hearse. Now it was time to be with the bereaved.

"I'm going to miss him terribly," she said. "First Russell, now Winston. My life's not going to be the same." We were speeding along the Long Island Expressway.

"Winston must have had a lot of friends."

"Oh, yes," she said more brightly. "He was very popular, especially with the ladies." She laughed. "But Melissa was his special friend. They've known each other since they were pups. She took it very hard, causing all that fuss back there. Yes, everyone at the service knew him in some way. The young girl with the blond hair was Winston's walker. His vet couldn't make it, but he sent lovely flowers. Even his first obedience teacher sent a card from Chicago. In his own way, Winston was quite famous."

"Who was the man with the beard?"

"That was Dr. Holtman. He was Winston's psychiatrist. The two of them got to be quite close by the end. Winston was never the same after we stopped showing him. He had a lot of trouble with the adjustment. All that attention, then suddenly nothing. So we took him to Dr. Holtman. He said dogs have identity crises just like people, especially show dogs after they retire." Her eyes were beginning to tear up. "I wish you could have known him."

"He sounds like quite a dog."

"I always wondered if there wasn't more to it though. I think it was a blow to his ego when they took him off the stud list at the New York Kennel Club. You know how sensitive men are about those things."

Up ahead of us loomed the Manhattan skyline.

"I wanted to have Winston buried with us in our plot, but they wouldn't allow it. Really," she said with disgust, "people can be so narrow. Don't you think it's silly to have segregated cemeteries? I mean, up in Heaven or wherever we're supposed to go, do you think people will be separated from their pets? I wouldn't accept afterlife if I didn't think Winston was going to be there to share it with us."

She sighed. "What does the church have to say about that?"

My collar was pinching like it used to in the old days. "To my knowledge, they don't have an official position on it, but I must say it would be hard for me to imagine any god worth his salt who didn't love animals."

"I'm glad you said that. Thank you. I wish there were more clergy like you. It serves them right for losing you."

As we approached the Queens Midtown Tunnel, she took out her checkbook. "I want to give you your honorarium now. You can't imagine how grateful I am for all you've done." She had already written the check, so she tore it out and handed it to me. "Here, this is for you and a little extra for being so nice."

"Thank you." I glanced at it as I folded it and put it in my pocket. $800! "Thank you very much, Mrs. Amory. You're very kind."

"You deserve every penny of it. Now tell me where you want to go and we'll drop you off."

"No need to go out of your way."

"I insist."

The limousine crossed Central Park to the West Side and dropped me off at my door. Feeling self-conscious in my clerical uniform, I darted into the building and dashed upstairs.

26

The longer my job search dragged on, the more I wondered if I was on the right track. Was I really cut out for the business world? Was the business world cut out for me? Wouldn't an astute employer have qualms about hiring somebody conditioned to view the accumulation of wealth with ironic detachment, if not outright disdain? "Do not lay up for yourselves treasures on earth, where moth and rust consume and where thieves break in and steal" and all that stuff? And wouldn't a full-time job in the business world be the kiss of death to a writing career, much less to my being the next Dante.

In the meantime, I watched Mike blossom. He loved his movie theater job and was now dating Mary Lou, one of the ushers. When they had the same time off, they went to other movie houses and saw more films.

"Can't you make me an usher like Mike?" I asked Ma on the phone. "That way I'd at least get to see some movies."

"Tom, this is not the time to lose heart. You're on the homestretch. Don't give up now. The finish line is in sight."

"If something doesn't happen soon, I'm going to have to go back and work for the church."

"Is that what you want?"

"No, not really, but . . . "

"Don't worry. You'll make it. Your luck is about to change. I feel it in my bones."

"Think so?"

"I know so."

My next interview was at the Universal Insurance Company on Third Avenue where I talked to a Human Resources officer by the name of Mr. Mannis. They had a job in their PR Department writing promotional material.

"We've had a number of former clergy work for us," he said, lowering his voice as if confiding a company secret. "One of our best salesmen here in the New York office was a Lutheran minister."

I shifted in my chair, uneasy at the prospect of getting thrown into a den of ex-clerics.

"A ministerial background is quite valuable in our business. We need to be in touch with people's deepest hopes and fears."

I wanted to work for Universal about as much as I wanted to work in the subway system, but I was broke and desperate and running out of time. Besides, it was a writing job. Sort of.

When I sensed the moment of truth arrived, I looked him straight in the eye and said with all the ministerial sincerity I could muster, "Human beings deserve a fair measure of physical and psychological security for themselves and their loved ones. It's their birthright."

Behind his glasses, he blinked in a way that told me I hit a home run. He wrapped up the interview and said he would contact me soon. The next day he called and told me I had the job. I was to start on Monday.

27

I assumed Harry Boland was still working on Wall Street, so I got his address from the alumni office and sent him a note to let him know I was in the city. A few days later his secretary called to say "Mr. Bolan" was out of town, but he wanted to meet me that Friday in the Oak Room of the Plaza Hotel at six o'clock. I told her I would be there.

I was surprised to find myself actually looking forward to seeing him again. It had been seven years since I last saw him and ten years since we roomed together freshman year. It was going to be interesting to see what he was like now. I had changed a lot since college, but then he probably had too. At least I hoped so.

On Friday, I walked over to the Plaza early to give myself time to look at the fountain in front where Zelda Fitzgerald is alleged to have frolicked. Then I went into the hotel and strolled around the lobby until six when I entered the Oak Room with its wood paneling and cocktail music. As I made my way to an empty table set against the far wall, I savored the feeling of being anonymous. Nobody knew I was "Father Reed" or "The Reverend Thomas A. Reed III." Now that I had a job, I was finally putting the church behind me. And who better to help me celebrate than hedonistic Harry?

"Rev baby!"

The unmistakable voice from the past carried across the room, followed by the familiar stocky figure in a light-gray modish suit making his way toward me. He had put on weight, lost some hair, and had a few more lines around his eyes, but otherwise he looked like the same old Harry.

I stood up, and he pumped my hand. "Long time no see, Tommio. I thought you'd be Pope by now."

"That's going to take a little longer."

We sat down, and he ordered Cutty Sark on the rocks.

"So what are you up to these days?" he asked me. "The last time I knew you were up in the boondocks somewhere."

"I had a small church in northern Connecticut, but I left."

"Why? What happened? Did they catch you with your hand in the till?" He laughed at his joke the way he used to in college.

"No, it was just time to move on. I'm supposedly on a study sabbatical at Union Seminary, but the program's very loose. I came to New York to explore other options, and to make a long story short, I have a new job."

"A new church job?"

"No, it's not with the church. Starting Monday, I'll be working for an insurance company."

He stared at me, then burst out laughing. "You? Working in insurance? That's funny. What the Hell do you know about insurance?"

"Nothing yet. They're going to teach me."

"But how can you do that? I mean, aren't you supposed to work for your church?"

"I can work for anybody I want. It's a free country."

Harry shook his head. "This is hard to believe. What are you going to do in insurance?"

I told him about the job as it had been explained to me.

Harry made a face. "That's a shit job, Tommio. With your education you should be able to do better than that. A lot better."

"I have to start somewhere."

Harry took a big swallow of his drink. "But you're still, you know, doing the clergy thing, right? I mean, they didn't defrock or deactivate or delouse you, or whatever they do to you?"

"Not yet. But now that I finally have a job, I'm going to leave. I'm going to write my resignation letter this weekend."

Harry whistled his amazement. "Oh, Rev baby, I knew if I lost contact with you, you were going to get into big trouble."

"I really missed your steadying influence."

Harry took another swallow and shook his head. "Poor ole Tommio." His voice trailed off.

"How about you, Harry? What are you up to? I saw in the Class News you're knocking them dead on Wall Street."

"Yeah, I'm doing good, and doing my own investments on the side is a big help. By next year, I should have my first million."

"Really?" I thought back to college and all the carousing he did. "That's hard to relate to. I'm trying to stay out of the poorhouse, but at least I have a job now.

But it will be a while before I get my first paycheck. So if we decide to get a bite to eat later, it will have to be a place that's real cheap."

"Don't worry about that. Tonight's on your ole roomie." He raised his glass. "Here's looking at you." He finished off his drink and ordered another.

"To be honest with you," he said, "I never thought it would come to this. I remember back in college how you used to talk about the meaning of life—Dante this, Buber that. What was it with all that bullshit?"

"Yeah, well, I was trying to find my way."

"Is that what it was? And what about that girl you were crazy about? What was her name?"

"Beatrice." Just saying her name made me go soft inside.

"You worshipped the ground she walked on even though she didn't give you the time of day. She was a real goodie-goodie too. Whatever happened to her?"

"She got married and moved to Boston and started a family. I still think about her a lot. In fact, I keep her picture on my bureau."

"She's married to somebody else, and you're still pining away? That's sick."

"Tell me more about you, Harry. How do you like your life of affluence?"

"Oh, I'm getting to be such a goddamn solid citizen it's disgusting. I should be a partner before too long if I play it right, but it's something anybody with half a brain can do."

"Are you engaged or anything like that?"

"Hell no. I'm having too good a time for that." He looked down at his drink, then back up. "But chasing the chicks isn't as much fun as it used to be. It's all such a big game. How about you? Got anything going for yourself?"

"Not really. In Pineville, there weren't any women my age to speak of."

"But you're in the Big Apple now. If you strike out here, there's something wrong with you."

"I'll be OK once I start getting a paycheck. Then I'll have some money to do things. There's a nice woman in my group, but I found out she's taken. A former nun actually."

"A nun?" Harry rolled his eyes. "You're in worse shape than I thought."

"But to answer your question, no, I'm not doing well on the female front. I can't even remember the last time I had a date."

Harry frowned. "Oh, Rev baby, don't do it to yourself. Don't punish yourself like this. This town is crawling with lovelies. What's the point of coming to New York if you're going to live like a monk?" He reached into the inside pocket of his jacket, took out a black address book, and began flipping through it. "I'm trying to think if I know anybody who might be your type."

The gallery of his "lovelies" who used to parade in and out of his room at all hours of the day and night passed through my mind. "Thanks, Harry, but . . . "

"Hey, I have a better idea." He put his book back in his pocket. "How about coming to my party next Saturday. A week from tomorrow. There will be lots of cuties there. Maybe you'll meet somebody you like. How about it?"

"Next Saturday?" I hesitated about getting involved with anything to do with Harry, but I knew it would be good for me to get out of my rut.

"Sure, why not? By then with a week of work under my belt, I should be ready for a party."

"Now you're talking. Let's drink up. I'm taking you to a little place not far from here. It'll help you shake off those church cobwebs."

"You don't have to do that."

"Relax. Let your ole roomie show you a good time."

"OK, Harry. Into your hands I commend my spirit."

28

The next day I wrote to Bishop Howard to break the news to him (and that way to my mother as well) that I was now working for an insurance company and decided to leave the ministry. "Since my decision is final and irrevocable," I wrote, "I trust you'll understand why I see no need to meet with you personally about this or in any other way prolong the inevitable." I revised the letter to get it just right, then put it aside, and took a long walk in Central Park, which was just down the street.

Sunday morning the church bells from the next block that woke me up seemed to be ringing more urgently than usual as if trying to summon me back home. As I lay in bed thinking about the momentous step I was taking, I began having serious doubts about what I was doing. Why the rush to resign? Why not wait until I have a better idea of what I'll be doing in the long run? Maybe I won't like the job. How fulfilling is it going to be to write propaganda for an insurance company?

I heard Ma's voice telling me this was no time to equivocate. I also imagined I heard Edward telling me it was time for me to move on to my next calling. He didn't mention my being the next Dante, but I assumed that's what he meant. I wondered what my father would think if he knew what I was doing. I already felt guilty about abandoning the church career my parents mapped out for me, but that was no reason to put the brakes on now. I had come too far to turn back. I said out loud Edward's and my favorite Talmud passage: "If I am not for myself, who will be? If I am only for myself, what am I? If not now, when?" When indeed?

After I read the letter one last time and caught a typo, I took it to the corner and mailed it before I could change my mind. Mike was at work, but I wanted to let him know the deed was done, so I went to the Y and left a note in his mailbox: "Mike, I just mailed my resignation to the bishop. Free at last. Let's celebrate. Tom."

That left one more matter I needed to take care of. Sacramentalist that I was, I wanted a rite of closure to mark this important turning point in my life. So when I got back to the apartment, I went to the bedroom closet and took out the box of my church gear for what I hoped was the last time. I removed my collar and put it in a brown paper bag that I took down the street to Central Park. I entered the park at West 81st Street and walked up past the Delacourt Theatre across the grass to the pond. The Belvedere Castle on the other side of the pond loomed up over it like a castle on the Rhine. It was an overcast, windy day, so there were fewer people around than usual. Just a few runners, strollers, and people walking their dogs.

When I reached the edge of the pond, I took my collar out of the bag and gripped it like a discus thrower.

After a couple of practice swings with a breeze blowing in my face, I tossed it out over the pond. However, just as I released it, a gust of wind blew it back, so it splashed down close to shore. Definitely not a good omen. Once a priest, always a priest?

Since the pond was shallow on that side, I took off my shoes and socks, rolled up my pants, and went out and retrieved the collar. I shook it off and brought it back to shore. This time after a couple of more practice swings, I tossed it harder and on a lower trajectory, so it landed farther out.

I sat down on the grass and used my handkerchief to dry my feet. I saw the collar floating in the water like an abandoned raft getting slowly blown back to shore. I put on my socks and shoes, got up, and headed for the exit. When I stopped and looked back one last time, the collar was much closer to shore. What was I afraid of? Did I think it was going to crawl up out of the pond and follow me home? I wondered what people were going to think when they saw it. Clerical suicide? Even though there was no identification on the collar, I wondered if it could come back and haunt me in some way.

That night I had a dream that I was on trial in front of my church world—my father, mother, grandfathers, Bishop Howard, the St. Luke's vestry, the ETS faculty, my seminary classmates, my father's parishioners, and everybody else. The presiding judge, who was wearing a white robe emblazoned with red crosses, was how I imagined the Grand Inquisitor looked when I read *The Brothers Karamazov* in college.

When the judge asked the jury, "Have you reached a verdict about the charges brought against the defendant?" Bishop Howard stood up and said, "Yes, we have, Your Honor."

"What is your verdict?"

"We find Thomas Aaron Reed III guilty on all counts."

The judge banged his gavel so hard it woke me up and kept me awake for the rest of the night until I had to get up and go off to my first day of work.

29

When I got there, my supervisor took me to a table in a large room where many of the secretaries did their work and brought me a stack of printed material to read "to get a feeling for what we do here." So that was how I spent my first day on the job: reading brochures, pamphlets, speeches, and other tributes to the benefits and glories of insurance that the PR Department churned out.

That night when Harry called to remind me about his party, I told him I didn't want him to tell anybody I was a clergyman. I also told him I didn't want him to call me "Rev" anymore.

"Sure, Tommio, if that's the way you want it. I know you have a hang-up about all that stuff."

That Saturday night I went across town to his party, not knowing what to expect. With a week of work under my belt, I was getting used to my new persona. Now when somebody asked me what I did, I could say, "I work in insurance" or "I write publicity."

Harry lived in a large, expensively furnished apartment near the top of one of the high-rise buildings near the East River. His party was what I would have expected a Harry party to be—lots of booze, catered food, and loud music. I ate, drank, danced, and ended up having a better time than I thought I would.

When Harry called the next morning, he said, "There's hope for you yet, Rev."

"I told you not to call me that." I had a hangover and was in no mood for his nonsense.

"Touchy, touchy. But you're absolutely right. We can't be careful enough about that big, dark secret of yours."

"Harry, knock it off. I don't feel good."

"I don't know why not. It looks to me like you're finally starting to live. I didn't even know you could dance. In college all you did was study and bullshit about Dante and Buber. It's good to know that collar of yours didn't squeeze all the juice out of you."

"Thanks."

"See how much fun life can be when you loosen up? If you don't watch out, you might turn into a human being like the rest of us."

He was getting on my nerves the way he used to in college. Him lecturing me about how to live. What a way to start Sunday.

"By the way, I think you turned Gloria on."

"Who's Gloria?"

"Oh, c'mon, you weren't that drunk. She's the one you were bumping and grinding with. She works in my department. She's a real sweetie. She just called to say what a good time she had and thanked me for the party.

She asked about you."

"I hope you didn't . . . "

"Don't be so goddamn uptight! You say you're through with all that church crap, but you certainly don't act like it. Minister, shminister, who the fuck cares? Relax and start living."

I didn't like the way Harry was appointing himself as my mentor. Some mentor.

"All I told her was I know you from college and now you're an insurance flunky."

"Thanks."

"Give her a call. I'll give you her number."

"Harry, I appreciate your interest in my social life, but . . . "

"No buts about it. Why are you living like a monk and hanging out with nuns? Did you take a vow of chastity or something? Give her a call."

"I'll think about it."

"That's your problem. You think too much."

After I got my first paycheck, I decided to pay Harry back for treating me to dinner and inviting me to his party.

"I can't take you out on the town," I told him, "but I can have you over for a drink. How's Saturday for you?"

"That's sweet of you, Tommio, but I'm doing something with Sylvia. You met her at the party. The model. Stylish as Hell."

"Yes, I remember."

"But if you let me bring her, you're on for Saturday. We have a cocktail party early, but we can swing by afterward. How's that sound?"

"Fine. The more the merrier."

"Hey, why not make it a foursome? Do you have somebody you can invite? Maybe one of those hot nuns?" He laughed uproariously.

"Don't worry about me, Harry."

"How about Gloria? Why not ask her? I see her at work every day. I can ask her for you."

My mind was adjusting to the idea of this expanding party. I thought of inviting Mike and Mary Lou, but the mix of Harry and Mike would never do. Mike might never recover.

"How about it, roomie? I'll see if she's free."

I hesitated.

"C'mon, Tommio. You only live once."

"OK."

"That's what I like to hear."

Harry called the next day to say Gloria was free to join us. He told me to call her and tell her what time to come over.

In the meantime, I didn't hear from the bishop. I would have liked at least an acknowledgment that he got my letter and was processing my request, but all I got was an ominous silence.

I could imagine my mother coaching him what to do to keep me in the fold. I had been around the church long enough to know that leaving it wasn't going to be easy. At least Mike's monastery was up front about it. They sent the goon squad. But that wasn't the way of Episcopalian bishops. Their ways were more insidious.

I thought Bishop Howard would probably try to contact me by phone, but the call never came. Instead, on Saturday afternoon when I was on my way out to buy food for the get-together that night, his letter was in my mailbox. I took it straight upstairs and sat down on the couch. I got bad vibes just looking at the envelope addressed to "The Reverend Thomas A. Reed III."

After the introductory niceties, he wrote, "Your comment that 'this may not be the work I want to do for the rest of my life' suggests to me that you have a longer way to go to resolve your vocational goals than you may realize. The tone of your letter was too urgent for me to be convinced that you have allowed yourself sufficient time to think through such an important decision. Can a lifetime of commitment and training be reversed so quickly?"

My spirits sank as I kept reading.

"So, Tom, I'm going to hold off on proceeding with your request until we have had a chance to talk. I would be remiss in my responsibility to you, to myself, to the church, and to your mother if I did not meet with you to discuss this most important matter. If it were simply a matter of a job change, that would be one thing. But at stake here is nothing less than the holy sacrament of ordination, the consequences of which you will live with for the rest of your life and for eternity. I'm certain you'll feel much better about whatever you decide to do after we have had a chance to talk about it.

"I'm very much looking forward to our meeting on Monday, June 8 at 11:00 a.m. as previously agreed. However, if that's not convenient and you wish to make it later (or sooner), call Lydia, and we can reschedule.

In the meantime, your mother and I would love to have you come up and visit us. Please know that you're in our thoughts and prayers.

"Finally, Tom, I want to assure you that in my capacity as your pastor, you have a special place in my personal devotions.

Faithfully your Bishop,

+Clark S. Howard"

Crunch! The church slams down its portcullis on yet another one of its prisoners trying to escape. That's all it takes—one episcopal letter—and suddenly all my escape routes are cut off.

I was in no mood to entertain Harry and his friends, but it was too late to call it off. Besides, it was probably better for me to be with people than spend the night staring at the goldfish and feeling sorry for myself.

30

I invited Gloria to come over early so I could get to know her a little before Harry came and took over the evening. The music at his party had been so loud it was impossible to have a conversation, and the psychedelic lighting even made it hard to see. So, when Gloria arrived, I felt I was meeting her for the first time.

She had frizzy black hair, moist red lips, and a compact, curvaceous figure that must have drawn me to her on Harry's dance floor. When she arrived dressed in a black leather skirt with a silver chain belt, red satin blouse, and fishnet stockings and heels, I hoped she wasn't expecting a real party. I had told Harry to tell his friends to eat before they came because I was only going to serve snacks and drinks.

I took her into the kitchen so we could talk while I finished getting things ready. I had already put out on the counter a large plate for the crackers and the dip and cream cheese I bought at Zabar's. When she asked me what I did before coming to New York, I told her I mostly did social work in Connecticut and left it at that. The ringing of the telephone saved me from having to say more.

"Want me to help with the snacks?" she asked as I headed for the bedroom.

"Yes, please do. There's more stuff in the fridge."

It was Harry calling from his cocktail party to tell me he and Sylvia were on their way. There was so much noise it was hard to hear him. He already sounded drunk, so I told him to eat something, but I don't think he heard me.

Just as I was starting to go back to the kitchen, the phone rang again. I thought about not answering it until I realized it might be Harry calling back to make sure he had the right address.

"Hello?"

"I just read your letter again. Tell me it's not true."

"Mother, I can't talk now. I have company."

"I can't believe you want to do this to me."

"I'm not doing it *to* you. I'm doing it *for* me. Just a minute." I closed the door.

"Mother, I asked you not to call."

"Did you get Clark's letter?"

"Yes, I got it this morning."

"He wants to talk to you."

"Dammit, Mother. Listen to me for a change. I can't talk now. I have company. Good-bye!"

I slammed the phone down and sat there fuming until I collected myself and went back to the kitchen.

"Sorry about that. Harry's on the way with Sylvia." Gloria had put more stuff out on the counter. "Thanks for helping out."

"I'm glad I could." She handed me a cracker with cream cheese on it, then picked one up for herself and ate it. "Hmm, I'm starved. The cream cheese and the dip are really good. And the tiny crackers are nice too."

Tiny crackers? Oh, my God! The box of wafers was on the counter, and she had already put some of the wafers on the plate with the crackers. She picked up a wafer and stared at it.

"I've never seen 'em so small and thin. Where did you get them?"

"I . . . I . . . I got them up where I used to work."

"They're nice. They must be for really little snacks."

"That's right. Just for special occasions."

She turned it over and kept staring at it. "Are they supposed to be good for your health?"

"Very good."

"Kind of like diet crackers?"

"Something like that."

"Trying to keep me nice and thin, eh?" She nudged me, then put the wafer in the dip and ate it.

Harry arrived with Sylvia, the slender, auburn-haired model I remembered from his party. He was as far gone as he had sounded on the phone. When I went back the kitchen, he followed me and made himself a drink while the women sat on the couch in the living room.

"Hey, Tommio," he said, putting his arm around me with the same unctuous camaraderie I remembered from college. "I've got a good one for you." He lowered his voice. "Why don't WASPs have sex standing up?" He was breathing Scotch fumes into my face.

"Have something to eat."

"C'mon, Tommio, you should know this. Why don't WASPs fornicate standing up?"

"Harry, I'm not in the mood for this."

He grinned and leaned closer. "Because it might lead to dancing." He guffawed and kept guffawing until he suddenly stopped. "Hey, ole buddy, you don't look so good. What's the matter?"

"They're giving me a hard time about leaving the church."

He slapped me on the back. "See, they really love you. They don't want you to go. Who knows? Maybe you'll change your mind and go back."

"Very funny."

"Why not? It would be better than the shit job you've got now." He gave me a mock punch. "Maybe they'll give you a second chance."

"Dammit, Harry. I don't want a second chance!"

"OK, OK, don't be so goddamn touchy. Let's have a good time without all this church bullshit." As he turned to go back out to the living room, he muttered, "Jesus H. Christ."

Asshole! I slammed the ice tray back into the freezer and took the plate of snacks out and put it down on the coffee table.

"Oh, nice," said Sylvia.

"The dip is delicious," said Gloria. "See what you think."

Sylvia leaned forward like a graceful flamingo and picked up one of the wafers. She dipped it in the mix and nibbled on it. "Hmm, you're right." She nodded at Gloria and ate the rest of the wafer.

I went back to the kitchen and made myself a stiff scotch on the rocks. With my mother's voice and the words of the bishop's letter buzzing around in my head like trapped mosquitoes, I bolted down the scotch and poured myself some more.

When I went back to the living room, Gloria and Sylvia were on the couch talking about movies while Harry was slumped in the chair on the other side of the table. He was staring at the tray with a funny look on his face. He leaned forward and picked up one of the wafers. He turned it over and looked at both sides.

"Hey, Tommio, what are these little fuckers anyway?"

"They're diet crackers," Gloria said, plunging a more substantial Wheat Thin into the dip. "Aren't they cute?"

"Lovely," purred Sylvia.

Harry held the wafer up to the light and squinted at it. "You can see right through these little pissers. Hey, Tommio, you know what? These are like those goddamn little fish-paste things you used to play with up there in . . . in . . . " He swung his arm around.

"Eat something, Harry."

He put the wafer in his eye like a monocle. "Ya, ya, das ist what it ist. Ein mass cracker!"

Sylvia and Gloria looked at each other.

"Ya, ya," he said, slapping his thigh, "you ran off with the mass crackers to start a black market." He laughed so hard he slid off the chair and hit the floor with a thud. Putting the wafer in his right hand, he crawled with over to the aquarium on all fours like a giant turtle.

Sylvia looked at me. "He wasn't going to say anything. He says you're very sensitive about failing in the ministry."

"I didn't fail!"

Gloria looked puzzled. "You were a minister?"

"He still is," Sylvia said staring at her nails.

Harry stood up and was now breaking the wafer into pieces and dropping them into the aquarium. "Here fishy, fishy, fishy. Eat the holy food, fishy, fishy, fishy."

"You're a minister?" Gloria asked me.

"Not really."

"Yes, he is," Sylvia said.

"I mean I am, but not for much longer."

"He doesn't want anybody to know. He's *very* sensitive." Sylvia put another wafer in the dip and placed it on her tongue.

Harry was making faces and funny, little sounds at the goldfish. "Hey, Tommio, the fish aren't biting. I think they're scared of Jesus."

Gloria picked up a wafer and looked at it suspiciously. "Oh, my God. It is, isn't it?" She put it down quickly as if it were a poisoned mushroom.

"Is what?" I asked her.

"It's what Harry said it is. I don't think this is funny. It's not funny at all."

"He's very strange." Sylvia said rolling her eyes in my direction.

"I'm shocked," Gloria said. "If you really are a man of the cloth, how can you make fun of holy things?"

"These are *not* holy things!" I picked a wafer up and turned it over so she could see both sides. "There's nothing holy about this. Life is holy, children are holy, animals are holy, but this is *not* holy. It's just a sliver of unleavened bread. No more, no less. It's not a holy object to be worshipped."

"Because it hasn't changed?"

"It doesn't change."

"Yes, it does. In our church, it changes into Christ's body."

It never ceased to amaze me how people through the centuries invested wafers with magical powers and paid homage to them with all sorts of genuflections, cross-ings, bowings, and scrapings. In the Middle Ages, peas-ants would pretend to swallow the wafer the priest gave them at mass so they could take it home and put it in their field to make the crops grow better. I had occasionally seen this kind of wafer adoration at my father's church, but I saw much more of it at St. Luke's. I once preached a sermon on "The Idolatry of Wafer Worship."

"Wait here," I told Gloria. "I'll be right back."

I scooped up the rest of the wafers and took them into the bedroom. With Beatrice looking at me from her photo which she inscribed, "To my beloved infidel," I put the wafers on the bureau, then closed the door and locked it.

I don't remember what happened next. All I know is that I was angry and upset. There I was on the brink of finally breaking out of my church prison, and my mother and her lover boy were doing everything they could to block my escape. By then I was intoxicated enough to do something irreverent like recite the consecration prayer, or at least parts of it, that I knew by heart because I had said it hundreds of times in Pineville and Darien. Or maybe I just made the sign of the cross over the wafers. I was certainly angry and drunk enough to do something irreverent and probably did. I just don't remember what it was.

There was loud knocking on the door. "Everybody wants to go," Gloria said. "What are you doing?" She tried to open the door.

"Just a minute." I picked up the wafers, opened the door, and took them out past her into the living room. Harry was on his back under the aquarium with Sylvia on her knees next to him prodding him to get up.

I held out the wafers for Gloria to see. "Here they are. Hocus-pocus. The holy wafers!"

She backed up.

"Oh, for God's sake, Gloria, they're not going to bite you." I dropped one on the rug.

"Don't do that!" She picked it up and put it back in my hand.

"Let's go, Harry," said Sylvia. "I want to go right now. I don't like it here. Get up!"

I took a wafer and tossed it farther out.

"Stop that!"

As Gloria went to pick it up, I took another wafer and gave it a good fling that sent it flying across the room like a tiny white Frisbee. It hit the wall and dropped into the aquarium, scattering the goldfish.

"He's crazy," Sylvia shouted and pounded on Harry's chest. "Get up! Get up! Get up!"

By now I was feeling trapped inside a nightmare of my own making. I took the rest of the wafers to the open window and threw them out into the night air. I flicked off the ones stuck to my hand and watched them flutter down like giant snowflakes.

Harry was now up on one knee. "Why's everybody shouting? What's going on?" He grabbed his head and groaned as Sylvia helped him stand up.

"Hey, Tommio, what do you say? How about one for the road?"

"No! No! No!" Sylvia shouted. "I want to go right now." She pushed him toward the door. Gloria helped get him out into the hallway, then slammed the door so hard it caused waves in the aquarium.

As an eerie silence settled over the apartment, I went to the window and waited for them to come out. Wafers were on the sidewalk and on top of parked cars. Moments later, they emerged and crossed the street with Sylvia and Gloria on each side of Harry propping him up. I watched them make their way down to the corner where they hailed a cab and disappeared into the night.

31

If any night would have been the time to have an Inquisition dream, that would have been it. But it didn't happen, probably because I was too drunk to dream.

When the phone rang the next morning, I didn't answer it because I thought it might be my mother. But when I realized she would never call that early on Sunday, I answered it.

"Hey, Tommio, that was some party you had last night. I mean, if you wanted to serve those little church crackers to have some fun, fine. I thought it was pretty funny myself. But, no, ole Tommio can't just have a normal party like other people. He has to have a black mass!"

"I didn't have a black mass."

"Gloria said you did. Here I bring my friends over to have a good time, so what does ole Rev boy do? He finds the thing that's going to upset them the most and then he does it! You should have heard them going on about it in the cab. Gloria says you're going to Hell."

"I'm going to Hell?"

"That's what she said. Sylvia thinks you must be very bitter about your church to do something like that. She chewed me out as if it was my fault. It's not like her to lose her cool like that."

"I'm glad something got through to her."

"You know what? You're an arrogant son of a bitch! I liked you better before when you at least acted like a nice person. But now the real you is coming out. No wonder your church doesn't want you anymore."

"Are you through?"

"And you know what else?"

"What?"

"I think you drove Gloria away on purpose. She went to parochial school and her uncle is a priest, by the way. Here I fix you up with her, so what do you do? You push her away. All you ever do is stare at your old girlfriend's picture and jerk off. When you're not panting after nuns. You know what I think?"

"What?"

"I think you're hung up on your mother."

"Thank you, Dr. Freud."

"Well, look at what happened. How do you explain it?"

"Gloria rubbed me the wrong way, making such a big fuss about the wafers."

"She made a big fuss?"

"Listen, Harry, I'm against the veneration of objects. So were the prophets. To make anything into a sacred object, whether it's a wafer or a flag or a country or anything else is idolatry."

"Idolatry, schmolatry. Who cares? You're so wrapped up in your goddamn little church world, you think these things are important. Besides, who are you to go around correcting people? That's always been your problem. Back in college, you used to float around above it all like you were the Messiah."

"Are you finished?"

"No, I'm not. You haven't changed one bit. You're still up in the clouds looking down your nose at the rest of us. Well, I've got news for you, Rev boy. The world is the way it is, and people are the way they are. If you don't like it, go find another universe."

Sunlight was streaming in through the window.

"Harry, I'm sorry if I upset your friends, but the truth is you have no idea what happened. You know why? You were passed out. Completely blotto."

"I didn't catch everything."

"That's putting it mildly. Let's get something straight, Harry, and this is the last thing I'm going to say to you this morning. You have a big drinking problem, a big, big, *very* big drinking problem. You had it in college, but now it's much worse. Lay off the booze, Harry, or it's going to kill you. Get some help and get it fast. That's all I have to say."

"Go to Hell!" Then he shouted it again more loudly, "*Go to Hell!*"

Slam.

"Harry?"

When I called him back, I didn't even get his answering machine. He probably unplugged his phone and was pouring himself a drink.

32

The two weeks before my trip to Hartford felt like the calm before the storm. I wrote Bishop Howard to confirm our meeting on June 8, but I hated that I had to go up there and talk to him, especially with my mother hovering around in the background.

The night before my trip, Mike called to wish me luck. "Don't be afraid of him because he's a bishop. He's just a person like anybody else."

"I know, Mike. Thanks. Don't worry about me."

"Do you have to meet with him? Can't you just mail it in?"

"I tried that, but it didn't work. He wants to talk to me in person, so that's what I have to do."

"Well, I guess if I can finesse a monastery, you shouldn't have too much trouble with one lousy Protestant bishop."

"No cracks, Mike. Remember the ecumenical movement."

"I have a favor to ask you though."

"What's that?"

"If you run into two fat Franciscans, let me know. I've got a score to settle with them."

"You're getting to be a real tiger. Working out at the Y is doing wonders for you."

"Yeah, it's great. I feel so much stronger now."

"Well, don't overdo it. We don't want you to get muscle-bound."

He laughed. "That would be nice. Maybe I'll turn into a Greek god."

"That wouldn't surprise me at all."

It was true. I had seen Mike change almost overnight. He had a job, he had a girlfriend, he worked out every day, and he now had a full head of wavy black hair. I sometimes had to remind myself that this was the same scared kid I took in that first night.

"Maybe you can come along as my bodyguard."

"Want me to? I can take the day off."

"Just kidding, Mike. Thanks anyway though. This is something I have to take care of myself. Don't worry. By the time I get back tomorrow night, this will all be history."

"Are you going to do anything dramatic?"

"What do you mean?"

"You know, like what Luther did? Nail something to the cathedral door?"

"Nothing dramatic, Mike. I don't even have a hammer."

"How about bringing me back a souvenir."

I was enjoying this side of Mike that had blossomed since his emancipation. "You're in rare form tonight, Mike. What do you have in mind?"

"You know, something to remember the old days. Like the cross on the altar. Something like that."

"How about the bishop's ring?"

"Yes! That's what I want. The bishop's ring!"

"How am I supposed to get it off his finger without him noticing?"

"I don't know, but if you bring back his ring, I'll treat you to all the beer you can drink for a year."

"I'll see what I can do. But seriously, Mike, don't worry about me. I'll call you when I get back."

"I'm lighting a candle for you."

"Every little bit helps."

I knew he was serious. Catholics like to light candles, so I appreciated the thought.

"But if it goes out while I'm up there, do me a favor."

"What's that?"

"Have Ma send the troops."

33

The next morning on the drive up to Hartford, I thought about how the church I was taking on was the same church that launched the Crusades and the Inquisition, burned witches and heretics, persecuted Jews, and condemned Galileo. That church would have squashed me like an annoying mosquito, but it didn't have that power anymore. Thank God.

When I reached the cathedral, I pulled into the diocesan parking lot and walked through the gate across the Close to the Synod House. Lydia said the bishop was in a meeting but would be back shortly. She handed me an envelope with my name written in a familiar script. Inside was a note from my mother.

My Dearest Tommy,

I'm sorry to have to miss you. I'm at a meeting in Bridgeport. Please tell Lydia, and she'll put you through. I need to talk to you. I love you.

Your Devoted Mother

I decided to get it over with, so Lydia took me to an empty room and put me through.

"Oh, Tom darling, I'm so glad you called. Have you seen Clark?"

"Not yet. He's finishing up a meeting."

"I want you to know I'm praying for you."

"That's very nice, Mother, but what exactly are you praying for?"

"For you. That you'll do the right thing by your family and church."

"Mother, I made up my mind."

"You're very stubborn. Just like your father."

"Oops, I think I hear something. Maybe he's back. I have to go."

"All right, dear. Have a good talk. Just remember I care about you very much. There's still time to change your mind."

"Mother, please."

"Miracles do happen."

"I have to go. 'Bye."

"Good-bye, dearest."

When I went back to the reception area, Lydia said the bishop was on his way and I should wait for him in his office. She opened the door and pointed to the chair next to his desk.

The room was as I remembered it from the time I visited my grandfather when I was four years old: English baronial with dark wood paneling, oil paintings and engravings on the walls, an oriental rug, and a large mahogany desk like the one in my father's study. The stone fireplace on the far side of the room was between two windows that looked out on the Close. The atmosphere was one of Anglican stability and continuity unruffled by passing fads and fancies. The ticking of the clock in the corner reminded me of the time my grandfather lifted me up so I could see the hands up close and touch them through the glass.

I sat down in the chair next to the bishop's desk. The writing area was surrounded by a small clock, a silver cup for pencils and pens, a pearl-handled letter opener, and a small rock I recognized right away. It was the rock my father brought back from the shore of the Sea of Galilee after my parents' trip to the Holy Land before I was born. Later I wondered if I was conceived in the Holy Land. Bethlehem? Nazareth? The rock had always been on my father's desk in his study, but now there it was on the desk of my mother's new husband.

There were also two large photographs. One was a group photo of the bishop, my mother, the bishop's two daughters and their husbands, several children, and an Irish setter. Bishop Howard has his arm around my mother the same way he did in the picture taken in front of the cathedral after his consecration. The other photo showed the bishop and my mother in their bathing suits relaxing on a beach somewhere, probably Hawaii where they went on their honeymoon. They're both aglow with a relaxed, sated look.

Suddenly the door opened, and in came Bishop Howard wearing his charcoal gray suit, purple shirt, and collar. The bronze cross hanging down from his neck reminded me of the cross my grandfather used to wear. Could it be the same one?

"Hello, Tom. It's good to see you again. It's been a while."

We shook hands, and he went behind his desk and sat down.

"So, tell me what's going on. This can't be an easy time for you."

There it was: the church's invitation to lay down one's burden dangled in front of heavy hearts.

"Things are going well, sir."

"Good. You'll be pleased to know that things have settled down up there at St. Luke's. They finally have a new rector."

"Anybody I know?"

"Sam Bassett is his name. He's from Ohio."

"I don't know him."

"I haven't met him, but I've heard only good things about him. He has a lovely wife and two fine children. From everything I've been told, he's very solid. Just what they need up there."

Unlike me who wasn't solid? Bishops aren't famous for their tact, but what do they care? They can't be voted out of office.

"As I told you in my letter, I've had a chance to do a lot of thinking."

"Yes, I want to hear about that."

"And my decision is now firmer than ever. I definitely want to leave the priesthood."

He looked at me closely. "You won't reconsider?"

"I've done all the thinking about this I want to. What I need now is for you to help me get the matter taken care of."

He kept staring at me, no doubt searching for a flicker of indecision. "As you might expect, your mother is very upset."

"She'll survive."

"In fact, she's heartbroken."

"That's understandable. She always expected big things of me church-wise. As you know, she's always been especially interested in the episcopate." I kept looking at him until he broke off eye contact.

"Are you absolutely sure about your decision, Tom?"

"Yes, sir."

"No doubts?"

"None."

He let out a long sigh. "I was hoping I could get you to think about a campus ministry. There's a challenging opening at Trinity College."

"Bishop Howard, I appreciate your interest, and I know you mean well, but I've made up my mind. I would like you to accept that."

He looked down at his folded hands, then leaned forward and put them on the desk. When I saw his ring, I thought of Mike's request and tried not to smile.

"Does this mean you now have questions about your original calling?"

Very clever, these bishops. They aren't chosen to be defenders of the faith for nothing.

"No, it's just that I feel God is calling me in a new direction."

"That's quite possible, of course. It's just that . . . well, I never think of our Lord as someone who changes his mind."

"But he has the right to do that if he wants?"

"Of course. He can do anything he wants to do. That's why he's God."

"He'll be pleased to hear that, sir."

Our eyes locked across the divide. Finding no give, he looked back down at his hands.

"Tom, I don't like losing a good man like you. We can ill afford to lose young clergymen with your background and training. The diocese won't be the same without a Reed around to keep us on track."

"I'm sure you'll do fine. People come and go, but the church keeps plodding along."

"Tom, it's not the church I'm concerned about. It's you. I'm obviously not going to twist your arm. Although if I thought it would do any good, I would. Your mother cares about you a great deal, and I do too. We don't want to see you make a hasty decision that you'll come to regret."

Silence.

"But if this is really what you want to do, I won't stand in your way."

"Thank you. That's good to know."

As if to signal that part of the talk was over, the bishop leaned back in his chair. "So tell me, how's your secular job working out?" In the secret language of clergy, the word "secular" denotes the lower order of work lay people do between Sundays. "Insurance, I believe."

"That's right."

"It must be quite a change from what you're used to. How's it going?"

Bishops are real pros at sniffing out discontent. It's one of the tricks passed on to them through the Apostolic Succession.

"It's very interesting work. There's a new challenge every day."

"Well, if that's what the Holy Spirit wants you to do."

Why do they always have to bring the Holy Spirit in on everything? "Sir, the Holy Spirit will have to speak for himself. I only know how I feel."

The bishop unclasped his hands, then folded them again. "As you probably know, there was a time when the official record didn't distinguish between a voluntary renunciation and a dismissal from the ministry. You would have been treated like anybody else who had been defrocked for reasons of immorality or even criminality. But fortunately, the canons now provide for a voluntary renunciation of the ministry, which I gather is what you're interested in."

"Yes, sir. That's right."

"I have to be honest with you. This will be one of the hardest things I ever had to do. And as I'm sure you know, this is going to break your mother's heart."

Leave my mother out of it, I felt like saying.

"I'll need to submit your name to the Standing Committee, and if it acts favorably on my recommendation, I'll notify you that the renunciation is official."

I didn't like the way this was dragging on.

"I have to honor your request, of course, assuming we're both convinced this is what God wants you to do.

I obviously can't keep you in the church against your will. As your bishop and pastor, all I can do is counsel patience and prayerful deliberation."

"I understand."

"Tom, now that your mother is my wife and you're my stepson, I would like you to call me Clark."

That made me want to stand up and leave, but I didn't have what I wanted. "I appreciate the sentiment, Bishop Howard, but I would like to finish up the matter at hand. I hope you understand."

"Of course. If this is what you really want, and apparently it is, what I need from you now is a statement in writing of your intention to renounce the ministry."

I thought my original letter should have sufficed, but I wasn't in a position to argue. Fortunately, I had anticipated this as a possible delaying tactic, so I brought a backup letter just in case. I took it out of my jacket pocket. "I already wrote it," I said and handed it to him.

"My, my, we are in a hurry."

He glanced at it, then put it down. "I thought you might want more time to tie things up, perhaps conduct a final Holy Communion service or whatever."

"I already did that." I was thinking of the "black mass" Gloria accused me of having.

"Oh, that's nice. At which church?"

"It wasn't at a church."

"Where was it?"

"It was in a private home."

"A house communion?"

"Yes, you could call it that."

"That's the wave of the future, Tom. I'm convinced of it." He looked back down at my letter. "I obviously haven't done a very good job of changing your mind. Your mother's never going to forgive me." He tapped my letter with his finger. "As much as I hate to do it, I'll send this over to the Standing Committee with my recommendation."

"Thank you, sir. I appreciate that. When will that be done?"

"The Standing Committee meets on the third Wednesday of the month, so the next meeting will be in two weeks. Don't worry. I'll take care of it. If and when it's official, I'll let you know."

"If?"

"Relax, Tom. It's highly unlikely the Standing Committee won't act on my recommendation. I realize you want to tie this matter up as soon as possible."

"Yes, sir, I do."

He frowned and looked down at his hands. When he kept his head down and didn't say anything, I sensed something was wrong. Was he worried what my mother's reaction was going to be to his letting me get away? I wasn't prepared for what happened next. He leaned forward, put his folded his hands on the desk, and glared at me without speaking until he finally said in a clam voice, "You're going to Hell."

"Excuse me, sir?"

"You heard me." He then said it much louder, "You're going to Hell!"

The frightful look stayed on his face and didn't change until he finally grinned and chuckled unconvincingly to try to make it look like he was just joking. But I knew he meant what he said the same way he meant what he said in the Inquisition dream when he told the judge I was guilty on all counts. I had no doubt that if there had been a button in front of him that would have sent me straight to Hell, he would have pushed it.

He leaned back in his chair with an idiotic grin on his face as if nothing happened.

"You know, Tom, not so long ago we would have conducted a funeral service here in the cathedral for your soul that had died and gone to Hell."

I knew about that medieval practice that had been an accepted cathedral rite for many years. There were rumors that it was still conducted secretly.

"Do you know who put an end to it?"

"Who?"

"Your grandfather."

"Really?"

"Yes. Thanks to him, we no longer conduct symbolic funerals for defrocked clergy. We're much more civilized about it now. We just shake hands and say goodbye like Anglican gentlemen."

"That sounds much better." I leaned forward in my chair. "Thank you, Bishop Howard, for your help. I don't want to take up any more of your time."

"You don't have to worry about that." He stood up and came around the desk. "C'mon," he said, putting his hand on my shoulder, "I'll walk you out."

"Your mother couldn't be here today," he said in the hallway, "but I know she would love to talk to you. I hope you'll give her a call before you leave."

"I already did. I talked to her before you got here."

"Oh, good, I'm glad."

I was surprised when he walked me across the Close and through the gate into the parking lot.

When we reached my car, he shook my hand. "Good luck and Godspeed, Tom. I wish you all the best for the future. We're going to miss you."

"Thank you, sir."

"You'll of course be in touch with your mother, so this won't be our personal good-bye."

I cringed when he raised his hand to give me his blessing. "The Lord be with you," he said and made the sign of the cross. The gargoyles on the cathedral behind him retched their disapproval.

"God bless, Tom." He shook my hand again.

"Thank you very much, Bishop Howard."

He went back through the gate, but instead of returning to his office, he stayed at the fence and watched me drive to the exit. As I waited for an opening in the traffic, I wondered if he was still preaching about sacrifice and bondage. Before I pulled out, I looked back one last time. He was still behind the fence lost in thought.

34

On the drive back to New York, I kept thrusting my fist into the air and shouting in my best Martin Luther King accent, "Free at last. Free at last. Thank God Almighty, I'm free at last!"

However, my upbeat mood kept getting punctured by the frightful look that was on the bishop's face when he told me I was going to Hell. I couldn't get it out of my mind.

That night I met Mike at the Y, and we went out for a beer to celebrate. I cracked him up with my story about how I wrestled the bishop down to the floor and tried to get the ring off his finger only to have him finally take it off, put it in his mouth, and swallow it! That was the part of the story Mike liked best.

There was nothing subtle about the dream I had that night. I was passing a newsstand on Broadway when I saw my picture, wearing my collar no less, on the front page of the *New York Daily News*. The headline over it in big, black letters was **EX-PRIEST GOES TO HELL.**

I wondered, what was it with all these Hell messages I was getting bombarded with? How was I supposed to not feel guilty about leaving the church when I'm peppered with dreams like that and with the likes of Harry, Gloria, and Bishop Howard telling me I'm going to Hell?

I didn't remember what Dante said about ex-priests. He put lots of clergy and even popes in the Inferno and set aside an entire circle just for heretics. I didn't remember anybody being down there just for leaving the church. That night I went to the *Inferno* to see what he said, if anything, about defrocked priests. I didn't find anything.

Four weeks later I received from the bishop's office what I had been waiting for.

RENUNCIATION OF

THE MINISTRY

Acting in accordance with the provisions of Title IV, Canon 8, Section 1 of the canons of the Protestant Episcopal Church in the United States of America, and having received in writing the voluntary Renunciation of the Ministry from

The Reverend Thomas

Aaron Reed III

and acting with the advice and consent of the clerical members of the Standing Committee of office, and that he is deprived of the right to exercise the gifts and spiritual authority as a Minister of God's word and Sacraments conferred on him in his Ordination.

Clark Stuart Howard

Bishop of Connecticut

That should have been the end of it, but my past wasn't going to let me get away so easily. It was often the little things that turned out to be most irksome like

263

the mail I kept getting addressed to "The Rev. Thomas A. Reed III." No matter how much I tried to get them to take me off their mailing list or at least change the "Rev." to "Mr.," the offending mail kept coming. Whenever I thought I solved the problem, I would get another letter addressed to "The Rev. Thomas A. Reed III."

My most persistent tormentor was the United Ministers' Life and Casualty Insurance Company, which specialized in selling low-cost insurance to clergy. When their mailings kept coming, I realized I had to take more drastic action. The next time I got a "Reverend" letter from them, I put it unopened in a larger envelope and sent it back. On the back of their envelope, I printed in big letters: **REVEREND REED IS DEAD—PLEASE LET HIM REST IN PEACE**. I never heard from them again.

Getting the official renunciation in writing turned out to be the push I needed to take the next step toward what I was now convinced was going to be my true calling. Writing PR material for Universal was a start, and it paid the rent, but I had bigger things in mind. So I signed up for a writing workshop at The New School for Social Research in Greenwich Village where I was living.

However, I still couldn't get away from my past. Everything I wrote tended to be connected to the church in some way or other. The first story I submitted to the workshop was about an Albigensian heretic burned at the stake in southern France (my guilty conscience showing?) while my second submission was a thinly disguised profile of CTS's Dean Parkington. When I went back to fiction, I wrote a story about a love triangle set in medieval England that involved a priest, a monk, and a nun. That got good feedback, so I revised it and ran it by the group again. I made some changes and sent it to *The New Yorker* and several other publications only to have form rejections trickle back to me weeks and months later.

The workshop instructor told me he thought I would have better luck breaking into print if I wrote an article, so I took his advice. Since I was curious about the wires, cables, and pipes under the streets of New York, I did research online and in the library and then sent out query letters about a possible article to *New York Magazine*, *The Village Voice*, and several neighborhood papers. I was pleasantly surprised when *The West Side Spirit*, a Manhattan weekly, expressed interest in the article I proposed, which eventually showed up in its pages as "The World Under the Streets of New York."

In the meantime, Beatrice came back into my life in a sadly unexpected way. In college I put her up on a pedestal the way Dante did his Beatrice, and for years I kept her picture on my bureau even after she got married. When one of my seminary classmates who knew her family sent me an obituary from a Boston paper about the death of her husband in a car accident, I wrote her a letter of condolence, and that summer on my way to New Hampshire I stopped in Boston and had lunch with her.

Seeing and talking to her again stirred up old feelings, especially after she told me she was starting a new job in the fall at an international children's aid foundation in New York and would soon be moving to northern New Jersey with her two sons. By then I had finally taken her picture off my bureau (Harry had been right about something), but when I got back in touch with her, back up it went.

"I'm not surprised you left the church," she told me at lunch. "As you know, I was never convinced you were on the right track with that. But it was obviously something you had to find out on your own."

"You were right, but I guess I had to find that out myself by drinking the cup of bitterness to the dregs." I stopped myself. "My God, I sound like Jesus."

She laughed. "Well, you always had a bit of a messianic streak, and I hope you still do. That's a good thing for a writer to have."

That fall after she moved to New Jersey and began her job, we would occasionally have lunch in the city, and once we went to a Broadway show. When I gave her a copy of my "Underground" article, she said, "Good for you. You're on your way. With all those Dante papers you wrote in school, you're obviously interested in what's going on down there."

35

One Saturday afternoon when I was browsing through Village Used Books down the street from where I lived, I came across Jules Verne's *Journey to the Center of the Earth*, a translation of his *Voyage au Centre de la Terre* published in France in 1864. It's a novel about a German professor and his nephew who go to Iceland and with the help of a local guide descend through "volcanic tubes" down into the interior of the earth. As I leafed through it, I thought, My, my, what an interesting coincidence that is! First Edward, now Jules Verne. Something was definitely going on, and all the signs were pointing in the same direction—*down*! I bought the book and read it that weekend.

It's the story of the adventures of the professor and his nephew down there coming across antediluvian bones, prehistoric animals, and a vast underground ocean teeming with ancient fish long thought to be extinct. The only human being down there is a mute giant who tends an animal herd. The novel ends with the professor and his nephew getting trapped and having to blast their way through solid granite, an explosion that sends them up one of the tubes and deposits them on the island of Stromboli near Sicily. They return to Germany where they're greeted as heroes.

Edward had told me at the end of his visit that that he was going to come back to see how I was doing with his invitation, but when weeks passed without that happening, I wondered if he and his invitation were for real and that maybe he didn't visit me. I just imagined he did. Or maybe the powers that be down there changed their minds about inviting me. When I searched my computer for the e-mail sent in his name that started all this off, I couldn't find it. Strange.

I also wondered about the timing of his visit. It was only after I started having Hell/Inquisition-type dreams and Bishop Howard told me I was going to Hell that Edward showed up. That was strange timing, *very* strange. Was I being set up, lured into some kind of trap? Maybe Edward was being used without his knowing it? I tried not to let my suspicions have the final word. I respected Edward and trusted him totally. As I waited for him to return, I tried not to be impatient. The only way to find out if his invitation was for real was to hang in there and go along with it. Not fight it, not retreat, not run away.

A few weeks later when he finally came back and I told him right away I accepted his invitation, his face lit up and he brought his hands together as if clapping.

"*Eccellente*, Thomas," he said beaming. "You made the right decision. I knew you would. This is going to be a great adventure for both of us. *Another* great adventure I should say."

"Will I be able to write about it when I get back, assuming it really happens? Or will I be sworn to secrecy?" I was already thinking about my book.

"I doubt that. The whole point of the visitors' program, as I understand it, is to get people who go down there to come back up here and spread the word. My guess is they'll be only too happy to have you write about your visit. That may be why they chose you."

"I never forgot what you told me at St. George's at the end of our last class about my maybe being the next Dante someday. Do you remember that?"

"I remember saying something to that effect, but now that you'll actually be going down there, it's not such a far-fetched idea. If you write about it when you come back, how can you not be the new Dante? Why not? If not you, who?"

We both laughed.

Before he left, Edward told me somebody by the name of Rinaldo would be contacting me about the travel arrangements, and sure enough, a couple of nights later, he called from Toronto where he was on family business (export-import). He told me I was booked on the night flight to Florence from Kennedy on the next Thursday.

"Your ticket will be waiting for you at the Alitalia counter. Make sure you bring your passport."

I was surprised he knew I had one. I wrote down the flight information on the pad I planned to take with me.

"It's a roundtrip ticket, I assume."

"No, it's actually one-way."

"One-way? Why? Won't I be coming back?"

"Of course, you'll be coming back. But as I understand it, you'll be coming back another way."

"What other way?"

"Thomas, I'm just the messenger. I don't have all the answers."

He said the first syllable of my name the way the word "tome" is pronounced.

One-way ticket to Hell? Edward or no Edward, I didn't like the sound of that at all. Now I was getting cold feet, very cold feet. What began as something of a lark was getting serious, too serious.

"Don't worry," he said. "You'll be in good hands. My cousin Carlo will pick you up at the airport and take you to Monteveggio." He explained that Monteveggio was the village in Tuscany where local tradition claims Dante began his descent into the Inferno. "That's where I was born. My family's from there."

When I asked him what I should bring, he told me just to bring myself. "That's all you'll need."

"Nothing else?"

"Just the clothes you'll be wearing, your passport, and a little pocket money. No luggage. No pajamas. No shaving kit. No toothbrush. Nothing except yourself. Oh . . . and the password."

"Password?"

"I doubt that you'll need it, but I'll give it to you just in case. It's *viaggio*."

"Let me write that down. V-I-A-G-I-O."

"Two Gs. V-I-A-G-G-I-O. It means 'journey.'"

"Got it."

"That's it, Thomas. Have a good trip. *Buon viaggio*."

PART 2

WELCOME TO THE UNDERWORLD

36

What in God's name was I thinking? How did I let myself get sucked into this trap? Am I really going to Hell like Bishop Howard said I was? Those were some of the questions I asked myself on the flight to Florence. I wanted to get some sleep for the full day ahead of me, but I was too keyed up to relax. I kept telling myself I could always change my mind in Italy. If this so-called *viaggio* turns out to be a hoax after all, at least I'll be able to spend the weekend in Florence soaking up the atmosphere of Dante's hometown. It was something I had always wanted to do.

However, my fantasy about spending a weekend in Florence strolling around the Piazza della Repubblica and visiting the Uffizi Gallery kept getting uncut by my suspicion that this so-called *viaggio* wasn't a hoax at all, but a cleverly orchestrated plot to get me down to Hell. I kept remembering my last meeting with Bishop Howard when as soon as I told him I was definitely leaving the priesthood and wasn't changing my mind, he glared at me ferociously and told me in no uncertain terms I was going to Hell. He tried to turn it into a joke, but I knew he meant what he said. And now there I was flying over the Atlantic Ocean going to where he told me I was going.

When nobody met me at the airport, I decided it really was a hoax after all. Although I felt like a damned fool for going along with it this far, I was relieved I didn't have to go along with whatever it was. I came out of customs wondering what I should do now when a short, partially bald man with heavily lidded eyes came up to me and asked me if I was Thomas Reed. He pronounced Thomas the same way Rinaldo did, but he put even more "tome" in it.

When I nodded, he told me he was Carlo, Rinaldo's cousin. "I'm your driver."

"*Buon giorno*," I said to him and shook his hand. Was this *viaggio* for real after all?

My saying *buon giorno* must have made him think I knew more Italian than I did because on the drive to Monteveggio he did the talking while I looked out the window at the Tuscan countryside. I would look over at him every so often and nod to let him know I was interested in what he was saying even though I didn't know what it was. The whole time I wished I was someplace else where I could catch up on the sleep I didn't get on the plane.

After the ride came to a merciful end in Monteveggio in front of the village church, Carlo took me to a small house behind it and knocked on the side door. A bent, wizened woman let us in and went off and came back with an old man dressed in a long-sleeved, black shirt and baggy trousers. He wasn't wearing a collar, so I didn't know if he was the priest or the sexton or somebody else. Carlo had a brief conversation with him, then said good-bye and left.

The old man, who knew even less English than Carlo, went off and came back with a ring of keys. I followed him out past the church to the road, which we walked along until we turned down a lane, which took us to a shop with a sign in front that said: "Entrance to Dante's Inferno—Souvenirs for Sale." Why was he taking me there? Did he want me to buy something?

The shop was full of Dante memorabilia—coffee mugs, postcards, buttons, posters, and T-shirts with messages like "Somebody told me to go to Hell—and I did!" and "Hell—it ain't as bad as you think." The shirt hanging in the corner had this written on it: "I went to Hell and all I got was this lousy T-shirt." The photos on the walls of tourists standing in front of a bolted door all had the same caption at the bottom: "Entrance to Dante's Inferno." I came all the way to Italy for this?

The old man rang the bell on the counter, but when nobody came, he rang it again.

When I asked him, "Where's the entrance?" all I got was a blank stare. I knew the Italian words for "where" and "entrance," so I asked him, *"Dov'e l'ingresso?"*

He motioned me over to the window and pointed at the hut with the bolted door where tourists paid to have their picture taken.

A tall, thin man with a pinched face came in from the back. "Welcome to our store," he said to me. "We have many wonderful gifts to remind you of your visit."

The old man took him aside, and they had a whispered conversation. The tall man kept looking at me as if trying to decide what to make of me.

"I've been in communication with Rinaldo," I told him. "He arranged the flight, and his cousin brought me here."

He didn't look convinced.

"Rinaldo gave me a password."

"What is it?"

"*Viaggio.*"

He smiled and shook my hand. "Welcome. My name is Enrico. We were expecting you, but I wanted to make sure."

Now it was my turn to be suspicious. He obviously made his living off the claim that the entrance to Dante's Inferno was on his property. I wondered if he was going to try to use me to promote his business in some way.

Since I was by myself and nobody knew where I was, I felt vulnerable. I could be robbed, although without luggage, I wasn't a promising target. Still, I had some American money, my passport, and a credit card.

"I'm supposed to meet Edward," I told him. "Father Edward. He used to be my teacher. He's the one who contacted me."

"I don't know anything about that. All I know is where I'm supposed to take you."

The photo on the wall above us showed a goofy young couple holding hands in front of the entrance. I pointed at it. "Is that where I'm going?"

"No, no. That's for tourists. The real entrance is someplace else. I'll take you there." He looked at his watch. "Are you hungry?"

I told him I had breakfast on the plane.

"You don't want a last meal?"

Last meal? I didn't like the sound of that at all. I shook my head no.

"Time to go then."

After the old man gave him the ring of keys and left, Enrico went to the back of the shop and came back with a flashlight. He took me out to the road, but instead of turning back toward the church, we went the other way. It was an overcast day, and it was getting darker. By the time we reached the cemetery, it was starting to rain. I followed him down a path past gravestones, mausoleums, stone crosses, and wilted flowers until we turned off the path and went through a grove of olive trees to a one-storied brick building.

He unlocked the front door with one of the keys, and I followed him into a large, dimly lit room full of lawn mowers, shovels, rakes, boxes, barrels, and other maintenance equipment. We crossed the room to stairs and went down to another locked door. He had me hold the flashlight while he tried different keys. When he found the right one, he pulled on the handle, but nothing happened. He kicked the bottom of the door and pulled the handle some more, but the door still didn't budge.

More kicking and pulling by both of us forced the door open and let us go into an even darker room where the air was stifling. He used the flashlight to take us deeper into the room, then stopped.

"This is where I'm supposed to leave you."

"Are you sure?"

He coughed and shined the light around at the grime, mildew, and cobwebs.

"Yes, this is it," he said as if he couldn't quite believe it himself. "You're very brave. It's been a long time since anybody tried to go down there. The last one . . . "

"What about the last one?"

"It was many years ago. He never came back. Later they found a corpse. They think it was his."

Oh, great, just what I wanted to hear. The light from his flashlight was giving his face a ghostly pallor.

By now, I was angry at myself for letting him bring me down to this dark, smelly basement. I knew Edward would never deceive me on purpose, but I couldn't stop myself from thinking that he was being used and didn't know it. I didn't like thinking that way, but I couldn't help it.

Enrico coughed again. "I have to go now, but I'll try to come back in case there was a wrong communication."

"Try?"

"Don't worry, I'll come back. I don't want you to get stuck down here and starve to death."

"When am I supposed to be picked up?"

"I don't know. All I know is this is where I'm supposed to leave you. I'll come back later to see if you're still here."

As I watched him go back to the door, I felt an urge to rush past him and get there first. But I didn't budge. I couldn't. I promised Edward. Besides, by now I was too invested in this so-called *viaggio* not to see it through to . . . to . . . to what?

When Enrico reached the door, he turned and looked back. "Good luck, Thomas. I'm glad I'm not going where you're going. *Buon viaggio.*" He stepped through the door and pushed it shut and locked it.

Bastard! Couldn't he at least leave the door open so I can breathe? Why did he lock it? To keep me from escaping?

I quickly made my way through the darkness toward the door, bumping into things on the way. When I reached the wall, I used my fingers to find the door. I pounded on it and shouted, but there was only silence. Couldn't he at least leave me the flashlight?

I felt like a complete jerk. Why did I let this total stranger bring me down here to this wretched dungeon? What in the world was I thinking? I wanted to cry.

As I groped my way back to where I had been, I heard scratching. Could it be a rat? Or two? Or more? To scare away whatever it was, I clapped my hands and shouted. I heard scurrying, then silence. By then, I was feeling so tired and defeated I was tempted to lie down on the slimy floor, rats or no rats.

I heard what sounded like moaning in the distance. Maybe the cries of dead souls seeping up from below? I thought of the sign over the gate of Dante's Inferno: *Abandon all hope, you who enter here.* Thanks to Edward, I also knew it in Italian: *Lasciate ogne speranza, voi ch'intrate.*

I had not prayed spontaneously since senior year in seminary when I got the letter from St. George's informing me that Edward died. The only prayers out of my mouth since then were the canned prayers I said at church services. But this was a matter of life and death, and I was desperate. If there really was somebody up there minding the store, I needed him or her to come to my rescue right away.

Almighty and Merciful God, if you hear this heartfelt prayer of your not-so-faithful servant, please come as soon as possible and deliver me from this hellhole. This is an emergency. Amen.

37

Trapped in that putrid hellhole with my prayer unanswered, I abandoned all hope as Dante's sign over the entrance to the Inferno instructed us to do. When I heard scraping and tapping coming from the other side of the basement, I wondered if my prayer really was being answered now. However, there wasn't anything welcoming about the shaft of light that suddenly came through a doorway on the other side of the basement. It was like I was watching a horror movie and the monster was about to push his way in.

"Thomas Reed?" said a voice. It was the same pronunciation of my name I was getting used to. "Thomas Reed, are you there?"

I saw a ghostly figure in the doorway, but I didn't answer him until I decided that if I didn't speak up, I might never get out of that miserable dungeon.

"Here I am," I shouted.

"I don't have a light, so you have to come over here by yourself."

I made my way through the clutter toward the door trying not to bump into anything. The smell at that end of the basement was even worse. Dead rats?

At first, the face of the figure in the doorway was blurry, but as I got closer, I saw he had what seemed to be eyes and fuzz on his head. His garment had a grayish hue like Edward's, but it also had legs and sleeves that made it look more like a jumpsuit than a robe.

When I approached the door, he moved back and motioned me to enter. Knowing I would be crossing the Rubicon and there would be no retreating, all my doubts came rushing back. Were Edward's visits what they seemed to be? Maybe they knew how to impersonate him. I heard yet again Bishop Howard telling me I was going to Hell, but this time I heard my mother's voice blending in with his in a macabre duet of damnation. The figure motioned to me again, but I didn't move.

Wondering what kind of reaction it would get, I said, "*Viaggio.*"

He stared at me.

"*Viaggio,*" I said again.

"Journey. Yes. Exciting journey." He looked amused. "My name is Guido. We're expecting you. Don't be afraid."

"Where's Edward? Father Edward. He's the one who got me to come here."

"You'll see him later."

That made me feel better. At least he seemed to know who he was.

"Where is he?"

"I'll take you there when the time comes."

When I finally got up my nerve and stepped through the door, he said, "Welcome to the Underworld."

I was now in what looked like the end of a tunnel cut into solid rock. The space had an amber glow that took my eyes a while to get used to. I looked at my watch that I had set to Italian time on the plane. Twelve noon. Amazing! That was the exact time Dante entered the Inferno on Good Friday in 1300. Was this really the beginning of the weekend Edward said it was going to be? "In and out just like Dante" he had said.

"Congratulations, Thomas. You made it. Follow me."

I quickly discovered the disadvantage of being a flesh-and-blood person down there as Guido glided effortlessly down the tunnel while I had to hurry to keep up with him. The cracks, fissures, and vents on the walls suggested that the tunnel might have once been used as a supply tunnel. We kept moving down the long incline—down, down, down.

"Are you a ghost?" I asked as I tried to keep up with him.

"You could say so. We're called all sorts of things—spirits, shades, souls, ghosts. We prefer spirits. This will all be explained later."

"That's what Edward is, right? A spirit?"

"That's right. I'll show you where we woke him up when we come to it."

He put his hand up and stopped. I was walking so fast I bumped into him. It was a soft, squishy bump, but it definitely was a bump. Spirits apparently have a physical core.

Guido motioned me to follow him into an alcove off the tunnel. Once inside, he had me stand back from the opening but didn't say why. After a long silence, he went to the opening and looked out.

"Seems OK," he said, but he had us stay there longer. When he finally told me it was time to go, I followed him back out into the tunnel.

"What was that all about?"

"Well," he said in barely a whisper, "you're already famous down here, but . . . "

"But what?"

"But not everybody's happy about it."

"What's that supposed to mean?"

He didn't answer me.

"Edward gave me the impression I would be welcome and safe down here."

"Don't worry. We'll make sure you're safe and you're certainly welcome."

"What are you making sure I'm safe from?"

He obviously didn't want to talk about it, or maybe he just didn't think he should.

"Who are you protecting me from?"

"The Crusaders."

"Who are they?

"They used to be in charge. It's a long story that I can't go into now. Save your questions for the orientation. I probably shouldn't have said this much. But you have a right to know."

"Right to know what?"

"That the Crusaders are upset that we chose you to be the first visitor."

"I'm the first visitor?"

"That you are."

"Why are they upset?"

"They're upset because you're . . . how do you say it? Deflowered."

"Deflowered?"

"A priest who leaves his church. De-de-"

"Defrocked?"

"That's it. Defrocked. Kicked out."

"I wasn't kicked out. I left voluntarily."

Guido had picked up the pace again, so I was hurrying to keep up.

"Did you know I left the church when you chose me to come down here?"

"We knew, but we had no idea the Crusaders were going to have apoplexy about it. Anyway, once the decision was made, Edward got his first assignment—to go and fetch you. And here you are!" He smiled at me for the first time.

I didn't like this cloud of Crusader disapproval hanging over me. "If I'd known I wasn't going to be welcome, I wouldn't have come down here."

"Thomas, you're more than welcome. We're grateful you came. In our eyes, you're a hero. Don't take it personally. The Crusaders are against just about everything we do. After they found out we chose you, they looked into your background and submitted a complaint to the Council. They claim you're a heretic."

"A heretic? Just for leaving the church?"

"That's how they think. They're looking for any way they can to discredit our visitors program before it even starts. They never liked the idea."

"Was that what our stopping back there was about?"

"That's right. I didn't want to take any chances. That's all we would need—to have something bad happen to our first visitor. Try not to be upset. I probably shouldn't have told you. I'm not going to say anymore."

We came to a ramp that took us down to a lower level where the tunnel was wider and had more side entrances and feeder tunnels.

"Is this really Hell? It certainly doesn't look like it. So far, it's just been empty tunnels."

"We're in the administrative area."

"Where's Hell?"

"Big, bad Hell? Oh, it's out there, I assure you. We're on the rim, and the Crusaders are on the rim on the other side. While you're down here, you won't actually ever be *in* Hell, or at least you shouldn't be. I don't know what you were expecting, but you're not going to be able to slog through it the way Dante did."

"Will I at least get to see it?" I was already thinking about the book I wanted to write.

Guido gave me a funny look. "Thomas, it's not something you want to see, believe me."

"Edward said my father's down here. Is that true?"

"I don't know anything about that."

"He said my father wasn't in Hell but was with good people somewhere."

"When we go to the Tech Room and I log you in, I'll see what I can find out."

He slowed down as we approached a platform in the middle of the tunnel that had a spongy black mattress on top of it. He stopped and pointed. "This is what we call our Lazarus couch. It's where we wake people up from the dead."

"Like Edward?"

"Like Edward. It's been seeing a lot of traffic recently because of the conference."

"Edward mentioned that. Famous thinkers from history, something like that?"

"That's right. It's time to take you to the Tech Room. Let's go."

38

I half-jogged down a dim corridor behind Guido and followed him into a large room filled with computers, monitors, screens, panels, and state-of-the-art hi-tech equipment set up on aluminum and Formica tables and counters. Wires, tubes, and pulleys crossed the room and hung down from the ceiling. Edward had mentioned renovations, but I wasn't prepared for this.

"This is the Tech Room," Guido said. "It's how we keep track of everything, or at least try to. We installed the system during the renovation, but the human population up there keeps expanding so fast, it's hard to keep up." He waved me over to a large computer and turned it on. "It's time to log you in.

Every visitor who comes down here will have to be logged in."

He pulled out the keyboard and started typing, but then he stopped and stared.

"What's happening?"

"I'm looking at your bio." He leaned closer to the screen. "Church family. Grew up in your father's parish. Interest in Dante. Hmm, this is interesting."

"What?"

"Mother problem."

"I have a mother problem?" I wondered how that got into their database. My therapy sessions were sup-posed to be confidential.

"That's what it says. Not true?"

"Well, there's a grain of truth in it, I guess. More than a grain."

"Let's see what else we have. St. George's Academy. That's where Father Edward introduced you to Dante. College. Seminary. Seven years in the priest-hood. Defrocked."

"Defrocked? Why do they use that word? It's misleading."

"Not right?"

"As I told you, I resigned voluntarily. I wasn't defrocked. Besides, defrocked sounds so . . . so . . . I don't know, it sounds so tacky."

"That's something else I'll have the fact checkers look into."

He turned back to the screen. "Let's see, after you left your church, you got a job with an insurance com-pany in New York. And that's where you're working now?"

"That's right."

"This is interesting. It says you're a writer."

"My job is to write promotional material, but I'm trying to branch out." I took the pad out of my pocket and showed it to him. "When I get back, I want to write about this—what do I call it? Visit? Journey? *Viaggio*? The chance to write about it was what convinced me to come down here. That plus the possibility of seeing my father. What's the story on him? Have you finished logging me in yet?"

"Almost. If your father's down here, he's probably in a Purgatory precinct."

"What's that?"

"It's a lot better than being in Hell, I can tell you that. This will all be explained later, so save your questions." He hit some more keys. "That does it. You're logged in. Let's see what we can find out about your father. What's his full name?"

"Same as mine. Thomas Aaron Reed. But he's Junior. I'm the Third."

"Let me enter that. Thomas Aaron Reed." He typed it in and watched the flashings on the screen.

"Thomas Aaron Reed. Dean of the Cambridge Theological Seminary. He would be your grandfather?"

"That's right."

"He was down here."

"Are you serious?"

"Not for long. In and out. Clean as a whistle."

There were more flashings on the screen.

"My, my, you really do come from a church family."

"That's the story of my life."

"I see your other grandfather was a bishop. Very impressive. He was down here too."

"Really? In Hell?"

Guido laughed. "No, no, he was also in a Purgatory precinct, but . . . "

"But what?"

"He was down here longer than your other grandfather."

"What's that supposed to mean?"

Guido kept staring at the screen. "Oops!"

"What do you mean 'Oops'?"

"Some financial funny business."

"Like what?"

"Nothing serious. Mostly creative financial record keeping and padded expense accounts. Small potatoes. Nothing to get him sent to Hell with the big boys. Ah, here he is. Your father. I found him."

"Good. I assume he's not in the Hell part of Hell. Edward said he wasn't."

"I can tell from his FS he's not. It's too high."

"What's FS?"

"Final Score. It's the score people have when they come down here. That's how we know what to do with them and how long to keep them." He typed something more. "No, your father's definitely not in Hell. He's probably in one of the Purgatory precincts like your grandfathers were. Although he could be over with the Crusaders."

"I hope not. He doesn't know I left the church. That's one of the reasons I'm here. I want to tell him some things I never got to tell him while he was alive. I don't want the Crusaders to be the ones to tell him his son is a defrocked heretic."

"That's understandable."

"If I visit him, will I be able to talk to him like I'm talking to you now?"

"I don't see why not."

"Will I be allowed to visit him?"

"That you'll have to take up with Umberto. He does the scheduling."

"Who's Umberto?"

"He's the Guest Master. You'll meet him at the orientation."

"Can you put in a good word for me before that? It's very important that I see my father."

"Well, since you're our trailblazer, why not? I'll ask him."

"When can you ask him? A weekend's not a lot of time. I don't want to go back without talking to him."

"Let me see if I can reach him now."

He moved away, talked to his hand, and listened. When he came back, he said, "Umberto says he'll look into it."

"What does that mean?"

"He says he'll try to see if he can find somebody to take you to your father when there's a break in the schedule. But he wants you to promise him you won't tell anybody. The last thing he wants is to have people come down here thinking they can visit their dead relatives. Does he have your word on that? That you won't tell anybody?"

"He has my word."

"Good. I'll let him know."

"Where *is* my father, by the way? Can you at least tell me that much? I'll feel much better if I know."

"That's information I'm not supposed to give out, but for you I'll make an exception. But promise me you won't tell anybody I told you."

"I promise."

He turned back to the computer. "Let's see what I can find out. The Purgatory precinct file uses a different set of passwords, so bear with me."

After more typing and waiting, he said, "Ah, here he is. Your father's in a precinct in the northern part of the southwest quadrant. Precinct 63. Not exactly walking distance, but we can take you there when the time comes. Oh my, this is interesting."

"What?"

"Your father."

"What about my father?"

"I probably shouldn't tell you."

"Tell me."

"He's coming to the end of his stay."

"What does that mean?"

"It means he's scheduled to be released. It could happen at any time."

"What do you mean 'released'? Released to what?"

"Released to . . . you know, to his eternal rest."

"My father's going to be terminated? Is that what you're telling me?"

"That's one way of putting it. He served his time, so now it's time for him to take the Big Nap. It's not really a nap, of course, because he won't wake up."

"What kind of reward is that? To come down here only to be terminated. Who decides these things anyway? Who decided it's time for my father to stop existing?"

"No one person decides, Thomas. These are policies that have been in place forever. If you're asking me if they need to be reviewed, reformed, even scrapped, the answer is yes. The Purgatory problem is right up there at the top of the list of things that need to be taken care of. Everybody agrees about that. You'll probably hear more about that at the orientation. Let me see how we're doing with that."

He moved away and talked to his hand again, then came back. "The California ladies haven't gotten here yet. They're having trouble with the living one, your counterpart. She doesn't want to come down here. I can't imagine why." He smiled.

He typed some more, then hit the keyboard with a flourish. "Finito! That's it, Thomas. Let's go find your friend.

39

We continued down the hallway, turned left into a narrow side tunnel, and went into a room with a long window on one side. All that I could see out of it was mist and lots of it. At the far end of the window was what looked like a telescope on a tripod. The wall opposite the window was gray with dark-brown vertical beams. The only piece of furniture in the room was a tan cushioned chair set off to the side. I wondered if it was there for me.

"Is this where I'm supposed to meet Edward?"

Guido nodded, then looked past me and smiled. "Speak of the devil. Here he is. The man of the hour. Ta-da!"

I turned and there he was—Edward! I felt a surge of relief. He looked like he looked in New York and even seemed to be wearing the same robe.

"My dear Thomas, it's wonderful to see you again. I wanted to meet you at the entrance, but they had other ideas."

"Gentlemen, while you two get reacquainted, I have to take care of something. I'll be right back. Don't go anywhere."

Poof! He was gone. I was getting used to the way spirits don't just leave—they vanish. I felt so much better having Edward there. I didn't feel alone anymore.

"You were right about my father," I told him. "He's down here, and they're maybe going to let me visit him."

"Oh, good. I would have felt bad if I misled you about that."

"I did get a big surprise though." I told him about what happened in the tunnel and Guido telling me the

Crusaders were against my being there. "Do you know anything about that?"

"I didn't when I talked to you, but I know more now. I've been assured you'll be safe."

"Well, I don't feel safe knowing they think I'm a heretic. We know what they do to heretics."

"Believe me, Thomas, if I thought there was any chance you might be in danger, I would have rushed right back up there and told you to stay put."

Guido came back. "I trust you two are having a good reunion."

Behind him was an imposing figure with large, searching eyes. He was wearing the same gray robe Guido was wearing, but his had more decorative trim. He looked overweight if it's possible for a spirit to be overweight.

"This is Umberto," Guido said.

"Hello, gentlemen. Good to have you back, Edward, and welcome to you, Thomas. The other visitors we're expecting haven't arrived yet, so it looks like we'll have to start without them. I hope you're both ready for the orientation I'm now going to inflict on you. You're my first victims, so bear with me." He nodded at Guido, who went back to a computer built into the wall.

Umberto said, "The first thing I'm going to do is show you Hell." He motioned us over to the window where all there was to see was a sea of soupy, gray mist. He spread his arms. "Feast your eyes, my friends. This is our panoramic view of Hell. Isn't it beautiful?"

Guido laughed.

"Right here I have my very own Berchtesgaden." Umberto spread his arms again.

I thought to myself, that's a strange thing to say. Berchtesgaden was Hitler's lair in the Bavarian Alps. Did Umberto fancy himself as the Hitler of Hell, even in jest? I could picture him as the Great Dictator in the Charlie Chaplain film, spinning the globe on his finger, but I couldn't picture him as Hitler. He was too good-natured. I looked at Edward and wondered what he was thinking.

Umberto pointed at the window. "You're no doubt disappointed you can't see anything because of the mist, but be glad, my friends. In the words of T. S. Eliot, 'Human kind can't bear too much reality.' To look directly at what's out there would be like looking at the sun. If you do, you'll go blind. The last thing we want our visitors program to do is upset people so they'll go back and tell everybody to stay away."

The mist is there is to hide Hell? Is that what he's saying? If people see it, they'll go blind? That's hard to believe. The *Inferno*'s most graphic images were forever imprinted on my memory like being boiled alive in blood and being buried alive upside down in a hole with your feet on fire. Yet I survived, and my eyesight is fine. Granted it's strong stuff, but I never thought of it as blinding. Dante doesn't blind people. He makes them see more clearly.

I looked at the telescope at the end of the window and figured it must be able to see something. Otherwise it wouldn't be there. I pointed at it and asked Umberto, "What's that?"

He smiled at Guido. "That's our miracle instrument that lets us see the mist magnified."

They both laughed.

Having Hell out there in the mist somewhere made me think of "Dover Beach," Matthew Arnold's poem about a world with "neither joy, nor love, nor light, nor certitude, nor peace, nor help for pain." The poem's final image is of a "darkling plain swept with confused alarms of struggle and flight, where ignorant armies clash by night." The mist was too thick for me to see any "ignorant armies," but I could imagine them out there somewhere.

"So there you have it, my friends. The vast graveyard of human hopes and dreams." Umberto let us stay at the window a little longer before he took us back to the center of the room. He pointed at the chair. "Thomas, feel free to sit down."

After all the standing and walking I had been doing, I was tempted, but I would be the only one sitting, so I stayed on my feet.

"First of all," Umberto said, "I want to thank both of you for being here. There are more visitors on the way, and hopefully there will be many more after that, but you're in the vanguard. No, let me correct that. You *are* the vanguard. You're Marco Polo, Columbus, and Neil Armstrong all rolled up into one."

His smile convinced me his gratitude was genuine.

"I had hoped the California ladies would be here by now, but since they aren't, let's begin." He pointed at the screen on the wall, then nodded at Guido. The light dimmed, and the word **Heaven** flashed up on the screen.

"As you know, Heaven is something millions of people have believed in through the centuries and many still do. But the truth is, my friends, are you ready for this?" He paused for dramatic effect.

"Heaven doesn't exist."

Edward and I looked at each other.

"That's right, gentlemen. Let it sink in. Heaven is kaput. Finis. Finito. Many were called to the heavenly banquet, but few came. So few that Heaven ended up like a big, deserted warehouse. Underused, to put it mildly. That's why it had to be shut down. Lack of attendance. Just as well, I say. People shouldn't have to be bribed to live loving, productive lives. Virtue should be its own reward."

I raised my hand as if I were back in school. Umberto called on me.

"What happened to the all people who were in Heaven?"

"Good question, Thomas. Let me give credit where credit is due." He pointed at the window. "When it came time to shut down Heaven, the Crusaders across the way agreed to take them in. *All* of them. I commend them for doing that. So to answer your question, everybody who used to be in Heaven is now in the Crusaders' care. It's really quite amazing. Not a single one of them was sent to the Big Nap. It was an impressive act of charity on their part. Whatever else one can say about them, they do take care of their own."

"And only their own," Guido said.

Umberto smiled. "A little editorial comment from the peanut gallery. What Guido's getting at, and he's right, is that while the Crusaders take care of their own, their compassion for others is limited, to put it mildly. It only extends to Christians in good standing and only to their kind of Christians. No salvation outside the church. *Their* church." He looked at the window again. "They're intolerant of pretty much everybody else and always have been—Jews, agnostics, unbelievers, atheists, apostates, heretics. The list of everybody they disapprove of is very long."

"Like me," I said.

When the three of them turned and looked at me at the same time, I imagined their eyes saying, *"Defrocked! defrocked! defrocked!"* Obviously my guilty conscience was being activated down there, and the Crusader disapproval was only making it worse. Whatever else my so-called *viaggio* accomplished, I wanted it to free me once and for all from the guilt I felt about leaving the church. I hoped that seeing my father and telling him would help with that.

When Edward asked Umberto a question about the Crusaders, I figured he was probably doing it for me.

"I didn't plan to go into that," Umberto said, "but since you bring it up, let me briefly explain the situation. Very briefly because we have a lot to cover." He motioned us over to the window again and pointed presumably in the Crusaders' direction.

"They ruled the roost before we took over. We call it the Reformation, so we're the Reformers, although they call us Rebels. They still don't accept us or the changes we're making, but there's little they can do about it except obstruct and complain, and they do plenty of that. Their goal is to preserve Christendom, what's left of it. They pride themselves on being the Defenders of the True Faith. In fact, the official name of their governing body is The Committee for the Promotion and Protection of the True Faith. In their eyes, all the rest of us are apostates, traitors, and heretics. So, Thomas, you're not alone. They disapprove of us and everything we do and stand for."

Edward asked, "Are they your enemies?"

"Not as much as they used to be. They're now on the Governing Council with us, although we outnumber them fortunately. We're getting along with them better now, but it's a fragile truce with long-standing resentments that can erupt at any time. It's like a bad marriage, but at least it's a marriage."

I told him, "I would like to include them in the book I plan to write. Would it be possible to visit them? You know, as a journalist?"

"Hmm, I don't know about that. That's something Tanya would have to agree to and arrange, but she might go for the idea."

"Who's Tanya?"

"She's the boss, the CEO, as it were. You'll meet her later. The problem with your idea is that the Crusaders would have to invite you, and I doubt they're going to want to put out the welcome mat for an ex-priest, especially after all the fuss they made about our inviting you down here in the first place. Anyway, enough about the Crusaders. Now that we've retired Heaven to the dustbin of history, do you have any questions before we move on?"

"I have one," said Edward.

"Yes, Professor Edward, what's your question?"

"When you told us about Heaven being closed down, you said people shouldn't have to be rewarded in the afterlife for living virtuous lives. Virtue should be its own reward. Did I understand you correctly?"

"You did. People shouldn't have to be bribed with eternal bliss, Paradise, 72 virgins, or whatever to live a good life."

"Did I hear something about virgins?" boomed a female voice. Standing next to Guido was a spirit dressed in tight-fitting jeans, a bright-red blouse, and black boots.

"Hello, Natasha," Umberto said. "Welcome to the other side of the tracks. Come here and meet our guests."

When she came over to us, Umberto pointed at me. "This splendid specimen from above is Thomas. And next to him is Edward, who was his teacher."

"Welcome to both of you. We're delighted to have you here."

Her face had movement, and her lips looked sort of like she was wearing lipstick. I also picked up a faint scent. Bath soap? Perfume? She looked more physical than any spirit I had seen so far. Was she some kind of hybrid?

"I'm here to welcome you on behalf of Tanya and let you know she's looking forward to meeting you." She turned to Umberto. "You were saying something about virgins? I hope you aren't corrupting the minds of our visitors with X-rated lectures." She looked at Guido, and they both laughed.

"Anyway, I just wanted to drop by to welcome you and thank you for coming. We're all looking forward to seeing you at the meeting. Umberto, I'm sorry I can't stay for the rest of your talk. Just when it was getting interesting."

She went back to Guido, who said something to her at the door that made her laugh. As she left, he tapped her on the tush.

40

As I waited for Guido to put up the next topic, I wondered what shocking new piece of information Umberto had in store for us. Heaven kaput. Now what?

I was glad that the next topic that flashed up on the screen was **Purgatory Precincts** because I wanted to find out more about my father's situation.

Umberto explained that after Heaven was shut down, Purgatory, which had served as the anteroom to Heaven, was moved down there and divided into precincts.

That puzzled me, so I asked him, "If there's no Heaven for Purgatory people to go to, what's the purpose of having Purgatory precincts?"

"Fair question, Thomas. Purgatory precincts function as sort of 'honorary societies' that recognize exemplary lives. Being in a Purgatory precinct lets a deceased person know he or she made the honor roll, so to speak."

That didn't square with what he said about not rewarding virtuous lives, but I let it pass.

"Purgatory precincts let dead souls exist as spirits, at least for a while."

Guido said something that made Umberto smile.

"Guido reminds me that Tanya doesn't want us to call them Purgatory precincts anymore. We're supposed to call them 'enhancement centers.'" He looked at Guido and rolled his eyes.

I asked him, "Is it fair to put people in Purgatory precincts only to terminate them when their time's up?" I wondered if he knew about my father's situation.

"Listen, Thomas, we all agree that Purgatory's an anachronism, but we're stuck with it for now. Besides, we can't let the souls of good people just die and dis-appear, especially the ones who were taught to expect something more. That wouldn't be fair. At least, when they're down here, they get more time to be conscious. We're all aware of the problem. I can't spend any more time on it now because we have to move on."

Umberto moved closer as if he was about to tell us a secret. "My friends, here's something more to wrap your minds around." He nodded at Guido, and **Hell Is Not Eternal** flashed up on the screen.

"That's right, gentlemen, you're reading that correctly. Hell doesn't last forever. It doesn't go on and on the way it used to and the way many people still think it does. Why not? The answer is simple. Space. We don't have enough of it. It would be nice if we could move to larger quarters, but we can't. I personally think they should have organized it the other way around and put Hell out in space where there's plenty of room and put Heaven down here where there's more than enough room for the chosen few. But then nobody asked me.

"So that's the problem pure and simple. Not enough room. To help relieve the problem, we instituted an early release program for old-timers, minor offenders, and those who show good behavior. And now we're releasing more and more of them early to relieve the overcrowding. With the population up there exploding—seven billion and counting—we had to find ways to remove the old to make way for the new."

"When you talk about releasing them," Edward asked, "where do you release them to?"

"To perpetual sleep. The Big Nap. To make a long story short, just as he decided he had to shut down Heaven, he decided to end the long tradition of eternal damnation."

He? Did I hear him correctly? I was about to ask when Edward beat me to it.

"Who's he?" he asked. "You said 'he' decided."

Umberto looked unsure how to answer the question, or even if he should. He glanced at Guido.

"He has a name," he finally said, "but nobody knows what it is. So he's simply 'The Name.' Hashem. That's not what we call him though. To us, he's 'The Chief,' so that's what we call him. He lives down here."

I couldn't believe what I was hearing. Edward also looked perplexed.

"Did you say Hashem lives down here?" he asked.

Umberto glanced at Guido, then turned back to Edward. "The short answer to your question is yes. He lives down here. After he closed down Heaven, he had to go somewhere, so he came down here."

My mind was racing to try to keep up with what he was saying.

"If he's down here," Edward asked, "where is he? Where does he live?"

Umberto motioned us over to the window and pointed out into the mist. "He's out there."

Edward looked incredulous. "Are you trying to tell us Hashem is out there now?"

"That's exactly what I'm telling you."

"Is he by himself?" I asked. "Does he live alone?"

"No, as a matter of fact, he doesn't."

Umberto went and had a whispered conversation with Guido. When he returned, he told us he wasn't authorized to say more. "Maybe he'll explain it later."

"What do you mean maybe he'll explain it later?" I asked. "Is that what you said? He'll explain it later?"

"That's what I said. Later when he talks to you."

"Hashem's going to talk to us?" asked Edward.

"Not to you. To Thomas."

"Me?"

"It's not finalized, so I'm not going to say anything more about it."

"Are you saying Hashem wants to talk to me?"

"It's quite amazing really. We don't even get to talk to him."

"Will Edward be with me?"

"Sorry, but Edward can't go." He looked at him. "You're a spirit, and no spirit knows where the Chief lives. I don't, and I'm not even sure Tanya does either. All we know is that he lives in the Northwest, but nobody knows exactly where."

"Are you sure he wants to talk to me?" I asked. "That's hard to believe."

"We're sure. After the Crusaders made such a fuss about our inviting you down here, Tanya ran it by him. Not only did he support our decision, but he said he wants you to visit him."

"How can I visit him if nobody knows where he lives?"

"Don't worry. If and when the time comes, we'll take you to the area, and somebody will pick you up. Probably Naomi. She's the only one who knows where he lives."

"Who's Naomi?"

"His wife."

I looked at Edward and asked him with my eyes: Is this for real? Or are they just playing games with us?

The normally unflappable Edward looked nonplussed. "Umberto, are you telling us Hashem has a wife?"

"She's not really his wife. He doesn't have a wife. That's just what we call her. She's his right-hand man, or rather I should say right-hand woman."

By now it was obvious that Umberto was more than just the Guest Master. He was the Teller of Tall Tales. The more he said, the harder it was to believe what he was saying.

"I have a question," said Edward.

"Yes, Professor Edward. What is it?"

"It's about Satan."

Oh, boy, I thought, this should be good. Let's see what Umberto does with this one.

Edward said, "The *Inferno* ends with Satan in the center frozen in ice, so here's my question. If Hashem is down here, does that mean Satan is too? After all, this is more his territory than Hashem's."

"Good question as usual, Professor Edward. Yes, Satan's down here. Come. I'll show you." He took us back to the window and pointed out into the mist again. "He lives out there."

Since he was pointing in the same direction he had pointed moments earlier, I said, "That's close to where Hashem lives, right?"

"That's right. They're neighbors."

Umberto looked at Guido, who smiled and shot us a thumbs-up sign. I wasn't sure why, but it was obvious the two of them were having fun telling us tall tales and sharing inside jokes.

"Is Satan active?" Edward asked.

"Oh, he's active all right, but he's much tamer than he used to be. He's still a handful though."

"Can't Hashem do something about him?" I asked. "After all, you just said he lives down here."

"He's down here, but he's not very—how shall I put it?" He looked at Guido. "He's not very active."

"He's retired," Guido said.

"I'm not sure I would put it quite that way," said Umberto, "but he's not all that involved. He's . . . what's the best way to say this?"

"He's discouraged," said Guido.

"Yes, I don't think that's too strong a word. But who can blame him? After all he's seen."

God is a depressed recluse living in Hell with a female companion? My theological training had not prepared me for this. This trip was fast getting to be more than I can handle, and it's just beginning.

"Gentlemen, a brief recess is in order. I want to find out what's going on with the ladies. Stay here. Guido and I will be right back."

Poof! They were gone.

41

Edward and I obviously had the same thing in mind because as soon as they left, we both went to the window and looked out into the mist.

Edward was the first to speak. "It's remarkable, isn't it, Thomas? It's hard to believe Hell is out there, but then there's a lot down here that's hard to believe."

"That's for sure."

"What do you think about Umberto saying Hashem wants to talk to you?"

"I don't know what to think. But why would he say these things if they aren't true?"

"I don't know what to think either. God and Satan living out there in the mist as neighbors? Are we really supposed to believe that?"

I pointed at the telescope. "What do you make of that? It must be there for a reason. Do you think we can see anything through it?"

"Go over and find out."

I glanced at the door, then went to the telescope with Edward following me. I put my eye to the lens, but all I could see was the magnified mist Umberto said we would see. However, as what I was looking at started to come into better focus, I saw what looked like a mass of wet, gooey worms until I realized what I was looking at weren't worms at all, but a tangle of human limbs, torsos, and naked body parts all squished together. At least, that's what it looked like.

"Yuck!" I said. "Dante's Inferno is alive and well. No wonder they don't want us to see it."

Edward made a face. "It's not a pretty picture, I know."

"Can you see out there?"

He nodded.

I tried to turn the telescope in a new direction, but it didn't move.

"It's probably operated by computer," Edward said. "Not manually."

Just as we returned to where we had been, Guido returned.

"Good news, gentlemen. The young one finally arrived, so Umberto's on his way with both of them."

Before he could say more, Umberto came through the door with two women—a spirit and a brunette dressed in jeans, a purple sweatshirt, and gym shoes. The spirit was smaller and thinner, but she had a pleasant glow that made her attractive in a ghostly sort of way.

"Here they are, my friends," Umberto said. "The California sunshine we've been waiting for. These two charming ladies are Professor Claudia Higgins of the University of California at Berkeley and her teaching assistant, Rachel Stein." He turned to them. "Claudia and Rachel, let me introduce you to Edward Tyler and Thomas Reed."

We all smiled and nodded at each other.

"Gentlemen, as you probably already know, Professor Higgins is the author of one of the most important Dante studies ever written."

Claudia made a little curtsy. "Why, thank you, Umberto. I may ask you to post a review on Amazon."

Edward laughed. "It's an honor to meet you," he said to her. "I know your book well and use it in my courses. The students love it."

"Why thank you, Edward."

I never read her book, but I always put it in the bibliography at the end of my Dante papers. "It's very nice to meet you, Professor Higgins."

"It's nice to meet you, Thomas. Please call me Claudia." She looked around the room and stared at the window. She turned to Umberto. "Where the Hell am I?"

Edward laughed again.

She went to the window. "Ugh. This looks like a foggy London day without London. I was hoping for something a little sunnier."

Edward was smiling, obviously pleased with the new addition.

"Is this really the afterlife?" Claudia asked Umberto. "I was hoping for something more . . . you know, something a little more uplifting." She looked at Edward. "Fog or no fog, being conscious is definitely more interesting than the alternative. Don't you agree?"

"Absolutely."

Umberto said he had to take care of something, but he would come back soon for the tour.

After he left, I asked Guido what tour was he talking about.

"He wants to show you his Dante museum. There's not a lot to see yet, but he has big plans for it. It's his pride and joy as you'll see. But first I have to log in Rachel."

"Log me in? What's that?"

"Everybody gets logged in," Guido told her. "Ask Thomas."

"It's just a formality," I said to her.

As I watched them leave, I thought Rachel would be a good person to interview for my book. Claudia too. Maybe I could interview them together and make it a chapter. Or it could be a separate article: "Hell Through the Eyes of Two California Academics: An Exclusive Interview." Something like that. I jotted it down on my pad. The longer I was down there, the more excited I was getting about writing the book that Edward said could make me the next Dante.

Edward and Claudia were talking about Dante translations, so I listened in.

"The problem," Claudia was saying, "not just with Dante translations but with poetry translations generally, is that the more accurate the translation is, the less poetic it's likely to be. And conversely, the more poetic it is, the less accurate it will probably be. How many Dante translations have there been that strike the right balance?"

"The way I see it," said Edward, "the problem, if we can call it a problem, is that Dante's poetry is in a class by itself. No translation can begin to do justice to it. If I had to choose between poetry and accuracy, I would opt for accuracy, even a literal translation no matter how unpoetic it might be. That's why I think footnotes that clarify the text are so important. Good footnotes are a close second in importance to—and I know this will be heresy to say—to the text itself."

"Edward, you are a heretic! Hell is a good place for you."

He laughed. "That's what I'm here for—heretical thinking."

I never saw Edward enjoying himself so much. Claudia was obviously good for him.

When Guido came back with Rachel, I took him aside and whispered, "When will I get to see my father?

He could be terminated at any time. I need to see him as soon as I can."

"Don't worry. Umberto is making the arrangements. He's a man of his word."

"And how about the other visit? You know, the one I'm supposed to have with the Chief, as you call him?"

"If and when that happens, Umberto will let you know about that one too. Frankly, it's hard for me to imagine that one taking place, but who knows?"

"I would also like to include the Crusaders in my book if that's possible. Can Umberto arrange something for me? A tour or at least an interview?"

"Thomas, you're going to be so busy with all your special trips, you're not going to have time for anything else."

"I know. That's the problem. I want everything to go into the book, but seeing my father is my top priority."

"Of course."

When Umberto returned, he took me aside, and with his back to the others, he whispered, "It's all set."

"My father?"

He nodded and put his finger up to his mouth to remind me that nobody else was to know. When he went back and told the others it was time for the tour, he said I wouldn't be joining them but didn't say why.

42

After Umberto left with the others, Guido took me downstairs to a tunnel that took us to the hangar where helicopters with black and brown stripes were lined up in rows. They looked like igloos on knobby stilts.

"This is our mighty air force," he said. "We call them beetles for obvious reasons. Not much to look at, but they get the job done."

"What is their job?

"Mostly surveillance and intelligence gathering. Sometimes we use them against insurgents."

"Insurgents?"

Before he could say more, a spirit materialized in front of us wearing burgundy knickers and a flight jacket that made him look like a World War I pilot. He and Guido made a fast, whirling motion with their hands that I assumed was some sort of organization handshake.

Guido said to me, "This is Pietro, one of our ace pilots. I'm now going to leave you in his capable hands." He wished me a safe journey, then disappeared the way spirits do.

Pietro took me to a nearby beetle. "As you can see, these weren't built with living visitors in mind. There's space for you on the passenger side, but it's not really a seat." He opened the door and motioned me to get in.

I ducked my head down and slid across the cabin. He got in and started the engine. After we taxied to the launch pad and were in place, he pulled a lever that sent us straight up into the mist. A sudden forward motion told me I was on my way to see my father, my dead father who wasn't really dead.

I wondered what was he going to look like. Would he look like he did at the end of his life? Or the way he looked when he was younger and healthier? The big question on my mind, of course, was what was his reaction going to be when I tell him I left the church.

Pietro interrupted my train of thought. "So how does it feel to be on your way to see your dad? Are you excited?"

"Very, but I'm also worried."

"Why?"

"I found out he's going to be terminated, and it could happen anytime."

"Yes, well, that's how the precincts are set up. Everybody gets sent to the Big Nap sooner or later."

"It's decided just like that? My father has no say in the matter? That doesn't seem right."

"Purgatory's been a problem ever since they moved it down here. I personally think they should have shut it down when they shut down Heaven. Having Purgatory without a Heaven for it to lead to doesn't make sense. The argument for keeping the precincts is that people who live decent lives have a right to some kind of afterlife even if it doesn't go on forever. They shouldn't just die and have that be the end of it. Take your father, for example. A good man I'm sure. Would it be fair to just let him die and that's it?"

"It might be better than putting him down here for a little while, then pulling the rug out from under him."

"Your point's well taken. There's a reform in the pipeline to make Purgatory precincts permanent, or at least more permanent, so people like your father can stay here as long as they want. But like so many other good ideas down here, it runs up against the space problem."

"When is this reform supposed to happen?"

"It's in the works, but then a lot of things down here are in the works. It's getting them implemented that's the challenge."

"Does my father know he's going to be terminated?"

"No, of course not. Telling him would be cruel." He pointed up ahead. "See what we're coming to?"

"I see something. What is it? It looks sort of like a river. Or maybe a swamp?"

"Both. What do you think it is? Take a guess."

"I don't know. The river Styx was down here in Dante's day."

"Very good. Guido said you guys are sharp."

Tall towers and dark walls came into view up ahead of us.

"Is that the City of Dis?"

"Very good again, Thomas. You're on a roll."

It looked the way I imagined the City of Dis would look when I read about it with Edward. Its towers and walls looked Germanic like something one might see on the Rhine.

When we flew over the wall, the mist got thinner and had more of an orange tint. We were now flying over a vast complex of square and rectangular walled areas that reminded me of the concentration camps I saw in a documentary about Nazi Germany. The similarity was chilling.

"Is this Hell? The real thing?"

"Pure Hell. Wall-to-wall."

"Who's down there?"

"This is mostly abuser country, but let me check to make sure." He looked at the coordinates on the control panel and pushed a button.

"Yes, that's what it is. Child abusers and animal abusers mostly. And not just those who do the abusing, but those who allow it to happen."

"Bystanders."

"That's right. That comes as a big surprise to a lot of people when they get down here. They're surprised to find out that letting evil happen and not trying to stop it is as bad as actually doing it. At the Processing Center, you should hear the whining and complaining when they find out."

"What's the Processing Center?"

"That's where they enter the system and get assigned. It's up ahead of us to the left. I'll show it to you when we come to it. Do you want to see it?"

"Of course."

As the beetle began losing altitude, I caught glimpses up ahead of us of a large, flat building that looked like an ugly power plant.

"There it is," he said.

"It's huge."

"It operates around the clock nonstop. Never a dull moment."

"Can you fly lower so I can get a better look?"

"I'm already flying lower than I'm supposed to."

"I won't tell."

"Well, OK, since you're our first visitor."

"Thank you, Pietro."

The towers and gate ahead of us reminded me of how Auschwitz looked in the documentary. The gate had a sign over it that I half expected to say *"Arbeit Macht Frei."*

As we got closer, I saw long lines going into the building through different entrances. Most of the spirits looked old and infirm as one might expect, but I was surprised to see so many children. I guess I shouldn't have been since I knew that millions of children around the world are constantly dying of disease, starvation, and violence.

Pietro pointed at the lines. "Look at those faces. People from all around the world. It's amazing to think they were alive hours, even minutes ago."

As we got closer to the sign over the gate, I asked him what it said.

"It says, 'All of life is sacred. Don't harm anyone or anything.'"

"Wow, that says it all." I took out my pad and wrote it down. I knew Edward would love it. Beatrice too.

Many of the dead souls in the lines were now looking up at us, and some of them were pointing and shouting as if they wanted us to rescue them. It reminded me of another documentary I saw about the fall of Saigon at the end of the Vietnam war when people on the roof of the American Embassy fought with each other to get on the last American helicopters.

I saw two more signs up ahead of us off to the right, but they were too far away to read. I asked Pietro about them, but he couldn't make them out either. So he banked the beetle and flew toward them.

"The one on the left says, 'As long as men kill animals, they will kill each other.'"

"That was one of Edward's favorite quotations, but I don't remember who said it. Is that a name under it?"

"Yes. It's by Pythagoras. The other sign says, 'The soul is the same in all living creatures although the body of each is different.'"

"Hippocrates."

"Very good, Thomas."

"That one was in Edward's office on the wall above his desk. I passed it on to Beatrice, my girlfriend in college, and it became one of her favorites too. Edward will love these quotations. He's very much in tune with their messages. Can we drop down for a quick visit? Maybe have a rest stop? Is that allowed? I'd like to stretch my legs and look around."

"No way, Thomas. Look at those lines. If you got caught up in one of them, you could end up somewhere you don't want to be with people you don't want to be with. Your visit would be a very long one."

"OK, I know you have your rules."

"I'm glad I got to show you this, but we do have to be on our way. I don't want Umberto to have a temper tantrum. I'll show you one more saying on the way, and that will be the last one. We're coming to it now. It's up ahead on the right." He pointed. "Do you see it?"

"Hmm, not yet. Wait! Yes, I think I see it now. What does it say?"

"Always do right. This will please some people and astonish the rest."

"Hey, I like that, and I know Edward will too. I'm pretty sure he doesn't know it. At least he didn't when I was his student." I wrote it down on my pad. "There's a name underneath that one too. What does it say?"

"Take a guess. He's one of your countrymen."

"I don't know. It sounds like something Mark Twain might say."

"Bingo again. Go to the head of the class."

As we pulled away, I settled back to be alone with my thoughts about seeing my father. I still wasn't convinced it was really going to happen.

Moments after I closed my eyes, Pietro shouted, "There they are!"

"Huh?"

"Over there!"

He was pointing at a group of spirits up ahead of us that looked like a herd moving across a plain. He flew toward them, and then when he got closer, he suddenly dove straight down at them. I was sure we were going to crash, but he pulled out of the dive just in time. The spirits scattered like frightened deer.

"Bastards!"

"What was that all about?"

"Rapists. I didn't know any of them were out this way. I never pass up the chance to strafe them. I only wish I could do more."

When he saw them regrouping, he circled back around, and with eyes blazing like a kamikaze pilot, he dove straight down at them and scattered them again. After he pulled out of the dive, he looked at me with a sheepish grin. "I always feel better when I do that. My sister was raped. As far as I'm concerned, they're the lowest of the low. I do everything I can to keep them from getting released. Termination is too good for them. If anybody deserves eternal damnation, they do. If I had my way, they would stay down here and be strafed and tortured till the end of time."

A light on the panel flashed.

"No more aerial acrobatics!" It was Umberto. "Stay on course to the assigned landing site. No more side trips. The code name of the contact is Augustus. Got it?"

"Got it."

"Once you drop Thomas off, stay there and wait for him. Remain on the alert at all times, understand?"

"Yes, sir."

"Over and out."

When Pietro was sure the speaker was turned off, he shouted, "Up yours, Umberto," and gave him the finger.

43

"You're looking very thoughtful," Pietro said during the descent. "Still worried about your dad?"

"Yup."

"I can understand you're upset, but you don't really know what he wants. He may not want to stay here. Not everybody does. After they put in their time, many of them are only too glad to take the Big Nap."

"You make it sound like a prison sentence."

"For many of them it is. We get requests all the time from people who want to end or shorten their stays. Enough is enough, they say. Some of them beg us to put them to sleep."

"What happens then?"

"Well, we don't kill them if that's what you're asking. The point I'm making, Thomas, is you have no idea what your father wants. You may be doing him a disservice if you try to get him to stay longer than he wants."

The terrain up ahead of us looked well cared for, and there were even patches of greenery. When I saw robed spirits alone and in small groups, I wondered if my father might be among them. Since it was unlikely they were rapists, it was good to know Pietro wasn't suddenly going to go berserk and start dive-bombing them. At least I hoped not.

"It doesn't look bad down there," I said. "There are even patches of color here and there."

"It's definitely better than Hell, but it's no great bargain. I've seen a lot of the precincts, and I'm not impressed. These folks shouldn't have to live this way. Is this what living a good life gets you?" He lowered the beetle slowly down until I felt the bump that meant we landed. Several spirits approached cautiously but kept their distance.

"Don't be afraid of them," Pietro said. "They're harmless. Some of them have never seen a beetle, much less a living visitor."

After Pietro got out, I slid across the cabin and got out behind him. When the spirits saw me, there was a ripple of excitement. I scanned the faces to find my father.

"They're obviously curious," Pietro said. "They've never seen the likes of you."

More spirits kept arriving, and soon there was a circle six or seven deep surrounding us. Pietro held up his hand to let them know he wanted to say something.

"My friends," he said pointing at me. "This is our guest from above. His name is Thomas."

A tall spirit emerged from the circle and came up to us. "Welcome to both of you. I've been expecting you. My name is Emile. I also go by the name of Augustus." He and Pietro made a quick, whirling motion with their hands.

I felt much better knowing Pietro was going to wait in the beetle for me. After I said good-bye to him, I followed Emile through the spirits who kept staring at me with great interest. I liked the vibes I was getting. It wasn't often I got to feel like a celebrity.

Emile took me down a cinder path through a russet-tinted grotto, then up a slope and into a small hut with file cabinets and a computer that he turned on.

"The first thing we need to do is find your father's number so we can know where he is. What's his full name?"

"Thomas Aaron Reed Jr."

"Yes, now I remember. You're III."

"That's right."

He pressed a button, typed, and looked at the numbers, letters, and signs flashing up on the screen. "Ah, here he is. His number is 78-214-758." He typed some more and waited. "He's in the west central section, which fortunately isn't that far away. That's it." He turned off the computer. "I've never heard of a living person coming down here to visit a relative. You must have pull."

"They're starting a visitors program, and I'm apparently the first one."

"Really? Congratulations. It's an honor to be of service." He bowed playfully. "Let's go find your father."

He took me down the incline to a gravel path that went through a maze of twisted, tree-shaped structures. I wondered what happened to the greenery I saw from the beetle.

Emile told me his instructions were to keep me in sight at all times. "So when you see me lurking around, don't think I'm spying on you or trying to eavesdrop on your conversation. When you see me coming toward you, that means it's time to wrap up your conversation, OK?"

"OK."

The open area we came to looked like a village common. Spirits were milling around mostly by themselves.

"Your father's in this section, so mix with them and see what you can find out. It will be best if you search for him on your own. He's around here somewhere, or at least he should be. If you don't find him, come back, and we'll try something else."

"Where will you be?"

"I'll be keeping my distance to give you your privacy, but I'll always try to be visible." He nodded toward the spirits. "Go find your father. Good luck."

By now, I wasn't sure I wanted to find him since I knew it was going to be upsetting to see him again. I dreaded telling him I ended up rebelling against everything he stood for.

I walked toward the spirits, careful not to approach them too directly or suddenly. I didn't want to scare them, or was it I didn't want them to scare me? I didn't connect to any of them. They either didn't see me or pretended they didn't. I said "Hello" to a couple of the spirits I made eye contact with, but they either turned away or kept moving past me without looking at me. I circled around the ones with their backs to me to see if they might possibly be my father. I was surprised to see some of them lying on the ground. Were they resting? Do spirits get tired the way living people do? I didn't think so.

When one of them I said "Hello" to actually said "Hello" back, I followed him in hopes of starting up a conversation. When I caught up to him, I told him I was looking for my father, Thomas Reed. He looked at me blankly, then turned away without saying anything and left. I thought, these are definitely not happy campers. The walking dead—that's what they are. Will my father be like that?

44

There was something about the tilt of the body of one of the spirits that reminded me of my father, so I circled around for a better look. He wasn't my father, but the intent way he was looking at something in the distance made me curious. All that was out there was a huge hole that looked like a dried-up pond or an artificial lake that had never been filled in. It reminded me of the pond behind my father's nursing home where I used to park him so he could sit under his favorite tree and look at the pond.

Going on a hunch, I walked out toward the empty pond, and I'm glad I did because as I got closer, I saw somebody sitting by himself on a bench facing the hole. I circled around him carefully in an arc so as not to startle him. When he turned toward me, I saw right away he was my father. He looked at me for a moment, then turned back and kept staring at the empty pond.

"Dad," I called. He didn't look at me, so I walked toward him. "Dad," I said louder.

He looked at me, but he still didn't react.

"Dad, it's me, Tommy."

He looked at me longer this time, but then when he turned away, I was devastated. I came all this way, and my father doesn't recognize me? This god-awful place is supposed to be a reward for living a good life? The gateway to Heaven? Ha! It's a grim, depressing hellhole— that's what it is. They all look like zombies, including my father.

I went up to him and said, "Dad, I'm your son. Look at me. Say something."

Finally, there was a flicker of recognition in his eyes. "Tommy, is it really you?"

"Yes, Dad, it's me."

He looked around as if noticing where he was for the first time. "Tommy, where am I?"

What could I say? You're in a Purgatory precinct in Hell?

"You're in the entrance to Heaven," I said, knowing it wasn't the entrance to anything except extinction. "I'm here to visit you."

He looked confused. "Where am I?" he asked again.

"You're in Purgatory."

As soon as the word was out of my mouth, I knew it was the wrong thing to say. My father had a strong Protestant disdain for superstitious Catholic beliefs, and he considered Purgatory one of the most superstitious. How ironical, I thought, that given his antipathy to Purgatory, that's where he ended up. I was glad to see that he grimaced when I mentioned Purgatory because it showed his face had some of the movement it had before his stroke.

"What are you doing here?" he asked me. "Are you supposed to be dead? You don't look dead."

"No, Dad. I'm not dead. I'm very much alive. I came to visit you."

He looked confused. "Is this Hell?"

That was another word I wanted to avoid. "It's the Underworld, Dad. It goes by different names." I tried to think of something encouraging to say, but I couldn't think of anything. "How are you doing, Dad?"

He looked back at the pond without answering. Oh no, I hope he's not going to tune out on me. I was relieved when moments later he turned back to me.

"I miss your visits, Tommy. Are you going to start visiting me again?" He looked at me as if seeing me for the first time. "Tommy, is it really you? How are you?"

"I'm fine, Dad."

"How's your parish?"

That would have been a good time to tell him I didn't have a parish anymore, but I couldn't bring myself to say it.

"How's Ruthie?"

I knew he was going to bring her up sooner or later. What could I tell him? That she married the man who beat him out of the episcopate and was already sleeping with him when my father was in the nursing home.

"She's doing fine, Dad."

"Glad to hear it, Tommy. What's she doing?"

Screwing the bishop, I felt like saying. Instead, I said, "She's busy with her diocesan work as usual."

He looked out at the empty pond and was quiet for a long time. When he turned back at me, he said, "Tommy, there's something I should tell you. It's something even your mother doesn't know, but it's time to tell you. I've protected you and protected myself for too long."

I had something to tell him too and knew I was running out of time. I looked at Emile in the distance and was glad to see he wasn't on his way, but I knew that could change at any time.

My father faced the pond and spoke without look- ing at me. "My senior year at CTS when I was doing my field work in Brookline, I got involved with Connie, the assistant parish secretary, and she got pregnant. When she decided to have an abortion, I didn't like that idea, but I didn't argue too much. She moved to California where she changed her mind. When she sent me a picture of the baby, it broke my heart."

I was mesmerized by what he was telling me and was glad Emile wasn't on his way to interrupt it.

"I sent her money from time to time, but I never met my son. Connie got married and had two more children. When she got divorced, she asked me for more money, and I sent her some. When I didn't hear from her for a long time, I thought that was the end of it, but when I became a candidate to be the new bishop, she asked me for a sizable sum of money. She said it was an emergency to take care of my son's medical problems. Without coming right out and saying so, she made it clear that if I didn't send her what she needed for my son and her other children, she would expose me, and I knew she meant it. That's the real reason I dropped out of the running. As you know, your mother never forgave me for that. She still doesn't know the real reason I did it." He turned and looked at me. "So, Tommy, you had a half-brother and never knew it."

"Where's he now?"

"He's dead. He died from a drug overdose." He turned back to the pond. After a long pause, he said, "I felt bad I wasn't more of a father to him. I didn't help him other than send an occasional check to his mother." He looked back at me. "Tommy, I'm glad you came. I've wanted to tell you this for a long time, but I couldn't bring myself to do it. I didn't want you to think less of me."

He looked around with sad, frightened eyes. "Am I in Hell? Tell me the truth."

"No, Dad, you're not in Hell."

"Does this go on and on?"

"Would you like it to go on and on?" Pietro was right. It was an important question. "Would you like to stay here?" When my father didn't answer me, I asked him again, "Dad, do you want to stay here or not? Tell me."

"I'm not sure." He said it so quietly I barely heard him.

"Dad, I have a confession of my own to make. There's something I want to tell you." No sooner did I say it when I saw Emile coming toward us. So, instead of telling my father what I had planned to, I said something else I had always wanted to say to him.

"Thank you, Dad, for being a good father. I never told you that while you were alive, so I'm telling you now."

"Thank you very much, Tommy, for telling me that. I'm proud of you and always will be."

After I said good-bye and walked toward Emile, I wondered how proud my father would be of me if I had told him the truth. That's what I should have done, but I was glad I didn't have to. It just didn't feel like the right thing to do.

I remembered the prayer I said at the cemetery as my father's casket was lowered into the ground that asked God to grant him "an entrance into the land of light and joy in the fellowship of thy saints." When I reached Emile, I turned and looked back at my father who was still sitting on the bench staring at the empty pond. I saw neither light, nor joy, nor fellowship.

45

Emile took me back to Pietro, and once we were up and on our way, I found out why he was in such a good mood. While I was with my father, he found out he had been chosen to fly me, pending a final confirmation, to my meeting with Hashem, or the Chief as they call him.

"I've never been to the Northwest," he said. "Very few of us have. So, I'm hoping it happens."

He must have sensed I wanted to be alone with my thoughts about my father because he was unusually quiet for the rest of the trip.

Guido met us at the landing platform, but instead of taking me back to Umberto's suite, he turned off the tunnel and took me to a large hall with marble columns, a high ceiling, and gold-leaf decorations on the walls. Young female spirits were bustling about, going in and out of rooms.

"As you can see," he said, "this is Tanya land."

"It sure is jumping. Umberto's side is deserted compared to this."

"There's never a dull moment over here."

Suddenly several female spirits burst out of a nearby room, chattering and laughing.

Guido pointed at them. "Plus, there are lots of pretty girls to look at."

"Who are all these energetic young women?"

"Tanya's girls we call them. You'll see lots more of them before you're through."

When he looked past me, his face lit up. "Well, well, well, look who we have here."

When I turned, I saw Rachel and Natasha coming toward us.

"How was the tour?" I asked Rachel.

"Claudia and Edward are still there with Umberto. The three of them are having a grand old time talking about Dante."

"Don't go anywhere," Natasha told us. "I'll be right back."

Rachel looked around the room. "I never cease to be amazed. I still can't believe I'm down here."

"I can't either. Although it's definitely beginning to sink in. So how was the tour? What's the museum like?"

"There's not much to see yet, but Umberto has big plans for it that he told us about. He apparently wants Claudia and Edward to be the guides."

"I'm not surprised. They're certainly qualified."

"And they'll be together, which is nice. Where did you go? All Umberto told us was that you were on a 'special assignment,' whatever that means. It sounded very hush-hush. Where were you?"

"I'm sorry, but I'm not allowed to tell you."

"Oh, come on. Don't be so mysterious. You're not James Bond. Or are you?"

"They don't call me 007 for nothing."

Natasha came back with Guido and a living, dark-skinned young man with a spectacular set of white teeth.

Natasha said to us, "I want you to meet our newest arrival. Sanjay's from India."

"This is Rachel and Thomas," she said to him. "They're from the United States."

We shook hands and smiled at each other, a conspiracy of the living.

"Sanjay did something quite amazing." Natasha said. "He came down here from northern India completely on his own. He didn't need anybody to fetch or guide him. He just came, and here he is! Isn't that something?"

"Amazing," I said.

"Very," added Rachel.

Natasha said, "OK, everybody, it's time for the meeting. Guido's going that way too, so he'll be tagging along with us."

"I'll be the caboose."

The auditorium Natasha took us to reminded me of St. George's auditorium, except there was no stage, no rows of seats, and it was much bigger. The only seats were chairs up front set out for us visitors. The auditorium was filling up fast, mostly with Tanya's girls.

On the way to our seats, Sanjay stopped to talk to a spirit he seemed to know. Maybe a friend or relative who died young? Natasha took Rachel and me to the front and sat us down on two of the chairs that faced the audience. The spirits filling the room stared at us as if we were from another world, which we were.

I was starting to tell Rachel about the book I wanted to write when Natasha came back with Sanjay and two Chinese women.

"This is Zhao Lijuan from Beijing," Natasha told us, pointing at the living one. "She came down here with her aunt, Qian Fenfang." She nodded to the spirit next to Zhao.

Natasha pointed at me. "Thomas was the first visitor to arrive, and Rachel was the second. And Sanjay here has the distinction of being the first visitor to come down here totally on his own."

Natasha looked at Zhao, "Tell us what you've seen so far."

Her face lit up. "Natasha take us to Chinese meeting. And you know who we see?"

"Who?" said Rachel.

Zhao tried to coax the answer out of her aunt until Qian finally said, "Kfouse!"

Zhao laughed. "Confuzius!" she said in her better English.

"Really?" said Rachel. "Confucius?"

"We not understand all he says because he speak in ancient way, but we have very big excitement to hear him."

The buzz was getting louder as staffers, most of them young and female, continued filling up the auditorium. Natasha sat Zhao down next to us and put Qian behind her.

"By the way," Rachel whispered to me, "I like your friend, Edward. He's cute. He and Claudia are hitting it off really well."

"That's quite something for a confirmed bachelor like Edward. Is Claudia married? Or rather was she?"

"She was married briefly when she was young, but she never remarried and has no children. She used to tell us she's married to Dante, which in a way she is."

With the auditorium now pulsating with energy and excitement, suddenly there was commotion in back that signaled the arrival of a spirit in a tight-fitting black body suit and boots. It was Tanya whose dark brown hair, deep-set green eyes, and hoop earrings made her look more hybrid than pure spirit. As she made her way forward, staffers cheered and crowded around her. She waved, pointed, and called staffers by name and said things that made them laugh and cheer. When she reached the front, Natasha gave her a hug and brought her over to us.

After Natasha made the introductions, Tanya said, "It's an honor for all of us to have you here. We can't thank you enough for coming. We'll be starting soon."

She went off to confer with staffers, then went to the center area and raised her arms to quiet the auditorium. "Welcome, welcome, everybody. It's time to begin."

Spirits were still coming in through the doors on both sides and in back. When I saw Edward and Claudia, I nudged Rachel, and we both stood up and waved. When Claudia saw us, she said something to Edward, and they both waved back.

"I'm happy to tell you what you already know," Tanya was telling the packed auditorium. "We have with us our very first visitors from above." There was sustained applause. After she called on Natasha to do the introductions and moved to the side, I thought, Tanya and Natasha are quite the one-two punch. It was hard to tell which one of them was more charismatic.

Natasha went out to the center. "Thank you, Tanya, and thank you, friends. I now have the privilege of introducing the very special people who had the courage to come down here and be with us."

That brought more applause as a young staffer in jeans and a 269 T-shirt went out and whispered something to Natasha.

"Thank you, Monique. I've just been informed that one of our visitors, Odiambo from Kenya, won't be joining us at this time because he's having too much fun at the African caucus. As we all know, the caucuses are very popular. Maybe too popular. He'll join us later."

She pointed at me, then said to the audience, "We're going to start with Thomas since he was the first one to come down here. Straight from New York City no less. Welcome, Thomas."

As I went out to the center, I saw Umberto come in a side door, so I waved to him, and he waved back.

Natasha said to me, "Thomas, start by telling us how you got here," then went to the side and stood next to Tanya. By now, every corner of the auditorium was filled.

"I can't believe I'm here," I said, then stopped. What a pitiful way to begin, I thought. Pathetic. I wasn't sure what to say next.

"Start at the beginning," Natasha said. "Who influenced you to come down here?"

"That's easy. It was Edward, or Father Edward as we knew him in school. He was my Latin teacher who taught me about Dante. Little did I know where that was going to take me." There were ripples of laughter. "Needless to say, it was a big shock when seven years after he died, he paid me a surprise late night visit and invited me to join him down here. I couldn't believe he was serious, but I soon found out he was *very* serious." I pointed at him. "Edward, please put your hand up so everybody can see you."

When he raised his hand, Claudia prodded him to raise it higher to laughter and applause.

I looked at Natasha, "So to answer your question, it was Edward who persuaded me to come down here. He's the culprit."

"Are you sorry you came?"

"Not at all. It's been—how shall I say it? It's been *very* educational." I looked out at the smiling faces and heard giggling.

"What's been the highlight of your visit so far?"

Visiting my father was the answer, but I wasn't allowed to say that, so I just thanked everybody for making us visitors feel welcome, "especially Umberto and his staff."

When I had nothing more to say, I looked at Natasha who came back out to the center.

"Thank you, Thomas. And congratulations on being our first visitor. You're making history."

As I returned to my seat, a "Thomas! Thomas!" chant started in back and quickly filled the auditorium.

46

Natasha pointed at Rachel. "I'm now going to ask lovely Rachel to speak. Like Thomas, she's an American, but she's from the other side of their country—California. It took some coaxing to get her to come down here."

The many smiles I saw showed that most of the staff members knew the trouble they had getting her to agree to go down there.

"Hello, everybody," she said and gave them a thumbs-up with both hands. "If I had known I was going to get such a warm welcome, I would have rushed right down here."

Natasha and Tanya laughed and applauded with everybody else.

"Like Thomas, I had a visit from my teacher, who happens to be the internationally acclaimed Dante scholar, Professor Claudia Higgins of the University of California. She's also here." Rachel pointed at her. "Claudia, would you please raise your hand?"

When she did and Edward playfully pushed her hand higher, she gave him a friendly poke.

"Behave yourself, you two," Rachel said with a big smile. "Claudia is the reason I'm here. It was her nighttime visit that convinced me after an Italian guy, who will go nameless, hounded me to the point that I almost called the police. I had made plans to be with my boyfriend and his family this weekend but . . . " She looked up at the ceiling and gave a little wave. "Have fun without me, Randy. You're not going to believe why I couldn't make it."

Looking in her direction again, she said, "Claudia convinced me there really was something to this. So thank you, Claudia, for not giving up on me." She made a little curtsy and gave another thumbs-up that brought a Rachel chant as she went back to her seat.

"Great," I told her and gave her hand a squeeze.

Natasha came back out to the center. "Thank you, Rachel." She looked at Zhao. "OK, Zhao, it's your turn. Come and tell us how you got here. Both Thomas and Rachel went to Italy and came down here the old-fashioned Dante way. But not you, right?"

Zhao blushed as she walked with little steps out to the center. "My aunt lead me," she said barely audibly. "She know everything." She smiled at Qian.

Natasha said to her, "Please speak up, Zhao, so everybody can hear you,"

"Excuse. I not talk to so many people."

Natasha explained to the audience that Zhao came down through an entrance near the Great Wall. "Isn't that right?"

"Yes, yes." She nodded and smiled but didn't say anything more.

"What has been most interesting for you so far?"

Zhao's face lit up. "Confuzius," she said and clapped her hands. When there were puzzled looks, she said "Confuzius" again.

"Confucius!" Rachel shouted.

"Yes, Confucius is here," said Natasha. "Does everybody know that?"

"Yes, yes," said Zhao. "He talk to us. We are very happy." She smiled at Qian and clapped her hands again.

"OK, thank you, Zhao. We're all very grateful you came so far to be with us. And we thank your aunt very much for bringing you."

The applause for them was the loudest yet. Zhao clapped her hands as she made her way back to her seat.

"Very good, Zhao." I gave her hand a squeeze. I liked squeezing living hands down there because there were so few of them.

Natasha turned to Sanjay. "That leaves Sanjay to hear from. Last but not least. Sanjay's from northern India. I say 'not least' because he did something incredibly bold that he's now going to tell you about. So, Sanjay . . . "

The door behind Tanya suddenly opened, and in came a young staffer with a large living man in lederhosen and hiking boots. Natasha signaled Sanjay to stay put and went to the side to talk with the staffer. As Tanya joined them, the large man looked around the room with his mouth open. When the conversation ended, Tanya was smiling and laughing.

Natasha went back out to the center. "The visitors program is certainly off to a flying start. Our newest visitor just arrived, and we'll hear more about that in a moment. But first, I want Sanjay to tell us his inspiring story."

"Thank you, thank you," he said as he went back out to the center. He flashed his brilliant smile as he waited for the applause to die down.

"My name is Sanjay Sanajuna, and I'm from Uttar Pradesh in India." He put the tips of his fingers together and made a slight bow. "For many years, I've been the student of Swami Rimiyananda, who is a great guru and a great man. He does not have a big following yet because he is still young. I'm honored to be one of his followers. Last year he took me aside and said, 'You're ready.' That's all he said. I didn't know what he was talking about."

By now the auditorium was so packed, the overflow was spilling out the doors into the hallways.

"I soon learned what he said I was ready for without his having to tell me. He had told us an ancient Hindu legend about a journey to the Underworld that fascinated me. When I told him I wanted to retrace the journey of the legend, he looked at me with an incredibly peaceful smile but didn't say anything. So I went ahead with my plan without telling him or anybody else.

"When I was ready to leave for the mountains, I told him it was time for my journey. Although he smiled without saying anything, I knew he understood, and I had his blessing. I went by myself to the foothills of the Himalayas, and when I found the legendary cave, I entered it and just kept going deeper and deeper and deeper into it. It was like magic, as if the earth was opening up just for me. I just kept going and going and . . . " He looked at Tanya and Natasha, then back at the sea of faces. He spread his hands out and said with a big smile, "Here I am!"

Natasha went out to the center and waited for the applause to die down. "Thank you, Sanjay, for your courage and determination and for sharing your inspiring story. Now it's time to hear from our newest visitor. Tanya and I have not had the privilege of meeting him, so we're very much looking forward to hearing his story. Please give a warm welcome to Herman."

"Helmut," said the staffer who brought him.

"OK. Helmut, please come out here and tell us about yourself."

He lumbered out in his lederhosen held up by leather suspenders. His bare legs were covered with scratches, and a pickax dangled from his belt. He looked like somebody preserved in ice from an earlier era who had just thawed out.

"So tell us, Helmut," said Natasha. "What gives us the pleasure of your company? Where are you from and how did you get here?"

Speaking with a thick German accent, he said he was from Hamburg and had been mountain climbing in the Andes with his hiking club when an avalanche swept him down into a deep crevice. He said the more he tried to get out, the more trapped he got. He told us he shouted as loudly as he could for as long as he could before he collapsed.

Tanya moved out to the center. "And guess who came to Helmut's rescue?" She paused. "Abdul! Our very own Abdul rescued him."

There was scattered applause.

"That's right. It just so happened that Abdul was in the Andes beginning to construct our first entrance in South America." She turned to Helmut. "So, Herr Helmut, you're a very lucky man."

"Ya, ya. Danke, danke. Aber wo am I?"

"Where are you?" Tanya laughed and winked at Natasha. "You're in Hell."

Helmut looked confused. "Hier ist Hell?"

"Ya, that's where you are, Helmut. You're in Hell. Can't you see how miserable we all are?"

Everybody laughed, and Helmut smiled for the first time. When a Helmut chant broke out, he grinned and clapped along with it. Tanya let it go on longer before she quieted the room.

"Thank you, Helmut, for choosing such an imaginative way to get down here. We welcome you." She moved to the center. "I'm sorry we don't have more time to spend with our wonderful guests, but we have to move on. We're getting some amazing people down here, aren't we?"

Loud applause was followed by a chant that had all the hyped energy of a football cheer. It sounded like "Newel! Newel!"

My, my, I thought, this sure is a fired-up group.

Tanya let the chant go on a while longer before she raised her arms and quieted the room. She turned to us. "Thank you, dear guests. Thank you, thank you." She blew a kiss to the audience and held out her arms. "Thank you all for your enthusiasm. If this doesn't express our spirit, I don't know what does."

That immediately brought an even louder chant of "New Hell! New Hell!" (not "Newel").

47

Tanya raised her arms. "All right, everybody. Now it's time for the part you've all been waiting for. The committee reports!"

A chorus of good-natured groans and hisses filled the auditorium.

"First, let's find out how the caucuses are doing." She looked out into the crowd. "Sonya? I saw you a minute ago. Sonya, are you out there somewhere?"

"Here I am!" came a voice from the side of the room. "The caucuses are doing great."

"Sonya, come up here. I want everybody to hear you."

When she made her way through the crush and emerged up front, I saw another flashy dresser in a crimson satin jumpsuit and black boots. Her chestnut hair was tied in a bun behind her head (do spirits have hair?), and a red bandana was around her neck.

In a voice loud enough for everybody to hear, Tanya said to her, "Tell us about the caucuses." She moved to the side, leaving Sonya in the center.

"First of all, having the caucuses this time was definitely the right thing to do. They're very popular."

"Any problems?" asked Tanya.

"A couple of little ones and one that's not so little."

"Oh?"

"The Greeks."

"What's the problem?"

"Well, as we all know, the Greeks like to have spirited discussions. But Dimitri called to tell me this one was getting out of hand."

"Why? What happened?"

"They're very upset that Dante put Alexander the Great in the Inferno, and he's still there after all these years with history's most notorious murderers. They're outraged he's trapped there with the likes of Genghis Khan, Pol Pot, and Hitler. Since he's on loan to us for the conference, he's the only one of the Greeks who will have to go back. They say it's an insult to Greek civilization that he's still there."

"He's actually scheduled to be released," Tanya said, "but he doesn't know it. And the rest of the Greeks don't know it either."

"And we can't tell them?"

"That's right."

"Too bad because that would solve the problem."

Tanya didn't say anything.

"Not all the Greeks agree about this, of course," said Sonya. "They never do. Socrates and some of the other Greeks think Alexander deserves to be in Hell and should stay there, but they're in the minority."

"Is the situation under control?"

"So far. Aristotle wanted to organize a protest and lead a march here."

I heard nervous laughter.

"And that still could happen."

"Keep them away!" someone yelled.

"Lock them in their caucus room!" somebody else shouted.

Tanya raised her hands to quiet things down.

Sonya said, "Dimitri is keeping an eye on the situation. He's Greek, so he knows how they think. He told Aristotle that since Greece prides itself on being the cradle of democracy, they should decide the matter democratically in assembly. So that's what they're doing now. They're discussing Aristotle's petition, and then they'll vote. But that will take time because in the assembly, everybody gets to speak, and Greeks tend to be long-winded."

"Can we assume then that the problem will be taken care of? That we don't have to barricade ourselves against an army of angry Greeks led by Alexander the Great?"

More nervous laughter.

"Dimitri thinks they'll vote for the petition, but it remains to be seen if Aristotle will lead a delegation that comes here to deliver it."

"Beware of Greeks bearing petitions," somebody shouted.

"Do thank Dimitri for us," Tanya said. "Anything else? How are the Muslims doing?"

"Better. Splitting up the Sunnis and Shiites was definitely the right thing to do. However, there's a problem in the Sunni caucus with the Wahhabis. They're difficult, to say the least. They issue fatwas right and left and condemn to death anybody who disagrees with them."

Tanya looked at Natasha and made a face.

"My thoughts exactly," said Sonya. "Next time we should give the Wahhabis their own caucus or, better yet, not invite them at all."

"I second that," someone shouted.

"They should be in Hell!" somebody else shouted to loud applause.

"Sonya, your point is well taken. We need to rethink our policy about them and also about inviting anybody who's in Hell like Alexander. It only asks for trouble. Thank you for filling us in."

Rachel and I exchanged smiles as if to say, isn't it amazing to be here taking this all in? I was tempted to take out my pad and make some notes, but I decided I better not.

Tanya moved back out to the center. "OK, so now it's time to find out how the panels are doing. Ingrid, come on up here and give us an update."

The crowd parted for a tall, stately blonde I could easily imagine as a Viking sea captain in a previous life. I learned later that she had a doctorate from the University of Uppsala in Sweden.

When she reached the center area, she moved back and forth and waved to spirits she knew in different parts of the room.

"Hi, everybody," she said. "I posted the panel schedule on the side walls and in back. And it's in the hallways too."

She gave copies to Tanya and Natasha, then told the audience, "This has all the latest changes. I'm not going to read it. It's posted everywhere."

Tanya smiled as she looked at her copy. "Ingrid, you've done an outstanding job with this. Very impressive." She held up the program. "Right here is the seed of our future university. Who's going to be able to resist studying with these great minds? Just look at the heavyweights Ingrid has assembled. How about this physics panel—Einstein, Newton, Niels Bohr, and Heraclitus?"

That brought applause and a loud "Ingrid! Ingrid!" chant.

"And how about this astronomy panel—Ptolemy, Copernicus, Galileo, and Carl Sagan. Ingrid, I want to compliment you and thank you for adding so many interesting new panels that we didn't have last time. And how about this one? 'Speaking Up for Animals Through the Ages' with Pythagoras, Leonardo da Vinci, Gandhi, Harriet Beecher Stowe, and Isaac Bashevis Singer. How's that for a lineup?"

Loud applause.

By now, staffers were crowding around the programs posted in the room.

"There are an awful lot of men on these panels," one of them shouted.

"Awful is right!" shouted another.

Tanya said, "Don't blame our patriarchal civilization on Ingrid." She turned to Ingrid. "Males or no males, my dear, you did a great job. We can't thank you enough. Were there any problems?"

"Oh sure. There are always those who resent having their beauty sleep interrupted. As one of them put it, 'One lifetime is enough. I'm not interested in an encore.'"

"Anybody famous turn us down?"

"Descartes. Infamous would be more appropriate in his case. He's in Hell with Claude Bernard, Harry Harlow, and the other vivisectors. We wanted him to be on loan to the conference like Alexander, but he refused. He's still mad at us for criticizing him last time for torturing dogs. He said he wanted nothing to do with our 'animal rights' conference. I don't know why we even bothered to invite him. We live and learn."

"Thank you, Ingrid, and congratulations again. Oh, I almost forgot. Tell them about the mix-up."

"Mix-up?"

"You know, the one with Marx."

"Oh, yes. That was amusing. Although it wasn't funny at the time." Those who were in on the story were smiling, and some of them were already starting to laugh. "As you see on the program, the political science panel has Plato, Machiavelli, Hegel, and Marx. Karl Marx."

"Anyway, when it came time to wake Karl Marx up, the intern on duty in the Tech Room entered "Marx" in the database."

Tanya was now laughing so hard she had to turn away. "Sorry, Ingrid. Go on with your story."

"The database listed Marx's brothers and asked if they should join him. The intern wasn't sure how to answer. He knew some attendees had gotten permission to have their wives join them. Since nobody was around to ask, the intern figured it would be OK to let Karl Marx's brothers join him if they wanted to. He certainly wasn't going to be the one to say no." Now even Ingrid was having trouble keeping a straight face.

"Try to imagine the shock around the Lazarus couch when it came time to wake up Karl Marx's brothers and up popped Groucho, followed in rapid succession by Chico, Harpo, Gummo, and Zeppo." By now everybody was in stitches except Umberto, who smiled sheepishly.

"I got called to the scene," Ingrid said, "so I knew about it right away. The Marx Brothers were sweet and, of course, very funny. They did their shtick and horsed around for our benefit. They're actually a lot of fun. Needless to say, they were thrilled to see each other again at their surprise family reunion. They begged and did everything they could to keep us from sending them back to the Big Nap. After talking it over with Umberto, we decided to let them stay for the conference. So they're around here somewhere. Has anybody seen them?"

A few hands went up.

"What happened to Karl Marx?" someone asked.

"Oh, he's around here somewhere. He's hard to miss. Big, bushy beard."

"Is he any relation to Groucho?" somebody asked.

"Not that we know of. Although, they could be distant cousins."

Tanya moved back out to the center. "That was a good decision to let the Marx Brothers stay and have more time together. I approve." She looked out at Umberto. "As we all know, Umberto has a big heart." This time when she gave him the thumbs up, the applause was louder.

"Thank you again, Ingrid. Let's hear it for Ingrid and the wonderful job she's doing." After the applause died down, Tanya said, "OK, everybody, it's time for a short break before we go on. Don't go away."

Seeing my chance, I quickly went over to Tanya and Natasha. "Before you go," I said to them. "I have a problem I need your help with. I found out that my father, who's in a Purgatory precinct, is scheduled to be terminated soon." I purposely didn't mention Guido because I didn't want to get him in trouble. "I'm very worried about him. It's spoiling my visit. Is there anything you can do to help us?"

It was obvious they had no idea what I was talking about. "It's not fair," I said. "He's a good man. He deserves better."

They looked at each other. Then Tanya said to me, "I'm glad you told us about this. We'll definitely look into it."

48

I was crossing the center area to go back to Rachel when Edward and Claudia emerged from the crowd.

"Welcome back, Odysseus," Edward said with a big smile.

"We missed you," said Claudia. "Where were you? We thought maybe the Crusaders got you."

"Don't ask where he went," Rachel told her. "He's doing cloak and dagger work that he can't talk about. He's the 007 of the Underworld."

Edward whispered to me, "Did you see . . . ? You know . . ."

I assumed he meant Hashem, so I shook my head no.

Claudia said to Rachel, "Can you believe all the energy in this room?"

Edward looked at me. "We never came across anything like this in Dante, did we?"

"That's for sure."

I never saw Edward in such good spirits. The mix of Claudia and New Hell was obviously good for him.

Rachel said to Claudia, "Tanya's a real dynamo, isn't she?"

"Dynamo is right. They're all great."

When Tanya and Natasha returned, Tanya went out to the center and raised her arms.

"OK, everybody. Time for some more reports." She waited for things to quiet down. "Let's start by finding out what's going on with the Entrances Committee. Abdul, you're here somewhere. At least, I hope you are. Abdul? Come out, come out, wherever you are."

There was movement at one of the side doors, and soon the crowd was parting for a short, stout spirit wearing a caftan and fez. He looked North African, possibly

Egyptian. When he reached the front, Tanya turned him around, so he faced the audience.

"Abdul is our engineering genius," she said. "Nobody works harder. Bring us up to date on your projects."

Abdul looked uneasy in front of so many people. "Our goal is to have entrances in every part of the world. At least one or two on every continent. If we don't have safe, easy ways for people to get down here, we're not going to have visitors. We can't expect everybody to go to Italy and use the Dante entrance." He looked over at us. "I understand one of you came down that way?"

"Two," said Natasha.

"Which two?"

Rachel and I raised our hands.

"The two Americans," Natasha said.

Abdul looked at us. "Not so nice, right?"

"You can say that again," I said, and Rachel nodded in agreement.

"When we get more entrances up and running, we'll be able to shut that one down. It's old and not worth fixing. Besides, too many people know about it. The local church has the keys. The last thing we want is to make it easy for souvenir hunters and thrill seekers to come down here."

Pointing at him, Tanya said, "Sanjay came down from the foothills of the Himalayas."

"That's a good entrance," Abdul said. "How was it?"

"It was very scary at first because I didn't know what to expect. It was safe though. But once Guido met me down here, we still had a long way to go."

"That's a problem," Abdul said. "The Italian entrance is the only one that comes here directly. The others need a long walk or a beetle ride. Someday I hope we can build a tram system that connects all the entrances."

While he was talking, Tanya crossed behind him and came over to us. Standing behind Zhao, she said to

Abdul, "Our Chinese friend here, Zhao Lijuan, used the newest entrance. The one near the Great Wall of China."

"Newest is right," Abdul said. "It's so new it's not even finished."

When he asked Zhao how it was, she stood up. "Many troubles, but nothing stop us from come here and talk to Confuzius." She smiled at her aunt, then looked shyly out at the audience that was applauding her.

"Thank you, Zhao," said Tanya. "Another visitor, Odiambo from Nairobi, who's not here now, came down through a mountain cave near Lake Tanganyika."

"He's lucky he made it," Abdul said. "That's not an entrance we recommend. Unless you like snakes and tigers."

"And you already know about our newest visitor, Helmut, because you rescued him. By the way, how are you going to get him back? I assume you're not going to send him back to the Andes."

"No, no. I couldn't return him that way even if I wanted to. It's nowhere close to being finished. He used it without authorization. I'm going to send him back through the Austrian Alps."

"OK," Tanya said, "we have India, China, Africa, Peru, Austria, and Italy, of course. Any other new entrances or exits we should know about?"

"The others we're working on now are in Russia, Indonesia, Japan, and Iceland."

His mention of Iceland made me think of the Jules Verne book. It was fiction, of course, but maybe there was some truth to it.

Rachel stood up and said to Abdul, "And the United States too, right? The Italian guy who contacted me told me there was a way for me to get back to California without having to come up in Italy and fly home from there. I hope he didn't say that just to get me down here."

"What he told you is right. We now have a usable exit that connects to the San Andreas Fault. You'll be the first to use it."

Rachel looked horrified. "Thanks, but no thanks. I have no interest in crawling around inside the San Andreas Fault."

"Don't worry. We know when earthquakes are coming."

Tanya said to her, "We would never send you back any way that wasn't safe." She turned to Abdul. "Thomas won't have to go back the long way either, isn't that right?"

"That's right. There's an exit for him in New Jersey."

That was very good to hear. I dreaded the thought of having to go back to that disgusting basement in Italy.

I stood up and said to Abdul, "You mention entrances and exits. What's the difference?"

"Entrances are also exits, but the exits are not entrances. Entrances are the passages we're developing for human traffic. Exits are cracks and tunnels that are ways to get to the surface but are not developed enough to be entrances. We hope someday to convert most of the exits into entrances."

"Nobody works harder than Abdul," Tanya said again.

Abdul said, "I think that's all the projects. Did I leave any out?"

"Egypt," shouted a not very friendly male voice from the middle of the room.

Dead silence.

"Egypt," the voice shouted again.

"Yes, of course," Abdul said. "Upper Egypt. Not far from where I'm from."

I heard murmuring around the room, but I wasn't able to pick up what was being said.

Abdul said, "I know some people think I'm building that passage just so I can visit my family."

"Well, isn't that true?" the same voice shouted.

Tanya quickly moved to the center and raised her hands. "This is not the time or place to put Abdul on trial. Bring your concerns up to him, or to me, after we're finished."

Sensing somebody behind me, I turned and saw Guido who had come in through the door behind us. He whispered to me, "Time to go."

"Oh, no," Rachel said. "Don't tell me Thomas is going off on another secret mission. Where's he going this time?"

When Guido didn't answer her, she said, "I understand. Everything James Bond does is top secret."

I said good-bye and kissed her on the cheek. Then I made a little wave to Zhao and Sanjay and followed Guido out into the hallway.

"It's definite with the Chief now," he told me. "But it still needs a final OK, which hopefully you'll get on the way."

In the tunnel on the way to the hangar, Guido said, "You're doing something that's never been done before, so we're all going to want to hear about it. But I suspect you'll be sworn to secrecy. The Chief likes his privacy."

He took me to Pietro and told us, "We'll give you the green light as soon we get it."

He wished me luck, and we said our good-byes. Then poof! He was gone.

49

After we were up and on our way, a flashing light on the panel signaled a call. It was Umberto.

"Stay on course. We're assuming the meeting's on, but we'll still need a final confirmation before we leave poor Thomas out there all by his lonesome. Proceed according to plan. Over and out."

Pietro frowned. "I hope this comes off. For your sake and for the sake of all of us."

"What do you think he wants to talk to me about?"

"Who knows? Maybe he's just curious. Or maybe he wants to talk to somebody else besides Naomi."

"His wife."

"More like a soul mate, companion, partner, significant other, whatever. Many think she runs the show behind the scenes through Tanya. She and Tanya are very close. Like mother and daughter."

The light flashed again.

"Good news," said Umberto. "We just got the green light, so it's official. Proceed to the landing site. You have the coordinates. And remember, after you drop Thomas off, leave right away. Don't hang around or go back to make sure he was picked up. Naomi won't show herself until you're gone and out of sight. Is that clear?"

"Yes, sir." Pietro stuck out his tongue and made a face. "How about after the meeting? Do you want me to pick Thomas up when it's over?"

"I'll let you know about that later. For now, just drop him off and leave. Over and out."

Pietro checked the speaker to make sure it was off. "Up yours, Mussolini," he said and gave him the finger again.

"So, my friend," he said turning to me, "you're on. This is very exciting. Nobody has ever had a personal talk with him or even knows where he lives. For us he's an absentee landlord. The only Chief we know is Tanya."

As the mist got thinner during our descent, I saw how forbidding the terrain was—mountains, gorges, canyons, bluffs, escarpments, ravines, cliffs all ominously dark and barely visible through the sullen haze. If Hashem wanted to get away from it all, he couldn't have picked a better place.

"This is the notorious Northwest. We don't call it the Wild West for nothing. Thanks to you, I'm finally getting to see it."

The canyon below us looked devoid of life and movement like the surface of a distant planet. I definitely didn't want to be left there. When I visited my father, Emile had been visible the whole time, and I knew Pietro was waiting for me back in the beetle. But now Pietro had instructions to leave without making sure I was picked up. It was all I could do to keep from telling him I changed my mind and wanted to go back.

"You look like you know where you're going," I said trying to disguise my anxiety.

"I'm just following the coordinates. I've never seen anything like this. Awesome. That should be the landing site up ahead." He pointed at a flat, elevated area in the middle of the canyon. "It fits the coordinates perfectly."

When we came to the site, he lowered us slowly down until I felt the bump that told us we landed.

"This is where I'm supposed to leave you." He didn't sound sure he was doing the right thing. "Somebody from headquarters—me or somebody else—will pick you up when you're finished. So, my friend, I bid you good-bye and wish you all the very best."

I thanked him and got out. As I watched him lift off and zoom down the canyon, I wondered why I thanked him. Thanks for what? For leaving me in this godforsaken place? Well, not godforsaken. At least, I hoped not.

As I circled the landing area, I looked up at the rocky slopes and cliffs. If I had been in a desert canyon up on the surface, there would be at least some signs of life—snakes, bugs, flies, something. But here there was nothing, not even a scorpion.

Will Naomi or whoever's supposed to meet me appear suddenly? Will I see her coming? I hoped I wasn't going to have to wait as long as I had to in that dreadful basement in Italy. Feeling alone and abandoned, I said to myself the Serenity Prayer that asked for help to accept the things I cannot change, the courage to change the things I can, and the wisdom to know the difference. Something like that.

The canyon was eerily silent, and it seemed to be getting darker. The large boulder nearby reminded me of the meteorite I once saw in the American Museum of Natural History in New York.

"Thomas."

I looked around but didn't see anybody.

"Thomas."

The woman's voice was louder and clearer the second time, but I still couldn't tell where it was coming from.

"Here I am," I shouted.

When I looked behind me to the left, I saw a tall, thin specter in a crimson robe coming slowly toward me. I was glad she didn't just pop up in front of me the way spirits tended to do. Her look was both haunted and haunting, as though she had lived through a great tragedy.

"I'm glad you made it," she said. "I'm Naomi. We don't have transportation for you, so you're going to have to walk. Ready for a little hike?"

I nodded and followed her up the canyon. I was glad she didn't drop back and try to talk to me, at least not yet. She turned up a path that curled around under a cliff and took us to a smaller but equally desolate valley. We crossed it and climbed up a long slope. Or rather I climbed. She glided, or was she floating?

Every so often she would look back at me and say something encouraging like "We're getting there" or "Not much longer." She seemed like a nice person, but then I wouldn't expect God's wife to be a shrew.

"There it is," she said, pointing up at an opening in the rocks. "Our humble abode."

Humble indeed. I followed her up to the opening and into a cave where there was barely enough light for me to see anything.

"Welcome, Thomas. We're here." She pointed at a ledge that jutted out from the wall. "Sit down and rest. You've had a long walk. Stay here while I go back and tell him you're here."

"The Chief."

She looked amused. "Are they still calling him that? I'll be right back." She left and disappeared into the darkness.

I felt much better now that I was in contact with her, but I was still feeling uneasy about meeting Hashem, or whoever he was. Was he really God or just somebody who calls himself God? I wondered if I should put this in my book. Probably not. It already had enough credibility problems.

50

When Naomi came back and said, "Come with me. He's ready for you," I got up and followed her down a dark passageway with twists and turns that made me think of the labyrinth in Greek mythology. I wondered if I would I be able to find my way back out if something happened and I needed to make a quick getaway. When we came to a doorway with a low arch, I had to duck down under it to follow her into what looked like a dark chapel or meditation room. The only light came through tiny, circular stained-glass windows.

"I'll be here the whole time," she told me, "but I'm only going to be a listener." She pointed at a cushioned chair with arms. "That's for you. I'll be right here behind you."

I would have liked to sit down after the long, uphill trek, but I decided to stay on my feet until I had a better idea what was going on. As I waited for the Chief, or Hashem, or God, or whoever he was, I felt again like the kid I was when I believed the world was in the benevolent hands of an omnipotent deity.

"Omnipotent I'm not."

Huh? Who was that? I looked around but didn't see anybody. Naomi was behind me, but it obviously wasn't her.

"I'm glad you're here, Thomas."

I looked into the darkness to try to see where he was. Or was he everywhere?

"When I found out you were coming down here, I told Naomi I wanted you to visit us. I don't get to talk to living people, so this is a special treat." He sighed. "As you can imagine, I get all sorts of communications directed *at* me. While most of the prayers are heartfelt, too many of them are acquisitive and self-serving. But enough of my kvetching. Sit down, Thomas. Thank you for coming."

When I sat down, I was surprised my body didn't press against the chair as much as I thought it would.

"Tell me what's on your mind, Thomas."

My father was on my mind, but I wasn't sure if I should start there.

"Begin with your father," he said. "You're worried about him."

"Very worried. I found out he's going to be terminated soon if he hasn't been already."

"Go on. I'm listening."

"I don't want him to be dead, and he doesn't want to be dead either. He deserves better. He helped people all his life." I felt like a lawyer pleading for my client on death row.

"I'm glad you spoke up, Thomas. Naomi, look into this, will you?"

"Done."

Done? Just like that? I turned around halfway and said to both of them, "I can't thank you enough."

"This is not something you should have to worry about while you're here."

His voice was strong and resonant, but there was a tinge of sadness in it that surprised me. I wouldn't expect God to be sad, but then why wouldn't he be?

"Anything else on your mind? Any questions?"

I had lots of them, but where to begin? "Yes, I have a question. I don't mean to be disrespectful, but are you . . . are you, you know, are you really God?"

"Apparently."

Apparently? He's not sure?

"What I am sure of is that different people and cultures make me into whatever they want me to be. They call on me to endorse and protect their way of life, but then if I don't do what they want or do it in a different way, they're disappointed and blame me. They create me in their image and then claim I created them in *my* image. Very circular and narcissistic."

"You don't sound happy about it."

"That's putting it mildly. But all accusation is self-accusation, so I take responsibility for my part. After all, I gave humans the capacity to dominate the earth and its other inhabitants, little knowing they would jump at the chance to do just that. I wanted them to be caring, responsible, compassionate partners, but instead they turned out to be bullies quick to exploit the earth and those who are different and vulnerable. Read *Eternal Treblinka*. It says it all."

"*Eternal Treblinka?*"

"The author is Charles Peterson."

"Patterson," Naomi said.

"Yes. Charles Patterson."

A long pause was followed by another sigh.

"I've seen it all, Thomas—genocide, war, racism, cruelty, greed. The last thing I wanted was an earth plagued by hunger, pollution, and cruelty with its oceans full of sewage, garbage, beer cans, and plastic. That's not what I had in mind. And now they're heating up the earth and aren't doing enough to solve the problem. Frankly, Thomas, I don't know how much longer the show up there can go on, or even should."

I had another question, but I didn't want to interrupt his train of thought.

"Ask your question, Thomas."

"OK, let me play the Devil's advocate for a moment." As soon as I said it, I realized I shouldn't have put it that way. "What I mean is . . . "

"Ask your question."

"My question is, did you or did you not give human beings dominion over the earth and its other beings?"

"I did no such thing."

"But it's in the Bible."

"So?"

"Well, that's your book, isn't it?

"No, it's not my book. People wrote it and then said I did. That's the problem, Thomas. People keep putting words in my mouth, then claim I said them."

"How about the passage in Genesis that says humans are made in your image?"

"That's the arrogance I'm talking about. They make me in *their* image, then claim I made them in *my* image. What they're saying is that because they're made in my image, they can commit any atrocities they want to. It's disgusting."

"How about that humans have souls and animals don't?"

"That's another example of what I'm talking about. When they say animals don't have souls, what they're really saying is it's OK to murder them. But you know what upsets me the most?"

"What?"

"What they did to the commandments. Originally there were twelve of them—the number of the tribes of

Israel—but the Jerusalem priests pressured the scribes to take out two of the commandments that had to do with protecting women, children, and animals. Then, as if that wasn't enough, they changed the Sixth Commandment.

"Thou shalt not kill."

"That's right. Originally it was 'Thou shalt not kill any living being,' but they dropped the 'any living being' part of it out because they didn't want anything to interfere with their highly profitable business of slaughtering animals in the Temple."

I felt his anger filling the room—not peevish, passive-aggressive, mean-spirited human anger but the righteous anger of the prophets. He was no impostor. He was the real thing.

"As you can see, Thomas, I've become jaded living down here. The souls in Heaven were more inspiring and much more enjoyable to be with, but unfortunately, there weren't enough of them to keep it going. That's why I had to close it down and move down here to this miserable hellhole."

Naomi giggled.

"Does that mean you've given up on us?"

"Not at all. There are many good, courageous, caring people up there doing their best to make the world more just and compassionate. They inspire me and give me hope. Bless their hearts. I wish there were more of them."

Naomi whispered to me, "He's been in an especially foul mood since the Holocaust."

"That showed how low people can sink. And it's not over. It's just more spread out. They keep doing it to animals and to the earth and to each other. Eternal Treblinka. I don't want to talk about it."

I wondered what my seminary classmates and professors would think if they could hear this. It would blow their minds.

"I don't mean to sound so negative, Thomas. I hope you don't go back and tell them I've given up on them. I don't want anybody to stop trying. We need all the help we can get. I fully support Tanya's plans to make the world better from down here—from the bottom up, so to speak. I'm not optimistic it will work, but at least she's trying. Bless her heart. We love her."

"Amen," said Naomi.

I had another question, but I didn't know if that was the right time to ask it.

"Ask your question, Thomas."

"It's about astronomy."

I had been doing a lot of reading and thinking about it and went to several Hayden Planetarium events at the American Museum of Natural History to get my head around the fact that this tiny planet we're on is just a grain of sand in the universe's vast ocean of galaxies.

"Tell me what's on your mind."

"My question has to do with the Big Bang that supposedly created the universe. If that's true, what came *before* the bang? There had to be something that banged. What was it? They don't talk about that."

Silence.

"Do you understand what I'm trying to say?

"Yes, Thomas, I hear you."

Naomi said something to him in a language that sounded like Yiddish.

"Thomas," she said, "I'm sorry we can't continue this conversation, but unfortunately, we have to stop. They have their schedule, and I promised them I would get you back on time. We loved having you here, even for such a short visit."

"It was our good fortune, Thomas," said the voice. "We don't get visitors, but if Tanya gets her way, maybe we'll have more."

"If Tanya gets her way," Naomi said, "we'll have so many visitors we'll have to open up a bed and breakfast."

Hashem laughed. That was good to hear because he probably doesn't get much of a chance to laugh down there.

I said good-bye to the darkness and followed Naomi back out through the cave to the path.

On the way to the landing site, I asked her, "What was the name of that book he recommended? *Eternal* . . . ?"

"*Eternal Treblinka*."

"Yes, that's the one. By Charles . . . Charles . . . "

"Patterson."

"I'm surprised he would recommend a book since it sounds like he doesn't even recommend the Bible."

"For good reason. All that business about the domination of animals and the earth, plus the commandments they tampered with that he told you about."

When we came to the end of the small valley that led to the canyon, Naomi stopped and pointed at the landing site ahead of us. "That's where they're going to pick you up."

"Will it be Pietro?"

"I don't know. It will be somebody. If it's all right with you, I'm going to let you go the rest of the way on your own. I hope that's OK with you. I want to get back to Moishe."

"Moishe?"

"I know he's the Chief to everybody else, but to me he's Moishe. It was wonderful meeting you and having you visit us. Thank you for coming. We both wish you the very best up there. Come and visit us again."

"Good-bye, Naomi. Thank you very much for your hospitality."

On the way to the landing site, I wondered what she meant when she said to come and visit them again. Did she mean visit them again before I leave? Or visit them later when I come down there? If I do end up there, will I be assigned to one of the Purgatory precincts like my father and grandfathers were? Or will Bishop Howard have his way and I get sent to . . . to . . . I didn't want to think about it.

51

When I saw what looked like a limousine coming up the valley floor, I wondered, Are they really sending a limo to pick me up? Now that's real service. As it got closer, I saw it was a sedan with black and brown markings similar to the ones on the beetle fleet. But why would they send a car? Were all the beetles in service?

The driver who got out was dressed in an orange jumpsuit and goggles. "My name is Bruno," he said. "I'm here to pick you up."

"I was expecting Pietro."

"He has another assignment."

He looked like he might be Italian, but his accent was hard to place.

I pointed at the car. "Will we be riding back in this the whole way?" I certainly hoped not. That would make for a very long trip.

"Part of the way."

"How long will it take?"

He shrugged without answering me, and we got in. He made a U-turn and headed back down the canyon floor without saying anything more.

"It's pretty desolate out here," I said, trying to get him to say something to give me an idea of who he was. But he just kept staring ahead without speaking. I thought, Oh boy, this is going to be a fun ride.

I took out my pad and jotted down some notes about my visit with Hashem.

"I understand you're a writer."

"Because of this?" I held up my pad.

"No, I knew you were a writer before I picked you up."

"How did you know that?"

When he didn't answer me, I wondered, Who is this guy anyway? He didn't look like what I imagined a Crusader would look like, but maybe he's working for them.

"Where are you taking me?"

"The boss wants to see you."

"Boss? I just talked to him."

"Not that boss. *Our* boss."

"I don't understand."

"That's all I'm allowed to say. I'm just following orders."

Oh, great. Where have I heard that before?

I went back to my pad and jotted down some more notes. When we approached a low, flat stucco building that looked like a transplanted ranch house, Bruno slowed down and turned onto a gravel drive that went up to the columned portico in front. He told me to get out and took me behind the building past a row of empty steel drums and up onto a porch with a brick floor. I followed him through the door held open by a cinderblock and down a narrow hallway to a small room that had an iron cot against the wall and a small sink in the corner. The only window faced the adjacent cell.

"Make yourself at home," Bruno said with a smirk.

"What's going on? I feel like a prisoner."

"You *are* a prisoner."

"Why? What are the charges against me?"

He left without even looking at me and locked the door. Now there was no question about it. I really *was* a prisoner. But whose? Who is Bruno's boss?

I looked at the cot and the bars on the window and didn't know whether to cry or pray or do both.

"Thomas."

The voice was familiar.

"Thomas, is that you? It's me, Rachel."

"Rachel?" I went to the window. When I saw the top of her head, I put my fingers through the bars, and we touched the tips of our fingers.

"I couldn't believe it when they told me you were going to be here."

"What are *you* doing here?"

"I was with Umberto when he showed the new visitors his museum-to-be. While he was giving his spiel, which I had heard before, I went off to look at other things. Somebody claiming to be on the staff started up a conversation with me. Then somebody else joined us. Before I knew it, they lured me away and brought me here."

"Who are 'they' and what do they want?"

"As I understand it, they want us to hear what Satan has to say."

"Satan?"

"That's what they call their leader apparently. He's obviously not Satan."

"Don't be so sure. At the orientation meeting, the one you missed, Umberto said Satan lives out this way, and he's still active. So who knows? Maybe he is Satan."

"Oh nonsense. Satan is just the name these guys give their gang leader."

"Guido says there are insurgents out this way, and they control certain areas."

"Oh great. So we've fallen into the hands of insurgents?"

"Looks that way."

"I had no idea where they were taking me, but I must say they treated me better than I expected. They're very interested that I'm from California. They asked me a lot of questions."

"Maybe they think we're celebrities, and they can get ransom for us."

"I don't get that impression. Do you know what I'm most worried about now?"

"What?"

"My mother. She must be worried to death. When I told Randy I wouldn't be able to join him this weekend, I never should have used the lame excuse that my mother wasn't feeling well. I should have known he would call her. By now, they probably called the police. Oh well, what's done is done. How did they capture you? The last I knew Guido was taking you off to one of your secret assignments. Where did you go?"

"Sorry, but I can't tell you. Besides, you would never believe me."

"Try me."

"I can't."

"Oh, come on. Where did you go? I won't tell."

"You're very persistent."

"Edward told Claudia you visited your father when you didn't go on the museum tour with us. Is that true?"

"My lips are sealed."

"I must confess visiting a dead relative seems weird to me. Sort of ghoulish. Did you go back and visit your father again?"

"If I tell you, you're going to think I'm crazy."

"Well, you *are* crazy." She laughed.

Why was I keeping all these secrets? I was starting to lose track of them.

"OK, I'll tell you if you promise not to tell anybody."

"I promise. Except . . . how about Claudia? Can I tell her? She won't tell. She's good at keeping secrets."

"I really shouldn't tell you."

"Oh, come on. What's the big secret? Where did you go?"

"OK, since you promised not to tell. Do you know about the Northwest?"

"No."

"It's a remote area Pietro took me to. He or somebody else was supposed to pick me up, but one of these jokers got to me first and brought me here."

"Why did Pietro take you to the Northwest?"

"To talk to somebody."

"Who?"

"I . . ."

"Thomas, tell me who you talked to. Please! It's not fair to torture me like this."

"You're right. OK, I'll tell you. I talked to . . . "

"Yes? You talked to . . . ?

"God."

"God?"

"Hashem. The one they call the Chief."

The silence on the other side of the window was deafening. Rachel missed the orientation, so she obviously didn't know what I was talking about.

"Are you trying to tell me you saw God?"

"I didn't see him. Nobody sees him. We talked."

"You talked to God? And he talked back to you?"

"That's right."

"Maybe he's just somebody who calls himself God. Like this guy who calls himself Satan."

Now I realized I should have kept my mouth shut. This wasn't the time to get into it with her, so I didn't say anything more.

After a long pause, she said, "So this god you supposedly talked to . . . what was he like?"

"Well, to be quite honest with you, he seemed a bit depressed."

"God is depressed?"

"He's discouraged about the way things have turned out. He thinks we're the bullies of the universe."

"It's hard to argue with that."

I heard a key turn in the door behind me. "Shush! Somebody's coming. I'll talk to you later." I stepped back from the window. It was Bruno.

"He wants to see you."

"Me?"

"Yes."

"Just me?"

"Both of you.

52

I followed Bruno down the hall to a large square-shaped room with wall hangings covered with what looked like runic characters. Up on the platform in front was an elaborately carved red chair that looked like a throne. Bruno took me to one of the two chairs on the floor facing it and motioned me to sit down. He then went and stood against the wall next to two guards also dressed in orange. Another guard came in with Rachel and took her to the other chair.

The big guy who came in next was also dressed in orange, but the stripes on his sleeves indicated a higher rank. At first, I thought he might be the leader, but he also went and stood against the wall with the other guards.

The door opened again, and in came somebody wearing jeans, boots, a lavender sports shirt, and a brown felt cowboy hat. No orange uniform for him. He swaggered over to the platform and got up on it as the guards chanted something that sounded like "Niko Quall Hymen Rustics." When he shouted "Bryn," they raised clenched fists and shouted "Farouche" three times.

The leader looked down at us. "If you're wondering why you're here, it's because your visit won't be complete if you only get one side of the story. You also need to get the other side." He looked at me. "Don't you agree?"

I didn't say anything, but when he kept staring at me, I nodded.

"I'm now going to sit down so you don't feel I'm lording it over you. Although lording it over others is what we're all about." He looked around the room at his men who laughed and smiled as if on cue.

When he sat down, his men chanted "Niko Quall Hymen Rustics" again.

He looked down at me. "You're Thomas Reed, and I understand you're writing a book."

How come everybody down here knows I'm writing a book? Even Satan.

"That's right, but it's only in the planning stage." I was tempted to show him my pad, but I decided not to. He might take it away.

"I like the entertaining way you left your church. You didn't just slink away the way most of them do. Some of the things you did were very amusing."

How did he know what I did up there? What amusing things did he have in mind?

"Since you're the first visitor down here, there's obviously going to be a lot of interest in what you have to say. Many people are going to read and hear about your book, so what you write needs to be fair and accurate, don't you agree?"

I didn't answer him, but when he asked me again, I said, "Yes, I agree." I glanced at Rachel, who was giving me a funny look.

"Good. I hope you'll leave out the tired clichés and stereotypes, especially of me."

"I intend to make my book as fair and as truthful as I can. I welcome different points of view. I obviously didn't plan on being here, but now that I am, I'm interested in finding out what you have to say."

Satan looked around the room at his men with a satisfied smile.

This is amazing. It sounds as if he might support my book if he thinks it's fair and accurate. He's certainly going to be in it. Maybe I can interview him or get a blurb. That would make it a bestseller for sure. How fortunate I'm here.

"By the way," I said to him, "what do you want us to call you?" I hoped to get a better sense of who this guy really was, or at least who he thought he was.

"I've been called lots of things. Lucifer. Beelzebub. The Devil. Prince of Darkness. You name it. And of course, Satan. Plus, any other name they can come up with to scare children and simple-minded adults. My men call me Boss. You can call me that."

I looked at Rachel. I certainly wasn't going to call him Boss, and I couldn't imagine she would either.

"How about Satan?"

"That's good enough."

He turned to Rachel. "And you're Rachel."

She didn't answer him or even look at him.

"Where were you, my princess, when we escorted you here?"

His men chuckled. It was hard to tell if they were laughing because they thought he was funny or because they were afraid not to.

"Ask your thugs." She turned and glared at them.

"My, my, aren't we the little spitfire." Satan and the big guy looked at each other and laughed.

"I don't like being kidnapped," she said. "And furthermore, I don't like your goons standing around gawking at me. Why are they here anyway? Are you trying to impress us with your macho militia? Or is your goon squad here to protect you because you're afraid of us?"

I liked Rachel's feistiness, but I didn't think this was a good time for it to be on display.

Satan went over to the big guy and said something that sounded like gibberish. By now several more guards had come in and were standing against the walls. After Satan finished telling him something, the big guy said something to the guards that made them all leave.

Satan looked at Rachel. "So, Miss Rachel, is that better?"

"Thank you, Boss!"

He pointed at the big guy. "By the way, this is Otto, my right-hand man."

Otto flashed a toothy grin and nodded.

Satan looked at me. "I understand you had a meeting with the so-called Chief. How is the old fart?"

Rachel was looking at me again with her funny look.

"You should have talked to me first. I've been down here from the beginning while he's a newcomer who doesn't belong here. He's only here because his grandiose dream of a Heaven full of adoring fans fizzled out. So he came down here to live in a cave with his mistress."

I thought, whoever this Satan character is, he's more articulate and intelligent than I expected.

"Don't misunderstand me," he said. "I don't hold it against him that he's a hermit. Who can blame him? These are not exactly his kind of people." He chuckled. "People assume we're mortal enemies, but that's not true. We're certainly not friends or allies, but we aren't really enemies either. We're rivals with different ways of looking at things."

I resisted the temptation to take out my pad and write down what he was saying.

"How do you see things differently?" I asked him.

"I'm a realist, and he's an idealist. More than an idealist, he's a romantic idealist. Or maybe I should say an idealistic romantic."

This guy could be a professor at one of our universities. He would fit right in.

"How is he an idealistic romantic?"

"He looks at the world as he thinks it should be, not as it is. He expects people to live up to his standards. Then his feelings get hurt when they don't. He goes into a funk when people think and behave the way *they* want to, not the way he wants them to. You were just with him, right?"

"That's right."

"Well, how did he come across to you? Did he seem like a winner?"

"What do you mean by winner?"

"Did he impress you as somebody who's playing a winning hand? Somebody confident that he's on the right side of history and history is on his side? That the cause he supports and believes in is the wave of the future?"

"He'll have to speak for himself about that. He's clearly disappointed if that's what you're getting at. He put a lot of faith in human beings to lead the way, but we haven't lived up to his expectations."

"That's exactly what I'm talking about. He sets his expectations unrealistically high and then feels hurt when people don't live up to them. He created Heaven to reward those who meet his standards, and look what happened. So few people qualified he had to close it down. He should know by now it's a waste of time to try to make people into something they aren't and don't want to be. Up there, and both of you know this better than I do because you live there, they're buying more into my way of thinking than his. That's why he's down here sulking in his cave."

Rachel said, "I have a question for you, Mr. Boss Man."

"Yes, what's your question, Princess Rachel?" He seemed to be enjoying their duel.

"What's your great way of looking at things that you claim people are buying into?"

"Might makes right, my dear. Pure and simple. It's a truth that's so basic, it's obvious. Strength is good. Weakness is bad. That's what it's all about, and the people up there know it. They don't need prompting from me. These days I just sit back and enjoy the show. All he does is watch and weep."

As much as I didn't like to admit it, that was pretty much what he was doing.

"So might makes right is what the world needs more of?" Rachel asked him. "Is that your uplifting message?"

"Look at history, my dear. Granted there has been too much war, crime, and violence, but look at the progress that's come with it: science, technology, medical advances, space exploration, the internet, etc., etc. The list of human accomplishments is endless. My point is you can't have progress without strength, power, assertiveness, and, yes, domination. The alternative is weakness, failure, passivity, and defeat." He stood up and shook his fist. "Might makes right!"

Rachel made a face. "Sounds fascist to me."

"Fascism, smascism. The meek do not inherit, my dear. The first are first, and the last are last. To the victors, the spoils!" He raised his fist again and looked at Otto. They both shouted "Farouche" three times.

Rachel rolled her eyes at me, then turned back to him. "So tell me, Mr. Boss Man, in your hierarchical view of things, where do women fit in? Forget the animals, as I'm sure you do. Where do women fit in?"

"Fear not, my Jewish princess. You ladies have a central, albeit subordinate role to play."

"There it is!" She shot up out of her chair, put her hands on her hips, and glared at him. "You give yourself away as the sexist fascist you are. I'm so glad I took the time to come and hear your inspirational message, Boss!"

Satan and Otto looked at each other and burst out laughing. Rachel sat down in a huff and looked away.

I thought Beatrice would like Rachel. I could imagine them being good friends.

One of the guards who had been in the room earlier leaned in the door and put his thumb and finger up to his ear.

"Keep an eye on them," Satan said to Otto. "I have a call. I'll be right back."

I would have liked to talk to Rachel, but with Otto hovering over us, I decided it was better to keep quiet.

When Satan came back, he was in a better mood. "You'll be interested to know your disappearance caused quite a stir. I assured them you're safe and are being well taken care of." He looked at me. "I told them we discussed your book, and since you promised to make it fair and accurate, I have no further need to detain you. They're sending someone to pick you up."

"They're coming here?"

"Not here. They'll pick you up at the landing site where they were supposed to pick you up before." He smiled at Otto. "But we beat them to it." They both laughed.

53

On the way back to the landing site, Bruno was his usual noncommunicative self. Living in Hell and working for Satan were obviously not conducive to improving one's social skills.

"This is the most barren landscape I've ever seen," Rachel said to me as we bumped along the canyon floor. "And I've seen some pretty desolate places. Like the Mojave Desert and the Dead Sea."

"It gets worse as we get closer to where I talked to God."

"I'm sorry, Thomas, but your saying you talked to God sounds . . . I don't know . . . I have a problem with it. I mean you didn't actually see this God person, right? Isn't that what you told me?"

"That's right."

"Then why not just say you talked to somebody who claimed to be God? I don't have a problem with that."

"If that makes you happy, fine. By the way, he was the one who requested to see me."

"God asked to talk to you? Is that what you're trying to tell me?"

"That's right. You might have gotten invited too if you had come down here when you were supposed to."

We rode back the rest of the way in silence.

When we arrived at the landing site and Bruno let us out, Rachel asked him, "What happens if nobody comes?"

He shrugged without answering her, made a U-turn, and headed off without even a wave or nod.

"Charming fellow." She looked around at the cliffs. "This is awesome. More than awesome. It's terrifying."

I soon heard the beetle, and moments later, it came through the mist and landed. I felt a tremendous sense of relief when I saw Pietro get out. He came over to us with a big smile.

"I understand you two had quite an adventure. And, Thomas, you've had an especially interesting time since I last saw you. Not everybody gets to hobnob with God and Satan on the same day."

I looked at Rachel as if to say, "See, Pietro doesn't think it's so strange that I talked to God."

"There's been a change of plan," he told me.

"Oh?"

"I'm not taking you back."

"Oh, no. Now what?"

"I'm taking you and Rachel to the Chief."

"But I was already there. Why would he want to see me again?"

"It's Rachel they want to see, or rather I should say who Naomi wants to see. Umberto says it's urgent."

"Who's Naomi?" Rachel asked.

"God's wife," I said.

"The person who says he's God has a wife?"

Pietro looked amused.

"It's a long story. I'll explain later."

I didn't like this change of plan. I had been counting on going back and talking to Edward whom I had barely seen. I also wanted to catch at least some of the conference, especially the Italian Renaissance panel that Dante was supposed to be on. Besides, I wasn't looking forward to a long trek back up to the cave.

Pietro must have read my mind because he said, "The good news is I have permission to fly you up much closer, so you won't have to walk as far."

We squeezed into the cabin with Rachel in the middle. It was a day for getting squeezed, but I didn't mind. In an Underworld devoid of physical contact, it felt good having Rachel's body pressed against mine.

Pietro flew straight up the canyon, keeping a close eye on the coordinates since this was totally new territory for him.

When I told Rachel what Naomi was like, she said, "She must be Jewish with a name like that."

"She doesn't seem all that old. By that, I mean I get the feeling she's only been dead for a few decades. I get the impression she's from Eastern Europe."

"Why do you say that?"

"Male intuition."

Rachel laughed. "Well, we all know how reliable that is."

Pietro asked me if any of this looked familiar.

"It's hard to tell from up here."

"According to the coordinates, we're right on course."

Rachel asked Pietro if he was going to wait for us.

"I'm not supposed to, but I'll be back, or somebody else will be to pick you up when you're finished."

"How will you know when we're finished?"

"Don't worry. We're in contact." As he lowered us down, he said to me, "I've never been this close to where the Chief lives. I doubt anybody has. Except you, of course."

After he let us off and wished us luck, he lifted off and headed back down the valley. I felt Rachel take my hand.

"Thomas, I'm scared."

I told her how Naomi showed herself to me earlier so she would know what to expect. A couple of minutes later, I heard, "Thomas," but I didn't see her.

It was Rachel who saw her first. "There!" she said, pointing behind me.

I was glad that Naomi was approaching as slowly as she did last time.

"It's good to see you again," I told her when she got closer. "And so soon. This is Rachel."

"Yes, I know."

"This is Naomi," I said to Rachel.

She looked at Naomi without speaking until she finally said, "I'm glad to meet you." She kept staring at her.

"It's a great pleasure to have you here, my dear. Both of you. Please follow me."

Naomi fell in beside Rachel as we headed up the path. I walked behind them but was close enough to hear what they were saying. Naomi asked her where her family was from.

"New York originally, then Cleveland. I now live in Berkeley, California."

"I was hoping you were going to come down here, so I was very happy when I learned you finally decided to come."

"It wasn't easy getting me down here, I admit. Not like Thomas." She looked back at me and smiled.

"He's a fine young man," Naomi said.

"Hear that, Thomas?"

"Yes, I'm here. Taking up the rear."

Naomi asked Rachel where her family was from before they came to America.

"You mean in Europe? My grandparents on my mother's side were from a village outside Minsk and my father's family was from Grodno. Most of my relatives were killed in the Holocaust."

When we reached the cave, Naomi took us through the opening and gestured to us to sit down on a bench that hadn't been there earlier. Naomi placed herself across from Rachel on the same level so it made it easier for them to talk.

"I don't want to leave you out," Naomi said to me, "but I hope you don't mind if Rachel and I talk a little about family matters."

"Not at all."

"Do you remember your grandmother?" Naomi asked her. "Your mother's mother?"

"Very well. She died when I was eight, but I have a lot of good memories of her."

I sensed something important was happening, so I asked Naomi if she wanted me to go off for a little while to give them more privacy.

"No, stay here," Rachel said to me. "I don't want you to go."

"There's no need for you to leave," said Naomi.

That made me feel better, so I just sat back and listened.

Naomi leaned closer to Rachel. "So tell me, my dear, what do you remember about your grandmother?"

"I have lots of good memories of her. She used to tell me stories about the old country, especially before the war changed everything. She talked about her family, school friends, shul, that sort of thing. Sometimes she talked about things that weren't so good like the bad things that happened to the Jews, but she didn't go into it that much. When she did, she would shake her head and say she didn't understand why the world was so full of hatred and war."

Rachel looked sad talking about her grandmother, and sometimes she and Naomi just looked at each other without saying anything. A couple of times I would have liked to ask a question, but I decided to stay in the background and keep quiet.

"My dearest Rachel, I hope you don't mind me asking you these questions."

"Not at all."

"I have a special interest in all of this, as I'll explain in a moment. But tell me more about your grandmother. For example, what did she say about her mother? Anything?"

"Oh, yes, she talked about her a lot—how she taught her to sew and cook and make clothes. Her mother was a seamstress who supported the family because her father was a scholar who didn't make much money. But Grandma said her mother loved him very much."

I now realized this conversation was the reason we were there.

"Did your grandma ever say what happened to her mother?"

"She didn't say anything about it until the last time I saw her. I'll never forget it. When I asked her why her mother didn't come with her to America, Grandma said she would have loved to come and be with us. She looked so sad, I didn't ask her any more questions. A little later, she told me what happened, and I'm glad she did because it was the last time I ever saw her.

"Grandma told me that just before the Germans came to their village, her mother arranged to have a Polish family take her in. When the Germans arrived, they rounded up the Jews and took them to the staging area supposedly to send them to a work camp. Grandma found out about it and went there to look for her mother.

When she saw her on the back of one of the trucks, she ran to it and tried to climb up on it to be with her. Her mother shouted at her to get down and pushed her back so hard Grandma fell down in the street. When the truck pulled away, Grandma ran after it screaming and sobbing. Her mother, who was also crying, waved good-bye to her, but Grandma was so mad at her for leaving her that she didn't wave back. She never saw her mother again.

"By the time Grandma finished telling me the story, she was in tears. I hugged her to try to make her feel better, but she just kept crying. I'll never forget it. When I was older, my mother told me what happened. The truck took Grandma's mother to Treblinka where the Germans killed her in the gas chamber."

Naomi lowered her head and remained silent. When she finally looked up, she said, "My dearest Rachel, I was the one who kept your Grandma from getting up on the truck when all she wanted was to be with me." Naomi looked down again, but then after a long pause looked back up. "My darling Rachel, your beloved grandma was my daughter. I was her mother. I'm your great-grandmother."

They hugged and cried, and I cried too.

54

After Naomi's dramatic disclosure, Rachel looked shaken but content. How many people get to talk to their dead great-grandmother?

Naomi took us back to the chapel-like room where I had been earlier. "Here she is," she said to the darkness. "This is my beloved Rachel."

"My pleasure and honor," said the voice.

Rachel looked around to see who was talking.

"He's here," I whispered. "God."

She looked at me but didn't say anything.

Still staring into the darkness, Naomi said, "While you two gentlemen solve the world's problems, Rachel and I are going to go off and spend some time together. You know where you can find us."

Off they went, leaving me alone. Well, not really alone. Hashem was there somewhere. By then I was feeling overwhelmed by it all—being with my father, then with Hashem not once but twice with time in between spent with Satan. All that followed by what Naomi told Rachel. What a weekend! Dante's weekend in the Inferno was a cakewalk compared to this.

"I'm very happy for Naomi," Hashem said. "Making contact with her daughter's family after all these years. It does my heart good."

"Speaking of family, I would like very much to see my father again before I leave if that's possible. As you know, I'm very concerned about him."

"Yes, Thomas, I know. After you left, Naomi looked into it."

"Does that mean it will be taken care of?"

"I'm sure it will be. Naomi's very dependable. What would I do without her? Did you know she was one of the six million?"

"Yes, I was with them when she told Rachel."

"Some Jews blame me."

"Blame you for the Holocaust?"

"They wonder why I didn't stop it. As if I didn't care." His voice trailed off. "Up there in certain theological circles, they talk about my 'eclipse.' 'The Crucified God' is how one German theologian put it. Some of them even claim I'm dead. Well, I'm not dead. Although sometimes, I think I might as well be."

There was a long silence. "Thomas, I owe you an apology about what happened last time you were here. Because we ran out of time, I never got to answer your question about the so-called Big Bang that scientists claim created the universe. Their theory contradicts the claim of many others who are certain that *I* created the universe. In six days, no less. Ha! They make me into a supernatural superman who can do amazing things like create the universe in six days and stop the Holocaust in its tracks."

He gave out a long sigh.

"Not only did I *not* create the universe like the Bible claims I did, I have no idea how it came into existence. I don't even know how *I* was created. I obviously exist, but how did I get here? It's a total mystery to me. Maybe I'm the result of some sort of supernatural big bang?" He laughed. "A cosmic coitus! That's what it was." He laughed again. "But enough about big bangs. Thinking too much about how it all started can drive you crazy. Speaking of crazy, I understand Satan corralled you on your way back."

"That's right."

"What happened?"

"I was waiting at the landing to be picked up when somebody I never saw before showed up in a car and took me to him. Rachel was there too."

"He's a feisty fellow. Misguided but feisty. What was your impression?"

"He's very different from what I expected."

"What did you expect?"

"I expected him to be more frightening, more evil, more powerful. More the way he's pictured."

"I know. Pitchfork. Horns. Tail. Jewish nose like mine."

"He says you two aren't really enemies. 'Rivals' was the word he used."

"Oh, we're not even that. He's as obsolete as I am. Maybe even more so. In some ways, we're mirror images of each other. Two sides of the same coin. Jinn and Jang. But if we talk about who's up and who's down, I'm the first to admit he's up. More people follow his way of looking at the world than mine. Many more."

I was glad Naomi and Rachel were off on their own. I didn't want them to come back too soon.

"I have no animosity toward Satan. He's a bit of a buffoon. How about that silly cowboy hat he wears? But I must confess that over the years, I've actually become fond of him. He's a colorful character. Narcissistic and narrow-minded, to be sure, but basically harmless. The world would be much less interesting without him."

"He's harmless?"

"His bark is worse than his bite. There are a lot worse down here, and up there, he would be an angel compared to some of them. Besides, he's very much on his good behavior these days because he wants to be part of the government."

"The Council?"

"That's right. I'm sure that's why he let you go so quickly. He doesn't want to hurt his chances of getting on the Council. He learned his lesson: If you can't beat them, join them. But enough of my rambling. I understand you're writing a book."

"That's my plan, but I haven't done any writing yet." I took the pad out of my back pocket and showed it to him. "I write notes in this, but it's hard to keep up with everything that's going on."

"Good for you. I thought about writing a book once. To counterbalance what the theologians and philosophers say about me, claiming I'm this or that or I'm for or against something they're interested in. I don't recognize myself in most of what they say. I thought a book might set the record straight."

"Many think such a book already exists."

Silence.

"The Bible."

"Don't get me started on that again. I already told you how people keep putting words in my mouth, and the Bible is the prime example. Speaking of books, does Satan know you're writing one?"

"Yes, I was surprised. And he wasn't shy about giving me advice. He told me he wants my book to be truthful and fair."

"Of course. Truthful and fair about him is what he means. He's always gotten bad press. They make him out to be more of an ogre than he is. I'm sure that's why he corralled you. He hopes you'll help him shed his bad boy image."

"How do the Crusaders fit into all this? I don't know what to make of them. I want to put them in my book even though they disapprove of me."

"They disapprove of everybody but themselves. By all means put them in your book. They're a strange bunch but interesting. As I'm sure you know by now, they used to be in charge down here, and now they're on the Council. But they're totally fixated on the past. They long for the restoration of the glory days of Christendom. By all means include them. They're still a big part of the scene down here."

"I would also like to write about my visits here if that's OK with you."

"Why not? Everybody else writes about me. And they haven't even talked to me."

"Do I have permission to quote you?"

"Feel free. Everybody will think you're crazy, of course, but don't let that stop you. Don't let anything stop you. Writing a book isn't for the faint-hearted."

Oh, damn! I heard voices that meant Naomi and Rachel were coming back. Moments later they appeared.

"I hope you two gents had a nice talk," Naomi said. "I'm sorry I have to interrupt, but it's time for Thomas to go. I've arranged to have Rachel stay longer so we can have more time together. It's not very often I get to be with my great-granddaughter. Thomas, I hope that's all right with you."

"That's fine," I said, although I would have liked to have more time to talk to Rachel.

"I told them I'll get you back to the landing area, the closer one. That's where they'll pick you up."

Naomi turned to the darkness. "Having Rachel here with me is a miracle. So thank you, thank you. And having her stay longer is an extra blessing."

I said to her, "I can go back to the landing area on my own if you want. I know the way."

"I won't hear of it. Our intern will take you. Come with me. Both of you."

"Good-bye, Thomas," said the voice. "Thank you for your visit and good luck with your book."

I waved good-bye to the darkness and followed Naomi to the entrance. She sat us back down on the bench and left.

Rachel had a faraway look in her eyes.

"Anything wrong?"

"She told me what she went through. Not everything, but it was enough." Rachel's eyes were moist. After a long silence, she said softly, "I know how he feels."

"Who?"

"God. You can hear it in his voice. Naomi told me she sometimes hears him crying."

That's ironical, I thought. For centuries they portrayed him as almighty, omnipotent, omniscient, Lord of Lords, King of Kings, mighty, powerful, invincible, etc., etc. If they could only see him now—the Crying God who lives in a cave in a remote corner of Hell.

"He has a lot to cry about," I said.

"Naomi says he likes to listen to the *Dies Irae*, the 'Wrath of God' part of Verdi's *Requiem*, because it expresses the powerful anger he feels."

Naomi reappeared with a thin spirit dressed in jeans and a Brandeis T-shirt. She looked like one of Tanya's girls, even younger. For a spirit, she looked very alive.

"This is Jessica," Naomi said to me. "Jessie, this is Mr. Reed. He's the one I want you to take down to the landing. Thomas, it's been a pleasure as usual. Please come back and visit us again. Maybe Umberto can find a place for you on his staff when the time comes. You'll have to brush up on your Italian, of course, but for some-body who read the *Inferno* in the original, that shouldn't be too hard."

Hashem's wife knows I read parts of the *Inferno* in Italian? My God, what don't they know?

I gave Rachel a hug and told her I would see her back at the conference. Then I followed Jessica out the cave and down the path. On the way she told me she was a junior at Brandeis taking spring semester off. "It came down to a semester at the University of Grenoble or this. Since I'm a French major, a semester at Grenoble would have been a big boost, but I couldn't pass this up."

"I'm surprised you're going back because you really do look like a spirit. I mean you don't have a physical body like Rachel and me."

She laughed. "Well, I'm not dead yet. I'm in what they call the spirit mode. It's just while I'm down here. It's in the agreement. When I go back, I'll return to the physical mode and be like you and Rachel again. Naomi says you're writing a book."

"I haven't written a word, but everybody down here seems to know about it. It's already an underground classic, no pun intended."

"Does it have a title?"

"Not yet. I'm thinking of *My Weekend in Hell*."

"Hey, that's catchy. How can they resist when they find out it really does take place down here and it's not just about an awful weekend with the in-laws or whatever?"

She pointed at the landing area ahead of us. "Naomi told me not to wait with you because if they see me, they might not land. So this is as far as I can go with you."

"That's too bad because I like talking to you."

"Thank you, Mr. Reed. It was very nice meeting you. Give my best to the gang up there and tell them to behave themselves. Have a safe journey back."

"Thanks, Jessica. Good for you for choosing this for your internship. In the words of Robert Frost, you took the road less traveled by."

"That's sweet of you to say that. Good luck with your book. I look forward to reading it."

PART 3

THE TRIAL

PART 2

55

Pietro got out of the beetle and came over to me smiling. "Good news, Thomas. Guess what?"

"What?"

"You're going to visit your Crusader friends. Tanya approved your request and made the arrangements. I'm taking you there now."

"Now?"

"Don't tell me you changed your mind."

"No, no. It's just that . . . "

"What?"

"It's just that this is getting to be one damn thing after another. I was hoping to go back and hang out with Edward. I've barely seen him. And maybe catch some of the panels. Besides . . . "

"Besides what?"

"I'm having second thoughts about visiting them. I want them in my book, but something tells me I should keep my distance. They think I'm a heretic."

"Don't worry. Tanya won't let anything happen to you. It's in the agreement. Trust her. This is a great opportunity. Don't pass it up."

"I know, I know, but . . . "

"No buts about it. Your book will be much better for it."

"No, you're right. Of course, I'll go." I thrust my arm up over my head. "Onward to the next adventure!"

Pietro laughed. "That's the spirit."

Once we were up and on our way, he told me how Tanya made it happen.

"Not only do you have an official invitation, but she hammered out an agreement with them that guarantees your safety. With the Crusaders, one can never be too careful."

I knew this was a journalistic coup, and I should feel good about it, but knowing the Crusaders had it in for me made me uncomfortable, agreement or no agreement. Also, I couldn't shake the feeling that Bishop Howard was involved in this somehow. I knew it was crazy thinking, but that's what was going on inside my head.

"Can you come with me?"

"I'm going to fly you there if that's what you mean."

"No, I mean will you at least wait for me like you did when I visited my father?"

"My instructions are to leave right away. It's in the agreement. Presumably I'll be back to pick you up."

"Presumably?"

"Well, it could be somebody else. Although I hope it isn't. I like being your chauffeur. You take me to such interesting places."

"Have you been to the Crusaders before?"

"Only once, and that was a long time ago."

I looked out at the mist and wondered if I was doing the right thing.

"What happened with the Alexander situation while I was away? Anything?"

"That's all taken care now. Tanya had him released from Hell, and once the Greeks were informed, the problem was solved. But something much bigger happened."

"What?"

"The protests that have been building in the caucuses came to a head. It turns out they all want to stay, and I do mean everybody. Nobody who came to the conference wants to go back to the Big Nap."

"That doesn't surprise me."

"They've been talking about it in their caucuses. They say that being conscious and mixing with others is much more interesting than being dead."

"Well, good for those geniuses for figuring that out."

"There was grumbling last time about having to go back, but it's a loud chorus this time, and they're better organized. They're demanding their 'right to life.'"

"So where does it stand now? What's going to happen?"

"Well, Tanya solved that problem as well in her usual, decisive way. I found out before I came here that she's going to let them all stay."

"Wow. That really is being decisive. So this place is going to be crawling with famous people?"

"Looks that way. It's certainly going to make life down here a lot more interesting, but . . ."

"But what?"

"But why does it always have to be philosophers and scientists and great thinkers? Let's have more variety, more entertainment, more fun. Bring on the celebrities!" He pumped his fist.

I never saw him so fired up. "The Marx Brothers are here."

"Yeah, but that was a mistake. How about people like Houdini, Greta Garbo, Babe Ruth, Mae West, Marilyn Monroe, Elvis, Michael Jackson, Madonna, Prince, people like that."

"Where are they going to put the conference people? Will there be room for them all?"

"Tanya and the Council will figure something out. My guess is they'll probably scatter them around in the Purgatory precincts since they're not all that crowded. If they do, your father could have some interesting company."

"I was just thinking about that. He would love to talk to Charles Dickens. He read and reread everything he ever wrote, so if he could sit on his favorite bench and talk to Dickens, he would be in Paradise, not Purgatory."

I saw up ahead of us a giant green lawn surrounded by trees, hedges, and bushes that was more verdant and easier on the eyes than anything I had seen yet. With a manor house in the distance, it was a scene straight out of an English novel that I knew my father would love. Maybe I can get him transferred here even though Pietro told me how fussy the Crusaders are about who they let in. Candidates have to be traditional Christians and the more Catholic, the better.

As Pietro lowered the beetle, I looked around at the vast green expanse. "This place is amazing, isn't it? Who's in charge? Do they have a Tanya figure?"

"You kidding? They would never let a woman be in charge of anything. Their governing committee is all male. It's run mostly by English Catholics like Thomas More and Cardinal Manning."

After we touched down, Pietro handed me a card. "Here, this is for you. It identifies you as an authorized visitor with journalistic credentials in case you need it. You never know when it might come in handy."

It was in Latin, which I could more or less read.

Pietro pointed at a row of trees on the other side of the lawn. "See the trees? That's where you have to go.

They have an unusual way of transporting visitors, what few visitors they have. See the cart next to the trees? It's on rail tracks you can't see from here. When you reach the cart, get in and tap the side three times to signal you're ready to go. That will send you on your way. Just three taps—that's it. You don't have to do anything else. Somebody will meet you at the end of the ride."

"Can't you come with me, at least to the cart?"

"Sorry. I'm not even allowed to stay and watch. In fact, I have to leave now."

"I'm already getting bad vibes. It looks peaceful enough, but it just doesn't feel right."

"Thomas, don't worry. They're on the Council with us, and Tanya worked out an agreement. Plus, you have your ID. Show it whenever you need to. If there's a problem, we'll send our mighty air force to rescue you. Good-bye, my friend. Good luck with your new adventure."

56

After I watched Pietro fly off, I set out across the lawn. The grass looked real, but when I bent down to break off a blade, I couldn't. It wasn't real grass. The cart on the rail track under the trees looked like a toy train, so when I got to it, I climbed up on it very carefully. Once I was convinced it was sturdy enough to hold me, I tapped the outside three times. When nothing happened, I did it again.

When still nothing happened, I moved to the other side and tapped that side three times. I felt a slight jolt as the cart began to move slowly away from the platform. As it picked up speed, I felt like a little boy riding on a miniature train.

Once the cart got past the trees at the end of the lawn, the terrain became more parched like my father's precinct. After a ride shorter than I expected, the cart came to a platform where a gaunt, scarecrow-looking spirit was waiting for me. He was wearing a brown Franciscan robe without arms or even openings for them. Didn't he have any arms?

"Thomas Reed?" he said with what sounded like a German accent.

I got off the cart. "Yes, sir." I clicked my heels and saluted him. "Reporting for duty."

He frowned. "Your attempt at humor is not welcome, Mr. Reed. Come with me."

I followed him up a path to a lawn with "grass" that was more brown than green. I didn't like the way I was being received. Didn't Mr. Scarecrow know who I was? That I was an invited guest?

"We haven't been introduced," I said to him. "My name is Thomas. What's yours?"

"Horst."

Horst? What a god-awful name.

"Nice to meet you, Horst." I showed him my ID. "This is my identification."

He took it (he had arms after all) and looked at it suspiciously, then handed it back. "This is no longer valid."

"What do you mean no longer valid?"

"Just what I said."

I was following him up a gravel path toward what looked like a Norman abbey.

"Where are we going?"

He didn't answer me.

"Where are you taking me?"

"You ask a lot of questions, Mr. Reed. Too many."

I followed him into the abbey past several spirits wearing brown mendicant robes and down the side of the nave to a narrow hallway that took us to a blue-tinted room with Celtic crosses on the walls and a statue of a saint in the corner. The only furniture in the room was a chair.

"Wait here," he said and left.

The bad vibes I had been feeling were now getting worse. A tall, willowy spirit came in the room wearing a beige silk garment that did little to disguise her anorexic figure.

"I'm Wanda," she said. "I'll be looking after you while you're here."

She motioned me to sit down on the chair.

"What's going on?" I asked her. "I came here to collect information for my book. This is not the kind of treatment I expected."

"It's not what they expected either."

"Who's 'they'?"

"The Committee."

I took out my ID and showed it to her. "I'm here on an authorized visit. I'm an official guest. I think I should be treated like one."

She leaned over and looked at the card without touching it. "I'm afraid this won't help you."

"Why not?"

She went to the corner and looked at a small box on the wall that looked like a square thermostat, then came back. "Your card was issued by the previous administration. There's been a change since then. It's a long story I can't go into now, except to say the new administration withdrew your invitation."

"What do you mean they withdrew my invitation?"

"You're no longer an invited guest."

"Now you tell me. Why didn't you let me know before I came?"

"They didn't inform you on purpose." She glanced at the corner again. "They wanted you to come here voluntarily."

"I don't understand. Do they want me here or not?"

"They want you here but not as a guest. There's going to be a hearing."

"A hearing about . . . ?"

"You."

"A hearing about me?"

She nodded.

"Why?"

"Well, for starters, you broke your ordination vow."

"Resigning from the priesthood is a crime?"

"To them, it's very serious. And apparently that's not all. It's how you left the church that seems to be an issue for them. They're looking into it now."

I had a sinking feeling that told me I should have taken the bad vibes I felt from the beginning more seriously and acted on them.

"I'm not an insider," she said, "so I don't know what's going on behind the scenes, but I do know they're looking into a lot of stuff about you. Tsk, tsk, tsk, Thomas. It seems you've been a naughty boy." Smiling for the first time, she leaned forward and looked at me closely. "You don't look so good."

She had more shape than I thought. Her lips were fleshy and purple.

At the sound of a beep, she straightened up and moved away to take the call.

Knowing my worst fears were coming true, I put my head in my hands. Did this mean I was really going to Hell? The real Hell?

She came back. "It's time for the hearing. They're ready for you. So now we're on the way to solving the puzzle. Who is this mystery man from above? Rogue? Saint? Heretic?"

"The hearing is just about me?"

"That's right. It's just a hearing for now, but something's definitely making them curious. Do you have any deep, dark secrets you're hiding?"

She was starting to get on my nerves. I didn't answer her.

"Thomas, time to go. Let's see what they have on you."

57

I followed her down a hallway with crosses and statues that made me think of the catacombs of ancient Rome and secret passageways under medieval monasteries. A spirit in a mendicant robe went by carrying a missal and rosary beads. The Gregorian chanting I heard in the background made me feel like I was going back to the Middle Ages.

The guards on both sides of the door we came to were dressed in blue jackets, black and white striped pants, and tricornered hats. They held their lances out with stiff arms out at an angle and stared straight ahead the way the Swiss Guards at the Vatican do. They saluted and clicked their heels as Wanda took me past them into a foyer with more statues and crosses and on into a large, windowless chamber surrounded by black curtains.

There was a raised platform in the front, and over it on the wall was a gleaming silver cross. Wanda took me to a chair in front that faced the platform and motioned me to sit down.

"I'll be right here," she said, pointing at the black curtains behind us. "When there's a recess, I'll take you back to our room. It should be starting soon. God bless."

When the lights dimmed, the luminescent cross on the wall glowed with even more intensity. Was the Gregorian chanting I heard in the background a recording, or were there spirits chanting somewhere?

Suddenly two beams of light shot out of the darkness. One lit up the gilded table on the platform, and the other one was on me. When the curtains opened behind me, I heard murmuring. Who are these people? Jury? Spectators? They can see me, but I can't see them.

Up on the platform a tall, skeletal spirit in a white robe moved into the spotlight and made a sign of the cross that quieted the murmuring. Who was he? Prosecutor? Judge? His robe was covered with black crosses, and he wore a pointed white hat that made him look like the Grand Inquisitor in my Inquisition dream, a nightmare I was now living.

I imagined Bishop Howard out there in the darkness somewhere with a triumphant grin on his face waiting to tell the judge I was guilty on all counts. And how about my father? Could he be out there too? Since he was already down there, maybe they brought him there to watch. I was now even more sorry I didn't tell him I left the church when I had the chance because this would be a horrible way for him to find out.

The judge raised his right hand and made the sign of the cross again. "*Pax nobiscum*," he intoned.

"*Et cum spiritu*" came voices from the darkness.

The judge banged his gavel on the table. "Let the hearing begin." He read a proclamation in Latin that I didn't understand even though I recognized many of the words.

"Thomas Aaron Reed III."

Why was he saying my name? What was I supposed to say? "Present" or "Yes, I'm here"? It was obvious I was there, so I didn't say anything.

"Are you Thomas Aaron Reed III?"

Of course, I am, you jerk, I felt like saying, but instead I said, "Yes, sir, that's right. I'm Thomas Aaron Reed III."

Seeing a chance to say more, I turned to my invisible audience and said, "There's something about my background all of you should know. Both of my grandfathers were leaders of the national church. My maternal grandfather was the Episcopal Bishop of Connecticut, and my father's father was Dean of the Cambridge Theological Seminary in Massachusetts."

The judge banged his gavel. "Out of order, Mr. Reed. We're well aware of the distinguished background of the family you chose to betray and dishonor."

The murmuring that was getting louder made them sound like a lynch mob warming up.

"Stand up, Mr. Reed. It's time for the oath."

As I got up, I thought of others before me who faced church trials like Galileo, Joan of Arc, John Wycliffe, and Jan Hus.

"Raise your right hand and repeat after me, 'I, Thomas Aaron Reed III.'"

"I, Thomas Aaron Reed III."

"Do solemnly swear."

"Do solemnly swear."

"To tell the truth, the whole truth, and nothing but the truth."

"To tell the truth, the whole truth, and nothing but the truth."

"So help me, God."

"So help me."

"So help me, God."

"So help me."

"Mr. Reed, we know you have a problem with oaths, but do your best to say the exact words of this one. So help me, God."

Silence.

"Say it, Mr. Reed. So help me, God."

"So help me, Hashem."

When the obviously flustered judge moved out of the spotlight, several robed spirits converged on him. Who were they? His advisers? Kitchen cabinet?

The judge returned to the spotlight and looked down at me. "The court is accepting your wording in the interest of moving on to the issue at hand. Be aware that our investigation is turning up evidence that goes beyond your abandoning the priesthood. We're finding a disturbing pattern of irreverent, even blasphemous behavior."

Feeling nauseous, I looked around for a place to vomit if it come to that.

"Mr. Reed, be aware that the case against you is strong and getting stronger. While Christian duty obligates us to treat you with mercy, we're committed to uncompromising standards of truth and justice. What began as a fact-finding hearing has now been upgraded to a trial. Your contempt for basic religious principles and practices left us no other choice."

When it felt like I couldn't hold it back any longer, I stood up and moved away from the chair. I bent over to throw up, but nothing happened.

"Sit down, Mr. Reed. You'll get a chance to speak later. There's going to be a break now. When we return, we'll present the charges."

The spotlights went off, plunging the courtroom into darkness. When I sensed somebody behind me, I assumed it was Wanda.

"Come with me," said a young male voice.

I followed the robed figure out the side door and down a hall to a small room that was completely bare except for a chair. I was getting used to being in places with a chair set out for me.

"My name is Brother Ignatius." He didn't look much older than 17 or 18. "I'm a court page. This is where I'll bring you when there's a break." He pointed at the chair. "You can rest here. Although the breaks tend to be short."

"I thought I would be with Wanda."

"When there's a recess, which is longer, Sister Wanda will take you back to your room."

I sat down in the chair. "So tell me, Brother Ignatius, what's going on?"

"You don't need to call me Brother Ignatius. Call me Iggie."

"OK, Iggie. Why am I being treated like a criminal?"

"I don't know, but even if I did, I'm not allowed to discuss it with you. It does sound serious though. Stay here and rest. I'll come back when it's time."

After he left, I pictured Bishop Howard out there with his idiotic grin, saying, "What did I tell you? Thumbing your nose at the church has consequences."

Moments later the light blinked three times, and Iggie came back. "I told you the breaks are short. Come with me."

I followed him out through the darkness to my chair and sat down. When I heard the curtains open, I wondered if Wanda was out there somewhere. I hoped so.

The spotlights shot out of the darkness again, followed by a scroll that materialized in front of the judge as if by magic. It was hard to tell if the next voice I heard was his or belonged to somebody else reading the scroll.

58

On the day Thomas Aaron Reed III was ordained to the priesthood, he took a sacred oath to be "a servant of Christ's Church forever." Mr. Reed's "forever" didn't last very long, however. Six years after he made his holy promise, he broke it and abandoned the priesthood.

My goodness, that doesn't sound very good putting it that way. I wanted to say something, so I raised my hand. When I wasn't called on, I stood up. "I have something to say."

"Sit down, Mr. Reed. You'll have a chance to speak later."

"But I want to speak now."

"Sit down, Mr. Reed."

Feeling trapped inside my Inquisition nightmare, I sat back down. Now I suspected more than ever that Bishop Howard and the Crusaders were connected in some way.

"Next!" said the judge.

The voice that continued wasn't the judge's because I watched his mouth closely and it didn't move.

Not only did Thomas Aaron Reed III break his ordination vow, but he also betrayed his pastoral calling. With a lifetime of support behind him in the way of church, family, education, seminary training, and the support and blessing of his bishop, he became the pastor of a parish at a very young age only to squander his chance to serve and nurture his congregation. He spent most of his three and a half years as the rector of his parish battling its lay leadership until he finally deserted his flock and went to New York to pursue his own agenda.

I stood up again. "You're slanting the truth."

"Mr. Reed, is it not true that you promised to serve your congregation?"

"I . . ."

"Yes or no, Mr. Reed. At your installation, did you or did you not promise to be a faithful shepherd of the flock entrusted to you? Yes or no."

I didn't like being putting on the spot like this.

"Answer the question, Mr. Reed. Yes or no."

"Yes."

"Did you not then break your promise and abandon the congregation entrusted to you? Yes or no."

"I resigned from my parish if that's what you're getting at. What's wrong with that? It happens all the time."

"Mr. Reed, you've said enough. Sit down."

"It was time to move on."

"You heard me, Mr. Reed. Sit down!"

Now a photo I never saw before was up on the screen where the cross had been moments before. It showed the three of us: Bishop Howard and my mother with me standing between them in my shiny new collar. We're on the lawn in front of St. Luke's on the day I was installed as the new rector. My mother usually took family pictures, but she obviously didn't take this one. I don't know who took it, and I didn't remember posing for it either. But there it was up on the Crusader screen as "evidence." Evidence of what?

"Mr. Reed, look closely at the picture that was taken shortly after you promised to lead, honor, and protect the souls entrusted to you."

I resented having to look at the nauseating picture of me sandwiched between my mother and her lover boy while I'm on trial in Hell with the happy couple smiling down on me.

"On this sacred day, Mr. Reed, you were given the pastoral responsibility you had been preparing for all your life. You were raised in a loving church family with your father and grandfather's exemplary models of clerical fidelity."

The judge pointed at the photo. "And there you are on that happy, holy day with your loving parents who are obviously very proud of you."

I stood up. "They're *not* my parents!"

A stunned silence was followed by loud murmuring. The judge banged his gavel and moved out of the spotlight to confer with his advisers.

When he came back, he said, "Mr. Reed, please be aware that you're testifying under oath. There are severe penalties for perjury. According to our records, your mother and your bishop are married."

I stood up again. "They're married now, but when the photo was taken, they were not married. The woman in the photo is my mother, but the bishop is *not* my father. He wasn't my father then, and he's not my father now."

"He's your stepfather."

"He's not my father."

"Mr. Reed, we don't have time to quibble over semantics. Don't try to distract us from the matter at hand. Less than four years after you made your sacred pastoral promise, you broke it and deserted your flock. You may sit down now."

I didn't want to spend any more time arguing with this nitwit, so I sat down.

The judge pointed back up at the photo. "Tell us, Mr. Reed, before we move on. I'm curious to know how you would rate your performance as a pastor while you were at your church? What grade would you give yourself?

Was he serious? I felt like I was back in elementary school getting graded for citizenship.

"What I'm getting at, Mr. Reed, is that we have looked at the evidence extensively and have given you our own grade. What do you think it is?"

"How should I know?"

"Look into your heart, Mr. Reed, and listen to your conscience. You know better than anybody because you were there. You lived it. What do you think your grade is? Your grade as the pastor of your parish."

I shrugged. "I don't know. What's passing?"

"Mr. Reed, you have mastered the art of being evasive. Shifty, to be more precise. I repeat, what do you think the grade we gave you is?"

"The grade just for my parish work? Or for my life? My FS?"

He looked surprised that I knew what Final Score meant.

"I can't tell you about my FS because I'm still alive. I'm a work in progress."

I heard tittering.

"Mr. Reed, I'm losing patience with you. This is your last chance to answer the question."

"Please repeat it."

"What do you think your pastoral grade is?"

"With all due modesty, I would give myself an A or A-."

Silence.

"Or B+."

More silence.

"B?"

"You're going in the right direction, Mr. Reed. In the interests of time I'm going to tell you what your grade is. It's F. You are in serious trouble before this court. Your making light of the proceeding will only sink you deeper into the hole you've dug for yourself. Look up at the picture and think about what could have been. You were given everything anybody could ever ask for in the way of family, education, and training, everything you needed to do grade A pastoral work. What happened, Mr. Reed?" He pointed back up at the photo. "There you are surrounded by all the support you could possibly ask for. Your loving mother and bishop. Man and wife."

I jumped up. "Correction! The woman in the photo is my mother, but as I just told you, she's not the bishop's wife. He has a wife, and she has a husband, my father. In the photo you're looking at, my mother and the bishop are both married, but not to each other. They're married to infirm spouses languishing elsewhere. The bishop's wife is dying of cancer, and my father, who suffered a stroke, is in a wheelchair in a nursing home. Up there in the photo my mother and the bishop are not smiling because of me. They're smiling for one reason and one reason only. They're smiling because they're happily screwing away while they wait for their infirm spouses to drop dead, so they can get married and do it legally."

"Mr. Reed, don't try to distract us with your salacious gossip. The point you're trying to evade is that you were given pastoral responsibility and you weren't up to the challenge. To put it bluntly, Mr. Reed, you failed. Sit down."

I stayed on my feet because I had more to say. "First of all, who are you to judge me? Judge not lest ye be judged. Secondly, do me and everybody else in this room a favor and take down that obscene picture. You talk about breaking promises. There they are fornicating away while married to people they promised to be faithful to till death do them part. There's a name for that, Mr. Crusader. It's called adultery. If you don't know what that is, look it up in the Bible, assuming you have one. It's the Seventh Commandment."

"Enough, Mr. Reed. Sit down! You talk too much. Next!"

59

The next charge against me was that I used my study leave of absence to seek employment outside the church rather than the purpose for which it was intended. "When Mr. Reed was offered a job with an insurance company," it stated, "he jumped at it and promptly abandoned the priesthood."

The two photos now on the screen were of Ma Brogan and Mike. The judge banged his gavel and pointed up at them. "These are two of Mr. Reed's accomplices. The one on the left is a notorious ex-nun who runs an underground organization that specializes in preying on church workers to get them to leave their churches. She arranged the interviews that eventually got Mr. Reed his job with an insurance company. The other photo shows the young monk Mr. Reed palled around with while they thumbed their noses at their respective churches."

Where in the world did they get these photos? I never saw either one of them. Looking at the two people I was closest to during that difficult time brought back a flood of memories.

Suddenly the judge said, "Next!" and the photos disappeared.

That's it? That's the charge? That I hung out with unsavory Catholic rebels? Guilt by association? Case closed?

Sick and tired of their attacks, I wanted a recess with Wanda, or at least a break with Iggie, but no such luck. The new photo that they put up on the screen was of Mrs. Amory with Winston.

Oh, no, don't tell me they're going to make a big deal out of this. Like Joseph K in Kafka's *The Trial*, I felt trapped inside a trial that never ends.

While Thomas Aaron Reed III was still an ordained priest, he conducted a funeral for a dog, and if that wasn't bad enough, he did it for money.

"Is that true, Mr. Reed? Did you conduct a dog funeral? And if you did, did you do it for money?"

Knowing my fate was in their hands, I turned and spoke directly to the invisible audience. "Yes, I did conduct the funeral, and yes, I did get paid for it. I wasn't going to do it for nothing. I was looking for work, and I needed the income. When the dog's owner asked me for my help, I agreed. Under the circumstances, it would have been wrong not to help her."

I was surprised when the photos were now replaced by a video that showed me in Mrs. Amory's apartment coming out of the side room and going over to Winston's casket to conduct the service. How did they manage that? I certainly would have noticed if somebody had been filming in Mrs. Amory's living room.

When it showed the pandemonium that broke out when the noon whistle sounded, it did my heart good to hear laughter.

After the video ended (the burial on Long Island wasn't filmed) and a recess was announced, Wanda came and took me back out past the guards and down the hall back to the room. She closed the door and smiled at me. "You certainly did some strange things up there."

Glad she wasn't offended, I was feeling more and more comfortable with her and intrigued by her skeletal figure that shimmered with a ghostly sensuality.

"So what happens now? Are there going to be any more charges?"

"Apparently."

"How many more of them do you think there will be?"

"I don't know. There have already been more than I expected."

"What do they want to do? Bring back the Inquisition?"

"They haven't had this much fun since they put Jan Hus on trial again. As if the poor guy didn't have enough trouble the first time."

"As I remember, he was burned at the stake."

"That's right. And he was a priest too."

"Thanks for reminding me. Is that what they want to do to me? Burn me at the stake?"

"I doubt it. They wouldn't know how to light a match, much less burn a heretic."

"I'm a heretic?"

"In their eyes you are. Not in everybody's though. Certainly not in mine. I was very moved by the funeral you did for the dog. It was sweet of you." She gave me a friendly tap on my head with her boney forefinger.

"In the convent we took in a stray dog, and I was in charge of feeding him. Sister Monica too. We named him Frankie in honor of St. Francis. I think about him a lot. Frankie, that is, not St. Francis."

Remembering him made her smile. "He had a mind of his own and was always doing things that made us laugh. At least, Sister Monica and I thought they were funny. The sisters complained that he barked too much, and they didn't like it when he sniffed them with his wet nose. Once he jumped up on Mother Superior and scattered her rosary beads over the floor."

She had a faraway look in her eyes. "The funniest thing Frankie ever did—it's funny now—was when we brought him to mass on the Feast of St. Francis to be blessed. Father O'Malley was the priest that day. When he went to give Frankie his blessing, Frankie started barking ferociously and jumped up on Father O'Malley and knocked him down. He sank his teeth into his robe and shook his head and wouldn't let go. It took some doing to rescue poor Father O'Malley.

We scolded Frankie, but only halfheartedly. We didn't like Father O'Malley either."

Wanda's eyes were tearing up. "I miss him terribly. I'm glad you did the funeral. I would have done the same thing if I had your courage."

"Why thank you, Wanda. It's nice of you to say that. You seem very young to have been in a convent."

"I was only there five years. I died young. Food poisoning. Because I was a nun, they assigned me here, but . . . " She went to the corner and checked the box on the wall. She came back and said in a whisper, "It would be nice to live over there."

"With Tanya's people?"

She nodded. "I'm Catholic, but I'm not Catholic the way they are here."

"Can you transfer? Is that allowed?"

"I can't right now. There's a reason I'm here." She looked at the box again. "There's more to say, but I can't talk now. Anyway, enough about me. You're the one we have to concentrate on now."

She went behind me and rubbed my neck and shoulders with her boney fingers. It was incredibly relaxing. When I felt a twitch in my groin, I thought, Oh, no, don't tell me I'm getting turned on by the boney fingers of a dead nun.

At the sound of a beep, she moved away to take the call.

I heard her say, "OK, we're on our way."

60

When the next charge accused me of desecrating the symbol of my priesthood, I had a feeling what it was going to be about. I found out my hunch was right when the room went dark and the video showed me entering Central Park with my collar in a paper bag.

I didn't remember anybody shooting film that day either, so how in the world did the Crusaders manage to get film of this when there's nobody around to shoot it? Did they have a way of making themselves invisible? Were they spying on me the whole time and I didn't know it? If so, their skills were right up there with those of Mossad and the CIA.

When the video showed me cross the grass and throw my collar in the pond, there was a loud chorus of boos and hisses. During the break when Iggie took me back to the side room, I felt like a fighter returning to my corner after another round of getting pummeled. I was taking so many punches I was beginning to feel punch-drunk.

I went straight to the chair and plopped down. "The accusations keep coming fast and furious. There's no letup."

Iggie didn't say anything at first, but then he smiled. "That was very funny. Your throwing your collar in the pond like that."

When I heard another laugh, I realized we weren't alone. Off to the side behind me was another spirit in a Franciscan robe. He was taller and older than Iggie.

"This is Brother Frankie," said Iggie. "He wants to meet you."

He came over to me and put out his hand, so I shook it. It was squishy but more solid than I expected. "Glad to meet you, Brother Frankie."

"You can just call me Frankie. I loved the funeral you did for the dog. It was a moving and powerful statement. I came here to thank you. You should be praised, not criticized. I wanted to tell you that in person."

"Thank you very much."

"There are more on your side than you might think. I'm behind the curtain, so I hear what they're saying."

"Do you know Wanda?"

Iggie laughed. "Oh, yes, he knows Sister Wanda."

I told them she used to take care of a dog named Frankie. "Did she tell you about that?"

Iggie and Frankie smiled at each other.

"Yes, we know about that," Iggie said.

"Did she tell you about the time they took him to mass to be blessed and he bit the priest?"

Frankie smiled. "Yes, she told us. I guess I'm partly to blame."

"Why?"

"She brought him to be blessed on my feast day."

Feast day? Now the pieces of the puzzle were beginning to fall into place. I asked him, "Are you by chance from Assisi?"

"Yes, that's my village."

"Are you . . . ?'

He nodded.

"Are you Saint Francis of Assisi?"

He waved his hand dismissively. "I'm no saint."

Iggie laughed. "Yes, he is."

"It's a great honor to meet you." I told him about the Blessing of the Animals service I once had at St. Luke's on his feast day. "I wanted to make it a tradition, but when the lamb pooped in the aisle and one of the dogs urinated on the baptismal font, the vestry said no more animal blessings. They also didn't like that I kept rescued animals in the rectory, but I did it anyway."

"Good for you."

The light blinked three times.

"Oops," he said. "I have to go. It was wonderful meeting you. No matter what some of them are saying, I'm very happy you're the first visitor." He gave a little wave and was gone.

"He has to get back before the lights go back on because he's not supposed to be here. It's time for us to go back too."

"On to the next charge. Do you know what it is?"

"I don't, but there's a rumor that it's going to be a real doozie."

Oh, no. I shuddered to think what they might come up with now. I followed Iggie back out for the next round of pummeling.

61

Thomas Aaron Reed III not only deserted his flock and abandoned the priesthood, but when he left his parish, he took his church's communion wafers with him to New York and conducted a black mass in his apartment to entertain his friends. This shocking sacrilege ranks as one of the most brazen acts of blasphemy in the two-thousand-year history of the Christian church.

Oh no, don't tell me they have evidence of that too. This charge was obviously more damning than all the others put together. But how could they have it on film? Or even a photo? Except for the four of us, nobody else was in my apartment that night.

As soon as the room went dark and the video showed Harry and Sylvia at the door, I knew I was doomed. Now I knew for sure they wanted to send me to Hell and were doing their best to make it happen.

The video began innocently enough showing the four of us talking and having drinks in the living room, but the tone and tempo shifted dramatically when it showed Harry crawl over to the aquarium with the wafer and break it up and feed it to the goldfish. When the film showed me scoop up the rest of the wafers and take them into the bedroom, the courtroom became deadly quiet as if they sensed I was up to no good.

When the video showed me come out of the bedroom and throw wafers around the living room, then throw the rest of them out the window, the courtroom exploded with boos, hisses, and shouts of "Atheist!"

"Heretic!" and "Send him to Hell!" After the video ended and the screen went blank, I was sure they were going to grab me and take me straight to Hell, which wasn't that far away. I pictured Bishop Howard out there with his sadistic grin enjoying it all.

When the lights came back on, Wanda took me back out past the guards. She didn't say anything on the way or even after we went into the room and she closed the door. When she didn't look at me, I knew I was in trouble.

Battered, beaten, and exhausted, I went straight to the chair and collapsed.

She came over to me. "You certainly did some *very* strange things up there."

"Well, I was very angry at my bishop."

"I should say so." She went behind me and started massaging my neck and shoulders.

"By the way," I said to her, "I met a friend of yours at the last break."

"Oh?"

"Frankie. Not the dog." That made her smile. "I can't believe I met the one and only Saint Francis of Assisi."

"Don't let him hear you say 'saint.' He doesn't like it."

"So I found out."

"He's a wonderful man and a good friend. We work together. Iggie too. He helped us start GETA."

"What's GETA?"

"Ghosts for the Ethical Treatment of Animals. I wanted it to be Spirits, but SETA was taken. We want to get the cruelty that people do to animals factored more into how they're judged and assigned down here. More the way they do it over there." She nodded toward the corner.

When her phone beeped, she moved to the side to take the call.

"Yes, I'm here with him now," I heard her say. After a long pause, she said, "OK."

She came back and handed me the phone. "It's for you."

"Me?"

"It's Tanya."

The phone was shaped like an aerosol can. I didn't know what to do with it.

"Say something."

"Hello?"

"Thomas? It's Tanya. Are you OK?"

"Yeah, I'm OK, but they're throwing the kitchen sink at me."

"I know. It's on TV over here. We're all watching. You're doing great. Are you sure you're OK?"

"I was shaken by the last charge, but I'm OK now. It's on TV?"

"It's the show trial the hard-liners have been hoping to have ever since you got here. That's why they were so willing to have you visit. I owe you an apology about that. I thought the agreement I worked out with them would keep something like this from happening, but the hard-liners staged a coup that put them back in charge before you got there. It goes back and forth with them a lot, so it's hard to know who's up and who's down. Anyway, the good news is that the moderates are trying to work something out with the hard-liners now, so don't lose hope. My apologies about getting you into this mess. I misread the political tea leaves. I didn't see it coming. Sorry about that."

"To err is human, to forgive divine."

"I like that. Thank you."

"It's one of Edward's favorite quotations. It's by Alexander Pope. Speaking of Edward, how's he doing? I haven't seen him in ages."

"He's fine, but he's worried about you. He blames himself for bringing you down here. I told him the moderates will work something out. They usually do."

"I hope so."

"We're all looking forward to having you back here safe and sound. You're a big TV star now. Everybody's glued to the Thomas Reed Show and quite a show it is. I don't know whether to laugh or cry. Anyway, I want you to know you have a big fan club. We're all pulling for you."

"Thank you, Tanya. That's good to know."

"And your favorite pilot sends his best. He can't wait to bring you back."

"Is he going to pick me up?"

"Of course. Who else? So hang in there. Relief is on the way. In the meantime, the trial will play itself out, which is just as well since it's too good a show to cut short. Over here it's like a soap opera that nobody wants to end. It's that good. By the way, Naomi said she and the Chief are also watching. They think it's a hoot."

I heard a click.

"Oops, sorry. Got to go. Put Wanda back on, OK? Good luck, Thomas. See you soon."

"Hope so. 'Bye." I handed the phone to Wanda. "She wants to talk to you."

After she finished, I said to her, "I had no idea you're in contact with Tanya."

She glanced at the box on the wall in the corner, then leaned toward me and whispered, "*Viaggio.*"

That was all she needed to say. That one word said it all. When she told me she was with the Crusaders for a reason, she didn't say why. Now it all made sense. She was there to spy on the Crusaders for Tanya.

The blinking light signaled it was time to go back to the next episode of the Thomas Reed Show.

62

Thomas Aaron Reed III brought his clerical career to its ignominious conclusion at his final meeting with his bishop. When his pastor and spiritual mentor reached out to him in the spirit of forgiveness and reconciliation transmitted through the Apostolic Succession, Mr. Reed rejected his offer. That's right. When Jesus offered him his outstretched hand of love and forgiveness, Mr. Reed bit it!

My God, who writes this guy's purple prose? I wanted to jot it down, but I knew if I took my pad out now, they could confiscate it and use it against me. As if they didn't have enough ammunition already.

The two photos up on the screen I recognized immediately as the photos I had seen on Bishop Howard's desk at our last meeting. One was a group photo of the bishop, my mother, the bishop's two daughters, their husbands and children, and the family dog. The other photo showed the two happy lovebirds on their honeymoon in Hawaii relaxing on a beach in their bathing suits.

Since the photos were presumably still on the bishop's desk, the question was how did the Crusaders get copies? This was the strongest evidence yet of collusion between Bishop Howard and the Crusaders.

What was the point of the pictures supposed to be? To show that Bishop Howard was my stepfather as well as my bishop and therefore all the more reason I should have been his grateful suppliant? They certainly didn't prove I bit anybody's hand, much less the hand of Jesus. And why show my mother and the bishop in their bathing suits? Are they trying to rub my oedipal complex in my face?

When the judge called for a short break, I followed Iggie back to the room. He told me the techs were setting up audio equipment for the next charge. Just when I hoped they were finally finished with me, they're coming up with something else. Now what?

Iggie stopped me at the door and whispered, "Somebody else wants to meet you."

"Who?"

"You'll see."

I followed him in and saw a short, trim spirit dressed in a tunic. Her hair was cropped so short it took me a moment to decide if she really was a she. She looked about Iggie's age, probably a little older.

"This is Jeanne," he said.

"Hello, Jeanne. It's a pleasure to meet you."

"*Moi aussi.*"

Iggie said to me, "You can call her Joan if you want. She goes by both names."

"*Oui.*" She nodded and smiled.

"I like Jeanne," I said. "It has a nice ring to it. Very French."

She looked at Iggie, and they both laughed.

"Yes," he said, "Jeanne is *very* French."

There was obviously some kind of inside joke I wasn't getting.

"I am very happy to meet you, Monsieur Reed. I like how you help the lady with the *chien*. I love them *aussi*. You touched my heart."

"Merci, Jeanne. Wanda loves dogs too. Do you know her?"

"*Oui.*"

"Jeanne is one of us," Iggie said. "She's one of the gang."

"The GETA gang?"

"That's right. How do you know about GETA?"

"Wanda told me."

I heard the opening bars of *La Marseillaise* that prompted Jeanne to take her cell phone out of her tunic.

"*Pardonne*," she said and left the room.

Iggie smiled. "What did I tell you? You have to be *very* French to have the French national anthem on your cell phone." He looked at the door. "She's under a lot of pressure."

"Why?"

"Tanya's people want her over there, but the Crusaders want her to stay here. Whoever gets her will have a big feather in their cap."

"Why do they want her so much?"

Iggie looked at me as if I just asked the world's most stupid question. "Why do they want Jeanne d'Arc?"

Suddenly it hit me. "Are you telling me she's Joan of Arc?"

"The one and only."

"She's so young."

"She was only nineteen when they burned her at the stake."

Same age as Mike, I thought. I smiled inwardly at the thought of the three teenagers hanging out together— Mike, Iggie, and Joan of Arc.

"That was Tanya," Jeanne said when she came back. "She wants me to speak at the conference before it ends." She looked at me. "It is always a big surprise when somebody wants to hear what an illiterate peasant like me has to say."

"You're no ordinary peasant," Iggie told her. "Are you going to do it?"

"I would like to, but I'm in enough trouble with the Committee already. Besides, I want to hear what Thomas is going to say when they finally let him speak. Tanya says it's on television over there, but I want to hear you in person."

The light blinked three times.

"Time to go," She gave a quick wave and vanished.

"We have to go too," Iggie said. I followed him out for another round of pummeling.

63

It didn't take Thomas Aaron Reed III long to show his true colors. As soon as he got down here, he paid a visit to Satan and had a long, friendly conversation with him. In the part of their conversation you're about to hear, Mr. Reed is telling his new friend about the book he plans to write.

I jumped to my feet. "I didn't visit him. He kidnapped me!"

"Mr. Reed, sit down!"

I glared at the judge.

"You heard me. Sit down!"

I felt squishy hands on my shoulders push me down into the chair. The two spirits behind me stayed there to make sure I didn't try to stand up again.

The judge said, "Let's hear what they said. Listen carefully. Notice how quickly they bond. Birds of a feather."

When the spotlights went off, I immediately recognized the voices that came over the loudspeaker.

"You're Thomas Reed, and I understand you're writing a book."

"That's right, but it's only in the planning stage."

"I like the entertaining way you left your church. You didn't just slink away the way most of them do. Some of the things you did were very amusing. Since you're the first visitor down here, there's obviously going to be a lot of interest in

what you have to say. Many people are going to read and hear about your book, so what you write needs to be honest and accurate, don't you agree?"

"Yes, I agree."

"Good. I hope you'll leave out the tired clichés and stereotypes, especially of me."

"I intend to make my book as fair and truthful as I can. I welcome different points of view. I obviously didn't plan on being here, but now that I am, I'm interested in finding out what you have to say."

There was a clicking sound, then silence. The judge looked out over my head. "So there you have it. A sampling of the love feast between Mr. Reed and Satan. It goes on. There's something else for you to hear. Thanks to our electronic subverbal monitor that picks up thoughts as well as voices, we're able to know what

Mr. Reed was thinking as well as saying. Listen to some of what's going on inside his head as he salivates over the prospect of getting Satan's support for his book."

A new voice came over the loudspeaker saying what I had allegedly been thinking:

"This is amazing. It sounds as if he might support my book if he thinks it's fair and accurate. He's certainly going to be in it. Maybe I can interview him, or get a blurb. How fortunate I'm here."

When the spotlights came back on, the judge said, "So there you have it. Mr. Reed is willing to be Satan's ally in exchange for his support for his book. This is as classic a case as you'll ever find of selling your soul to the Devil. How ironic and telling it is that the very first visitor the Rebels invite down here is nothing less than a modern-day Faustus." He pointed at me. "Because that's exactly what you are, Mr. Reed. You sold your defrocked soul to the Devil. Shame on you. Shame!"

"Shame! Shame! Shame!" erupted out of the darkness and quickly became a deafening chant.

When I went to stand up to protest, the bouncers pushed me back down into the chair. The judge banged his gavel until it became quiet again.

"Mr. Reed, now that you've heard the conversation, I trust you're not going to try to deny that it took place. Did the conversation take place or not?"

I was too upset to answer. I didn't like the way they go around spying on people, filming and bugging whoever, wherever, and whenever they want. Not only do they film and record what people do and say, but they even spy on what they're thinking. Big Brother is watching, listening, and judging all the time. It's the totalitarian world George Orwell warned us about. I wondered if he was at the conference. If he wasn't, he should be.

"Mr. Reed, we're waiting for your answer. Did the conversation we heard take place or not?"

"Did what take place?"

"Was that your voice on the tape talking to Satan? Yes or no."

"It sounded like me, but it's hard to know for sure."

"I take that to be *yes*. Case closed."

64

By the time Wanda showed up, the bouncers were gone. She took me back out past the guards who were as usual standing at attention and staring straight ahead.

When we got back to the room, I went straight to the chair and plopped down. "This marathon is wearing me out. Are they done?"

"I think so. Unless . . . " Wanda went behind me and began massaging my neck and shoulders. "Unless they uncover something else, or unless you want to confess something more." She gave me a playful tap on the head. "That last charge about talking to so-called Satan was just plain silly. I don't know why they even bothered with that one. Probably to show off their audio equipment and remind the rest of us that everything down here is bugged, as if we didn't know that already." She nodded toward the box in the corner. "In fact, I don't even know why they bothered having this so-called trial at all. All the charges are a joke except . . . "

"Except what?"

"Except, you know, the one about the communion wafers. That's obviously more serious. Everybody's talking about it."

Her kneading the base of my neck and shoulders was just what I needed. Her back rubs, plus meeting Iggie, Frankie, and Jeanne made being on trial down there almost worth it. If I come down here after I die, maybe I can get a staff position and have Wanda be my personal masseuse. I could be Edward's assistant, and if I bone up on my Dante, maybe I could be a museum guide. Or Pietro can teach me how to fly a beetle, and I can give aerial tours. Doing anything down here would be better than being dead.

"So what happens now?"

"You get to say something."

"Until he cuts me off."

"He's not supposed to. He's supposed to let you make a final statement."

"I'm not sure I like the word 'final.' What happens after that?"

"They'll decide if there's enough of a case against you to proceed toward a verdict. Tanya doesn't think it will get that far, but around this nutty place you never know. Things can change quickly and usually do."

Wanda came around to the front and gave me another playful tap. "Try to relax, Thomas. What will be will be."

I rubbed my eyes and stretched my arms. "I met one of your GETA friends."

"Frankie. I know. You told me."

"No, somebody else just as famous."

"Jeanne."

I nodded.

"Oh, good. Iggie said he was going to try to arrange it."

"I almost flipped when I found out she was Joan of Arc. She's so humble and unassuming."

"Don't be fooled. She may look humble, but she's passionate about what she believes. Even the Committee has to watch its step with her. After all, she led the French army to a string of victories, so she's obviously not somebody to be trifled with. Guilt also figures into it since it was a church court that condemned her to death."

"I know. In high school, I was in a play about her trial. It was Bernard Shaw's *Saint Joan*. Guess who I played?"

"Joan." She tapped me on the head and laughed.

"I played Bishop Cauchon who had her burned at the stake. But don't tell her."

"Don't worry. She wouldn't hold it against you. The church will never live down what they did to her."

"But they made her a saint later, right?"

"That's right. They canonized her in 1920." Wanda glanced at the box in the corner, then lowered her voice. "First, they burn you at the stake, then they make you a saint 500 years later to make up for it."

"That's two saints in a row I've met, Frankie and Jeanne. Not bad for a heretic like me, eh?"

The light blinked three times.

"Speaking of heretics, they want you back." She tapped me on the head a couple of times as if playing a drum. "Let's go."

We went back down the hall past the guards into the courtroom. She took me to my chair.

"Do well, Thomas." She gave me a good-bye tap.

After the two spotlights shot out of the darkness, the judge looked down at me and said, "Mr. Reed, you now have a chance to speak if you so choose. Do you have anything you want to say?"

I stood up. "Yes, I do." I looked out at my invisible audience, gave them a little wave, then turned back to the judge. "I came here to include the Crusaders in my book and was led to believe I would be welcome. Instead, you broke the agreement and put me on trial. You owe me an apology."

"Mr. Reed, we don't have time to listen to your self-serving ramblings. Please use the time you have available to explain your behavior. That's what we're here for."

"OK, let's begin with my leaving the priesthood. I make no apologies about that. I was born into a church family and went along with it to please my parents. That early momentum swept me into seminary and on into the clergy. I don't blame my parents or anybody else. I take full responsibility for what happened. Like many people, I put what my family and other people expected of me ahead of what I wanted for myself and was best for me. When you live your life to please others, you don't become the person you were meant to be and deep down want to be. In the words of the Talmud, 'If I am not for myself, who will be? If I am only for myself, what am I? If not now, when?'"

"Here, here," somebody shouted.

"Mr. Reed, we don't have time to listen to you lecture us about how to live. Do us a favor and address the charges brought against you. You're using up valuable time."

"Valuable time? Do you call all the time you spent on your ridiculous, mean-spirited accusations valuable?"

"He's right!" somebody yelled.

"Let him talk!" somebody else shouted.

"Mr. Reed, do you really think the charge that you conducted a black mass in your apartment is ridiculous?"

"I don't deny something happened that night. I just don't remember what it was. Whenever my college roommate is around, it's bad news because . . . well, because Harry is Mr. Trouble." I heard somebody snicker.

"I'm not blaming him. I take responsibility for whatever happened. I drank more than I should have and more than I usually do. And I was definitely in a bad mood. I had asked my bishop to be relieved of my clerical duties, only to get a letter from him that morning denying my request. That was the last straw. So yes, that night I was angry and upset. *Mea culpa, mea maxima culpa.* Nobody's perfect."

"What about the dog funeral?" somebody shouted. I wondered if it was one of the GETA people trying to take advantage of the chance to get the GETA message out.

"The dog funeral. Yes, I'm proud of what I did. I'm only sorry I didn't do more of them. Dogs deserve respect. Cats do too, and so do cows, pigs, chickens, horses, whales, and all of God's creatures. They deserve protection. They weren't created to be used and abused."

There was a burst of applause, no doubt from the GETA contingent, but it was quickly drowned out by boos and hisses.

By then I was so fed up with having to defend myself, I decided I had enough. "I've had a full weekend," I told them, "so I'm going to stop. Any questions?"

"Mr. Reed, it's not your place to invite questions. We've heard more than enough from you already."

"Here I stand," I said, echoing what Martin Luther said at his trial. I gave them a little wave and sat down.

There was scattered applause and even the beginning of a Thomas chant, no doubt from the GETA people, but boos and hisses quickly drowned it out.

The judge banged his gavel and kept banging it until order was restored.

"Thank you, Mr. Reed, for your closing statement. May the Lord have mercy on your soul."

The curtains closed, and the courtroom went dark.

PART 4

LIGHT AT THE END OF THE TUNNEL

65

I felt Wanda's boney hand on my shoulder. "You were great," she whispered. "C'mon. Let's go."

As I followed her out through the darkness, I couldn't shake the feeling that my father might have been out there the whole time. Why did I think that? Probably because it was my worst fear.

We passed the stony-faced guards, but instead of taking me back to the room, Wanda took me in the opposite direction and picked up the pace. By the time she turned off into a small, dark tunnel, I was hurrying to keep up with her.

When she finally slowed down, she said, "They certainly let you have it back there, but you handled yourself beautifully. By the end, you had them eating out of your hand."

"Really? It was nice to hear the applause, but there was a lot of booing and hissing."

"I think you won most of them over."

"Think so? The booing was very loud. So are they going to arrest me? Can they?"

"Not without a conviction they can't. I doubt they'll try to lay a hand on you, not with Tanya breathing down their necks. My guess is that the most they'll do is file a complaint with the Council and press for better visitor background checks. The worst is over, Thomas. You survived your ordeal. How do you feel?"

"Much better. I was glad they let me speak at the end, and overall, the trial wasn't as bad as I thought it was going to be. Besides, I like being the center of attention. That's how I was raised. I was the prince of my father's parish, and now . . . well, now I'm the Prince of Hell!"

She laughed and gave me a friendly tap. "If I'm right about it not going any further, you get to go home now."

"Back to being an insurance flunky."

"Oh, I don't think you'll have to worry about that for very long. Your book's going to make a big splash and get lots of attention. You're going to out-Dante Dante."

"From your lips to God's ears. Or maybe I should say to Tanya's ears."

She laughed again. I was going to miss her. We were moving more slowly now knowing it was the last time we would be together.

"So, tell me the truth. Did you really conduct a black mass?"

"I'm not sure what I did that night. I was definitely angry and inebriated, so I probably did something irreverent, or at least tried to. I just don't remember what it was. Maybe because I don't want to."

"Tsk, tsk, Thomas, you're a naughty boy." She gave me another playful tap.

"This tunnel's very long. Where are we going?"

"I'm taking you back where you belong."

When a beep sounded, she put her hand up to her face. She smiled and nodded. After she finished, she turned to me.

"Good news, Thomas. Just as I thought. There wasn't enough support to take it to the next level."

"Great!"

"You'll be interested to know that somebody with a lot of pull went to bat for you."

"Oh? Who was that?"

"Guess."

"I don't know. Who?"

"Dante."

"Dante? Really? I know he was supposed to be on a panel, but I didn't know for sure if he was here. Did he really put a good word in for me?"

"That he did, and when he speaks, they listen. He apparently put the fear of Hell into them literally. He told them that if they didn't release you, he was going to reinstate his Inferno and put them all in it."

"That must have gotten their attention, and he would know where to put each and every one of them. I can't wait to tell Edward. I hope I get a chance to thank Dante before I go. Maybe I can interview him for my book. Or better yet, maybe I can get him to write the Foreword."

She held up her hand to signal she had another call and turned away to take it. She again mostly listened. I heard her say, "I agree."

She turned back to me. "That was your fan club. Iggie, Joan, and Frankie send their love and congratulations. They wanted to say good-bye in person, but they said I whisked you away too quickly. They want you to know we're making you an honorary GETA member."

"That's very nice. Thank you. And I'm not even a ghost."

"Not yet, but your day will come. Then you'll get to be a real GETA member, not just an honorary one."

"Is there any way I can thank them and say good-bye?"

"Sorry, but we don't have time. Besides, I don't want to risk tipping off our location any more than we have to."

"What do you mean?"

"That's the not-so-good news. The hard-liners are upset you're getting away. They want your scalp, and unfortunately, they control the military, such as it is."

"They have an army?"

"If you want to call a bunch of old fogies who like to parade around in uniforms an army. It's a ragtag crew made up mostly of Charlemagne's troops and Teutonic Knights, but they're always ready to fight infidels."

"Like me."

"Like you."

When we came to the end of the tunnel, I looked out at the vast green lawn where I started. I heard the beetles approaching.

"Talk about good timing," she said, pointing at them as they came toward us over the trees. One by one they came through the mist. Six in all.

"Wow!"

"Tanya doesn't mess around."

While they circled above the lawn, the lead beetle lowered itself and set down where Pietro landed earlier.

"That's your ticket home, Thomas. You made it."

"Thank you, thank you, thank you. I can't thank you enough for looking after me." I raised my arms. "I haven't felt this good in a long time. I feel, I don't know, I feel sort of . . . "

"Cleansed? Purged? Forgiven?"

"All of the above."

"I'm not surprised. Your life was spread out for everybody to see. It was like a cathartic confession."

"That's what it felt like."

"As absurd as some of those charges were, it was probably good they came out into the open and didn't just fester. In the words of somebody, 'The unexamined life is not worth living.'"

"Socrates said that."

"Oh, no," she said with mock horror. "Don't tell me I quoted one of those pagan guys."

"That you did, so now it's your turn to go on trial."

"Thanks." She gave me a poke.

I was sure Edward will like Wanda when he meets her. Since he was staying down there, their paths are bound to cross sooner or later. At least I hope so.

"Time to go, Thomas. All good things must come to an end. It was a great pleasure knowing you."

"It was a pleasure and honor for me. Thank you very much for everything. You're an angel." I kissed her on her purple lips.

"Have a safe trip home and good luck with your book." She tapped me on the head one last time and then poof! She was gone.

Feeling light and free, I ran across the lawn to the beetle.

66

Pietro was the pilot of the lead beetle as I hoped he would be. It was only right that he should be the one to take me back.

"That was quite a show you put on," he said as we lifted up into the mist and headed back in formation with the other beetles. "We had great fun watching it in the hangar rec room. The dog funeral was hilarious. So was your throwing the collar in the pond. As for your tossing those little church crackers around, well it was it was bizarre! More than bizarre."

"I hope they didn't show that in my father's precinct."

"No, no. The precincts don't have TV. Although they're talking about it."

"I want to talk to my father again before I go, assuming he's still there. Will that be possible?"

"I don't see why not. It will need an OK, of course, but it's on the way when I take you to the exit. We'll just have to leave earlier."

Guido met us at the landing site. "Well, well, well," he said with a big grin, "the arch-heretic has returned. We didn't know if you were going to make it."

He told Pietro he would bring me back as soon as Tanya was through with me. "It shouldn't be too long."

In the tunnel Guido asked me how it felt to be a celebrity. "You had everybody, and I mean everybody, glued to the screen."

"I'm glad I didn't know. I would have been self-conscious. I've never been on TV before."

"Well, it won't be the last time, I assure you. Not with that book you're going to write."

"What's the latest on my father?"

"Nothing's final yet, but Natasha entered Tanya's order in the system."

"What does that mean? Entered in the system?"

"If it doesn't get entered, it won't get done."

We went into the auditorium through the same door we left by. It was full of the conference people mostly in the center and staffers in the back and on the sides. I saw Zhao and Sanjay, but when I didn't see Rachel, I figured she was probably still with Naomi.

Tanya was telling the conferees they would be staying in their caucus rooms for the time being until more permanent arrangements could be made. I recognized some of the ones Guido pointed out to me earlier when he took me past the caucus rooms and let me look down at them through the windows. It was hard to miss Alexander the Great since he towered over everybody else. He looked glad to be back with his fellow Greeks instead of with the likes of Hitler and Attila the Hun.

When Natasha saw me, she waved and went out and said something to Tanya who turned to me and shouted, "You're back!" She rushed over to me and gave me a big spirit hug. She then took me out to the center and held my hand up like I was a boxer who had just won the fight.

"Here he is, everybody. Our beloved infidel has returned!"

The applause was deafening with both conferees and staffers cheering and chanting my name. Did they all see me on TV? I recognized or thought I recognized Gandhi, Freud, Queen Elizabeth, Lincoln, Einstein and some of the other better known conferees. The Marx Brothers were halfway back not far from Karl Marx, or somebody with a bushy beard who looked just like him. They were obviously in good spirits carrying on in the middle of what looked like a comedy caucus—Charlie Chaplin, Abbott and Costello, Lucille Ball, and Danny Kaye. It was Pietro's dream come true. I can't wait to tell him about all these celebrities.

When I saw Edward and Claudia come in one of the back doors, I waved at them, and they waved back, an exchange that set off more chanting and cheering.

Tanya went back out to the center and raised her arms. "OK, everybody, it's time for this love fest to end. Thomas has to go. I'm glad we got to welcome him back before he leaves. I know I speak for all of us when I thank him for providing us with such entertaining TV watching."

That brought a roar of laughter and a Thomas chant so loud I put my fingers in my ears. When I saw Rachel join Edward and Claudia, I flashed a V sign in their direction, and they V-signed me back.

This time Tanya raised her arms like she really meant it. "Thank you, everybody, thank you. Now we're going to hear from Thomas, but before we do, I want to thank all our guests for coming down here and helping our visitors program get off to such a good start." She nodded and smiled at Zhao, Sanjay, and Helmut. "I want all of you to say something about your visit," she told them, "but I'm starting with Thomas because he has to go."

She said in a voice loud enough for everybody to hear, "Thank you very much, Thomas, for being our first visitor, and what a first visitor you were! You've had quite an amazing weekend down here. We already know about *The Thomas Reed Show* that shut down the conference." She smiled at me to let me know she didn't hold that against me. "Please say a few words before you go." She then went to the side and stood next to Natasha.

That put me in an awkward position again because I wasn't supposed to mention my meetings with my father or Hashem. And they already knew about my Satan "visit" because it was one of the televised charges against me.

"Thank you, Tanya. Without doubt, the high point of my visit was making it through the trial without getting burned at the stake or sent to Hell."

That brought a wave of laughter, cheers, and another Thomas chant that Tanya let go on for a while longer before she went out to the center and silenced it.

"Another high point for me," I said, "was seeing Edward, my teacher and dear friend. He was the one who introduced me to Dante and talked me into coming down here. I only wish I had been able to spend more time with him." I saw that Claudia was next to him, but when I didn't see Rachel anymore, I wondered what happened to her.

I called out to Edward and thanked him for convincing me to go down there "even though your two unannounced late-night visits were unsettling. More than unsettling."

When I looked over at Guido, he drew his finger across his throat to let me know I should wrap things up.

I looked back out at the sea of faces. "Thank you everybody for all the good vibes you sent my way. They really helped. So good-bye and thank you again." I waved to all the corners of the room, then went over to Guido and followed him out into the hallway. I was surprised to see Rachel.

"I can't let you go without saying good-bye." She gave me a hug, not a squishy spirit hug but a solid living one. "Claudia and Edward told me to say good-bye for them and let you know they wish you a safe return."

"I'm sorry I didn't get to say good-bye to them." When I looked at Guido to see if there might be some way to say good-bye to them, he must have sensed what I was going to ask because he shook his head no and drew his finger across his throat again.

I asked Rachel, "Did Edward and Claudia see, you know, the show?"

"Oh, yes, they saw it like everybody else. Claudia said you deserve an Oscar."

"And they're staying down here for sure, right?"

"That's right. It's all set. Umberto made it official."

"Good. By the way, I was told Dante put in a good word for me with the Crusaders that helped get me released. Do you know anything about that? I would have liked to thank him personally, so if you happen to see him, please thank him for me and tell him he's my hero. I would have loved to meet him and maybe even interview him for my book."

"I'm sure with all your James Bond adventures, you'll have more than enough to write about."

Guido kept looking at me impatiently.

"Good-bye," I said to Rachel. "It was great meeting you. Let's stay in touch. How can I reach you?"

"The Department of Comparative Literature at Berkeley will know where I am. Why are you leaving early?"

"I have to take care of something."

"Of course. Agent 007 has his secret assignments right up to the bitter end. I bet I know where you're going."

"Where?"

"To see your father."

"How did you know?"

"Female intuition. I had the same idea about seeing Naomi again, but Umberto said it was in the opposite direction from where I'm going, and besides, I was just with her."

Guido came closer. "Thomas, we have to go. Now!"

I gave Rachel a quick hug and kiss, then turned and followed Guido down the hall. Before we turned into the tunnel, I looked back at Rachel, who waved and gave me a thumbs-up with both hands. I waved back and blew her a kiss, then hurried to catch up to Guido.

The Tech Room was empty except for a spirit working in back. I followed Guido to the main computer and watched him type in a password and punch some keys.

"Your father is Thomas Aaron Reed."

"Junior. That's right."

He typed it in and stared at the screen.

"Sorry, Thomas, there's no change. It still says Natasha's order is *pending*. If there's no final word by the time you leave, we'll call you in flight."

"What time is it up there, by the way?"

"Up where?"

"Up in New York where I live."

"Ah, now that's a good way to use this damn machine. Let's find out." He typed in a command. "OK, let's see, up there in New York it's now 2:40 their time. Sunday afternoon. We're on schedule, so you'll get back when you're supposed to."

"Will Rachel be coming with me?"

"She's leaving later. Why?" He typed something and waited. "She's not available."

"What's that supposed to mean?"

"It means she's not available. She's getting married next year."

They not only know our past, but they know our future too?

"To Randy?"

"Yup, and they're going to have two children." Guido stroked the computer as if he were petting a cat. "This baby knows everything. Wait, now here's something interesting. If you're willing to wait, they're going to get divorced in eleven years."

"Are you serious?" His attempt to be amusing was getting on my nerves.

"That's what it says."

"I'm more interested in finding out what's going on with my father."

"Of course." Guido gave me a little salute, then turned back to the computer. "Let me try one more time before I go to the backup." He did some more typing and waited. "Still *pending*. There could be a problem, but fortunately we have a backup system to get us past glitches. Let's try it."

He went over to what looked like a large safe set in the wall and turned the dial back and forth a few times.

When he opened the door, a computer slid out. He turned it on and typed something.

I couldn't bear the thought of letting my father down as I watched Guido do what seemed like a futile search.

"Bingo!" he shouted and gave me a thumbs-up with both hands. "Good news, Thomas. The termination order is terminated. Your father's safe."

"For sure?"

"For sure."

"Thank you, Guido. Thank you very much. Wow, what a relief!"

When we high-fived each other, I felt something physical the same way I felt Tanya's hug and Wanda's back rub.

"Congratulations, Thomas. You saved your father. If it hadn't been for your perseverance, he would have been a goner. Kaput. Finito." He hit a key that made the screen go blank. "That's it, my friend. Let's go."

67

On our way to the hangar, Guido asked me if there was anything I didn't get to see or do that I would have liked to.

"Well, now that the trial's over and they didn't send me to Hell, I have no complaints. Although it would have been nice to spend more time with Edward. I was under the impression he was going to be my Virgil down here, but I barely got to see him. I had my special visits, of course, and he had his own companionship."

"Claudia."

"Yes. Don't get me wrong. I'm very glad she's here. She's obviously good for him. I'm happy they're going to stay down here and work together."

"Anything else you would have liked to do?"

"I would have liked to meet Dante, or at least see what he looks like. Was he in the auditorium?"

"Oh, yes, he was there cheering and chanting your name with everybody else."

"Really? Dante was cheering and chanting my name?"

"That he was."

"Are you sure?"

"Yes, I saw him."

"Where was he?"

"About halfway back on your right. He was with the rest of the Italian Renaissance panel—Raphael, Michelangelo, and Leonardo da Vinci."

"What a great panel that must have been. I'm sorry I missed it."

"Well, thanks to you, it never took place. Like the other panels, it couldn't compete with the Thomas Reed Show. As for missing Dante, don't worry. You can talk to him next time."

"Next time?"

"You'll be back, or do you have other plans?"

We both smiled, but I didn't answer him.

When we were up and on our way, I told him about Tanya's hug and the physical feel of Guido's hand when he high-fived me.

"The physicalization is definitely taking place, but it's happening too fast. I mean, do we really want to have to deal with what goes on up there? All the eating, sleeping, pissing, shitting, screwing, burping, farting, vomiting, and all the rest of it? That's where we're heading, and the momentum's picking up. It's not going to be easy to slow it down, much less stop it." He paused. "I probably shouldn't tell you this."

"What?"

"I've told you more than I should."

"Tell me."

"I really shouldn't."

"Oh, come on. I promise I won't tell anybody if you don't want me to."

"Well, since you're going home, I guess . . . " He checked the control panel to make sure there wasn't an open mike. "This is off the record, of course."

"Of course."

"It seems that some staffers are beginning to pair off."

"What do you mean pair off?"

"You know, pair off. Meet privately. Romantically. My guess is that not much happens because there's not enough juice down here, at least not yet. Again, this is just between us."

"Of course."

"A few days ago, I walked in on two of them. They were in an empty room going at it."

"What do you mean going at it? What were they doing?"

"I'm not sure. They were dressed and upright, but they were definitely in an embrace doing something, or at least trying to do something. And these weren't lowly staffers either."

"Who were they?"

"I can't tell you."

I fixed my cat stare on him. At home when my cat Madonna wanted something, she stared at me until I did what she wanted me to.

"I promise I won't tell. Who were they?"

"Guido and Natasha."

"That doesn't surprise me. There's definitely chemistry there."

"Guido told me that if things keep going at this rate, they'll be able to have a kid."

"Are you serious?"

"We're still a very long way from that, but still . . . "

"You don't sound happy about it."

"I'm not. I'm all for the physical renovation going on. This place certainly needs it, especially if we want visitors to come down here. But things are changing too fast." He looked at the control panel. "We're almost there. Remember, you're not going to have as much time with your father as you did last time, so make sure you tell him what you want to tell him right away. Don't wait."

When the common came into view and beyond it the pond, I saw two spirits on the bench where my father liked to sit. I hoped he was one of them because there wasn't going to be time to go looking for him. Pietro landed far enough away so as not to startle them.

"I'll wait for you here. When you see me get out and begin walking toward you, it's time for you to wrap up your conversation. Like last time. OK?"

"OK."

I got out of the beetle and walked back toward the bench in an arc to keep from approaching them too directly. When I got closer, I was relieved to see that my father was one of the spirits. The other one was a female in a pastel robe who seemed to have hair, albeit short hair. She said something to my father that made him turn and look at me. This time he recognized me right away.

He stood up and shouted, "Tommy, you're back!"

I went up to him. "Yes, Dad, it's me. I'm back."

"I was afraid you might not want to talk to me anymore." He pointed at the spirit next to him. "Here's somebody you know."

"Why, hello, Tommy."

I didn't recognize her.

"Your father told me you visited him. I wish my children would visit me."

"Do you remember Nancy? Mrs. Stephens? She was on the Altar Guild, and her husband, Art, was on the vestry."

"Our Jimmy was confirmed with you, remember?"

Yes, now it all came back. Jimmy Stephens. He and his friends used to throw stones at cats and dogs, and on the Fourth of July, they threw firecrackers. I hated the little bastard.

"Nice to see you again, Mrs. Stephens."

"Your father talks about you all the time." She stood up. "I'm going to leave and let you two have some privacy."

"You don't have to do that," my father said.

"I insist."

"Well, don't go far away. When Tommy's through, I want you back here."

"Good-bye, Mrs. Stephens," I said as I watched her glide off. I sat down on the bench where she had been sitting.

"Dad, I've got good news for you. You can stay here. They're not going to send you away. I came here to tell you that."

"Good. I'm not ready to be put out to pasture."

"I'm glad you have somebody to talk to now. Somebody you know."

"I like talking to Nancy, but do me a favor."

"Sure, Dad. What is it?"

"Don't tell Ruthie. Don't tell her about Nancy."

How ironic, I thought. Here my father is concerned about my mother knowing he's talking to a former parishioner while she's up there married to the man she was sleeping with while he was in the nursing home.

"Don't worry. I won't tell her." I turned and looked back at the beetle. "Dad, I have something I want to tell you."

"Yes, Tommy, tell me how you're doing. Last time I spent so much time talking about me, I never got around to finding out how you are. How things are going up there at . . . at . . . "

"St. Luke's."

"Yes, St. Luke's."

"I'm not there anymore."

"What?"

"I'm not there anymore. I left."

"Why? What happened?"

"It's a long story. I needed time to sort things out, so I took a leave of absence and went to New York."

Seeing Pietro get out of the beetle made me realize I had less time than I thought.

"This is what I came to tell you. I left the church. Not just the parish. I left the ministry."

"You're not ordained anymore?"

"That's right, Dad."

He turned and looked at the empty pond without saying anything more. He didn't look upset, just stunned and confused.

"Dad, I have to go now. I'm sorry I can't stay longer."

"So soon?"

"I came back to tell you I don't have a parish anymore. I thought you should know. It's been on my mind a long time. And I wanted you to know that you're safe here. They're not going to send you away."

"This is forever?"

"Yes, Dad."

"Will Nancy be staying too?"

I obviously didn't know, but I said yes to give him one less thing to worry about.

"Will you come and visit me again?"

"Not right away, but maybe someday I'll be able to visit you like the old days."

Pietro was getting closer.

"I'm proud of you, Tommy, and always will be. I want you to know that whatever you decide to do with the rest of your life, it will be the right thing."

"Thank you, Dad. Thank you very much. I appreciate that."

Pietro stopped and nodded to let me know it was time to end the conversation. I stood up, and so did my father.

"Good-bye, Tommy. God bless you."

"Thank you, Dad. Good-bye. I love you."

I gave him a hug, but when I started to choke up, I pulled back and said good-bye again. On my way to Pietro, I gave him a thumbs-up to let him know I told my father what I wanted to tell him. When I got to him, I turned and looked back at my father one last time. He was sitting on the bench looking at the pond, waiting for Nancy to return.

68

Back up in the mist, I felt good, very good. I finally got to tell my father the truth and was heading home with his blessing and enough material for a book or two.

I told Pietro how the hug I gave my father felt more physical than I expected. When I told him the woman he was with had hair, he made a face.

"That's all we need. Hair salons for women and men getting haircuts and shaving. Or not shaving and growing beards and mustaches." He shook his head. "Where's this all going to end? I told you about Guido and Natasha. Now Tanya's girls are starting to wear frilly, sexy tops and have little boobies that jiggle. And that's nothing compared to . . . " He stopped.

"Compared to what?"

"Forget it."

"Tell me."

"I can't."

"Yes, you can." I fixed him with my cat stare.

"I'm not allowed to talk about it."

"Oh, come on. I won't say anything."

Silence.

"What are you not supposed to talk about?"

"Tanya's plan."

"What is it?"

"It's secret."

I knew if I pressed him too much it could backfire, so I let it rest for the time being. But I kept turning and looking at him the way Madonna looks at me.

"It's a simple plan," he finally said. "Radical but simple."

More silence.

"OK, Thomas, since you promised not to tell anybody, Tanya's plan is . . . is . . . "

"Yes?"

"Her plan is to close down Hell."

"Huh?"

"Yup. Hell will be kaput the way Heaven is. Instead of punishing the bad guys down here after they die, the plan is to have them just die and stay dead. That will make everything a lot simpler."

Wow, another bombshell. A super bombshell.

"So no more Processing Center?"

"That's right. Umberto can have fun turning it into a museum."

"But what about the Purgatory precincts? What's going to happen to them? What will happen to people like my father?"

"The plan is to let Purgatory people stay here as long as they want, but they won't be required to stay. If and when they've had enough, they can opt out for the Big Nap."

"What about people living up there now who have lived good lives and expect to be rewarded in some way? What will happen to them? They won't be able to come down here and be in a Purgatory precinct anymore?"

"That's under discussion. There's a big debate going on about that very issue now. Some say that good people like your dad should be allowed to come down here after they die. But others say we should be consistent and not have an afterlife for anybody. No Heaven, no Hell, and nothing in between."

"This is mind-boggling. If Hell and maybe even the Purgatory precincts aren't going to be here anymore, what's going to happen to all this space?"

"Ah, that brings me to the heart of Tanya's plan. That's the part that really is secret."

"What is it?"

"I'm not allowed to tell you."

"Oh, come on, Pietro. Don't stop now. You're on a roll."

"I'm not authorized to talk about this with outsiders. Although it's hard to think of you as an outsider anymore what with all your special visits and now with your rock-star fame as a television personality."

"Yeah, it's quite amazing, isn't it?"

"It really is. When Dante came down here, he was a passive spectator compared to you."

"Tell me about Tanya's plan. I promise I won't tell."

I had already decided I wasn't going to have anybody else read all or parts of my book while I was writing it since I didn't want what I was doing to leak out. That's why I could tell Pietro I wasn't going to "tell" anybody. Writing it in a book that would come out later was another matter.

"Trying to coax the secret out of me, eh?"

"I can try, can't I?"

He checked the panel again to make sure the mike was off.

"OK, Thomas, you win." He lowered his voice to barely a whisper. "Tanya's plan is to get people to come down here, not just to visit, but to settle."

"What do you mean 'settle'?"

"Just what I said. She wants people to live down here permanently—start businesses, raise families, build schools, the works. She wants them to come down here while they're still alive. Not wait until they die. She wants life down here to be safer and better than what's up there now."

He was sounding more and more like Umberto. He obviously picked up his talent for telling tall tales. The more shocking, the better.

"How does Tanya expect anybody to live down here? It's not the most inviting place to visit, much less settle." I pointed out the window. "Who wants to live in all this mist?"

"Once there's no more Hell, the mist won't be needed anymore because there won't be anything to hide.

And it will definitely look better with all the improvements that they're planning. Plus, there will be incentives to get people to come and live down here. Not just the fear of bad things happening up there like global warming, nuclear war, famine, disappearing rain forests and coral reefs, melting glaciers, species extinction, asteroids crashing into the earth, etc., etc."

"What incentives do you have in mind?"

"Leave me out of this. Her plan is much too grandiose for me, but then nobody ever accused Tanya of thinking small. The challenge will be to persuade people to live down here, not just have them come down here to visit the Dante museum or attend a conference and then go back home."

"How are you—how are they—going to lure people down here? You mentioned incentives."

"Greed, Thomas, greed. That's always the biggest motivator when it comes to people. If they think they can make money, they'll come flocking down here."

"How are they supposed to make money?"

"One idea is to let people know there are mineral deposits here for the taking—gold, silver, oil, gas, lead, zinc, precious metals. The plan is to whip up a kind of California Gold Rush frenzy that will make everybody want to come down here and get rich quick. Another idea is to circulate rumors that there are exotic animals down here ripe for exploitation—skinning, shooting, racing, fighting, experimenting on, and, of course, eating."

"Are there animals down here?

"No, their Hell is up there."

"Let me make sure I have this right. Tanya's plan is to close down Hell to keep bad people out and get good or at least better living people to come down here and settle?"

"That's it in a nutshell. Some think she wants to make life better down here to keep Naomi and the Chief from leaving. She's very close to them, especially Naomi. It's no secret that Naomi and Tanya rule the roost."

"Her plan is obviously very ambitious."

"It's a utopian vision all right, but that's Tanya for you. She wants to turn all of this into a huge permanent retirement village." He looked out at the mist. "Can you believe it? With all the amenities."

"Like what?"

"Oh, they're constantly coming up with ideas for fun and games to keep people busy and happy. Sports, recreation, exercise, lectures, films, dance classes, hikes, yoga, and, as they say, much, much more. They're even planning a golf course."

"Are you serious? A golf course in Hell?"

"Why are you smiling?"

"I'm thinking about my dad. Whenever his parishioners got him out on the course, he would hook, slice, and dub more shots than he hit straight. Once he even whiffed the ball on the first tee, no less. So golf isn't going to be much of a draw for him."

"No, it doesn't sound like he's going to rush to sign up."

"He'd rather sit on his bench and stare at an empty pond."

"Just as well. The golf course doesn't exist, and it probably never will. At this point, it's just an idea that's floating around."

When I saw Pietro checking the coordinates on the panel, I asked him what he was up to.

"There's an insurgent group out this way called Animal Avengers you might be interested in for your book. Some of them used to be on Tanya's staff, but they left."

"Why did they leave?"

"They got fed up with the slow pace of bringing animal abusers to justice. They don't want to have to wait for them to die and come down here to be punished. They want to catch them in the act and zap them while they're doing it. Or better yet, zap them before they do it."

"What do you mean 'zap' them?"

Pietro drew his finger across his throat.

"Kill them?"

He nodded. "They already started. A couple of months ago they zapped two animal researchers in your country. It was in the news."

"Yes, I read about it. At Oregon State University."

"That's right."

"How did they manage to do that from down here?"

"They're in contact with activists who feel the same way they do."

"As I remember, the Animal Liberation Front claimed responsibility for it."

"The ALF carried it out, but it was the Animal Avengers down here who planned and directed it."

"They're allowed to kill people?"

"They're not supposed to, but Tanya and Natasha aren't about to shed any tears when animal abusers get what's coming to them." He drew his finger across his throat again.

I took out my pad and wrote down what he was saying.

"They're the most tech-savvy group down here. Most of them have some kind of scientific or engineering background. Bella, who's their leader, has a doctorate from MIT."

"That's impressive."

"Their hi-tech sophistication lets them take their activism to levels other activists can only dream of. Take hunting, for example. They're designing rifles and shotguns that will fire backward, so it will be the hunters who get shot, not the animals. They're going to start with pigeon shoots and canned hunts and take it from there."

"So the hunter will aim his gun at an animal and . . . ?"

"*Bam!* It blows his brains out or his heart or his genitals." He laughed. "I kid you not. Bella has made no secret that she wants guns that will blast the balls off hunters in the spirit of symbolic retribution à la Dante. But that may be beyond even her formidable skills."

"So where are these Animal Avengers now?"

"Their main camp is up ahead off to the left."

"Can we swing by? I'd love to visit them. Maybe I can interview Bella for my book."

Pietro gave me a you-must-be-crazy look.

"I'll make it short. I promise."

"No way, Thomas. We don't have time. I think I spoiled you when I broke the rules and showed you the Processing Center."

"I'm glad you did. It's definitely going in my book. Thank you. You're a wonderful guide.

69

When a buzzer sounded and a red light flashed on the control panel, Pietro looked startled.

"That's strange," he said. "It's not from Headquarters. It's an outside call."

"What does that mean?"

"It's from outside the system." He stared at the flashing light. "I'm not sure I should answer it. It could be hackers."

I never saw Pietro so indecisive. I wondered if it might have something to do with my father. Some last-minute change. I hoped not.

"Maybe it's an emergency," I said.

When the buzzer sounded again and the light kept flashing, Pietro looked at me. "What do you think?"

"I think you should answer it."

Pietro hesitated some more, then shrugged. "OK, keep your fingers crossed." He picked up the phone. "Hello?"

I couldn't hear what the caller was saying, so there was a long silence.

"Yes, just a minute," he said and handed me the phone. "It's for you."

"Me?"

He nodded.

I cautiously took the phone and put it to my ear. "Hello?"

"Hello. I want to talk to Tom Reed. Do I have the right number?"

"Who shall I say is calling?"

"Beatrice Stein."

"Beatrice?"

"Tom, is that you?"

"Yes, hello. This is quite a surprise."

"Tom, we have a terrible connection. Where are you?"

"I . . . I'm in a place with bad reception."

Pietro had his earphones on and was listening in on the call.

"I looked up the area code in the international directory, but it's not there. Tom, can you call me back? Maybe we'll get a better connection."

Pietro shook his head no.

"I can hear you fine. If we lose this connection, we won't get it back. How did you reach me?"

"Somebody by the name of Rinaldo called and gave me this number. He said you want me to meet you at the Barnes and Noble in Dover at seven. Is that right?"

Pietro nodded yes.

"Yes, that's right."

"The trip you mentioned in the message you left sounded very mysterious. Did you really go to Italy?"

"Yes, I actually did."

"That was very adventurous of you. How was it?"

"Very interesting."

"I want to hear all about it but not on this lousy connection. I just wanted to check with you to make sure I got the right information. Barnes and Noble in Dover at seven."

Pietro kept nodding.

"Yes, that's right. I'm looking forward to seeing you. How are the boys?"

"They're with my folks, but they'll be back later. I hope we're still on for tomorrow." She had invited me to join them on a trip to Washington on Memorial Day. "They're really looking forward to it. By the way, you can stay here tonight if you want. That will save you having to go back to the city and come back in the morning."

"Thank you. That sounds like a good idea." I had never been to her house, let alone stayed overnight.

"The traffic shouldn't be too bad if we leave early. I hope this isn't going to be too much traveling for you for one weekend."

"No, no, it's fine."

"Tom, I can barely hear you. I'll see you at seven, OK?"

"Very good. If I'm late, don't give up on me. I have your cell number. See you soon." The line went dead.

Pietro took off his earphones. "Abdul never ceases to amaze me. This is his doing. Not only does he have an exit for you near where you live, but he arranges to have somebody meet you. He's amazing."

"He arranged to have Beatrice meet me?"

"Absolutely. Is her name really Beatrice?"

"Yes, that's her name."

"I get it. Like Dante's Beatrice, she's waiting for you at the end of your journey so she can lead you to Paradise."

"I wish."

"Well done, Thomas. Is she your girlfriend?"

"I should be so lucky."

"I hope she's not married the way Dante's Beatrice was. It didn't sound that way."

"She was married, but her husband died in a car accident."

"Sorry to hear that."

"She used to live in Boston, but after she got a job in New York, she and her sons moved to northern New Jersey. She was my girlfriend in college, so I'm glad to be back in touch with her."

"Don't give up on her, Thomas. There's a reason she's meeting you. Trust me. She's going to lead you to something better. Maybe not Paradise, but a better life. Her name isn't Beatrice for nothing."

"How do you know all this? Is that in the data bank too?"

"I wouldn't know. We lowly pilots don't get to poke around in it the way Guido does. I just have a gut feeling."

"I see."

"Anyway, it's nice you have a Beatrice to meet you. A perfect way to end your *viaggio*. Does she know where you went?

"You kidding?"

"You going to tell her?"

"I don't know."

70

As the mist got thinner, I saw that the space we were flying through was closing up. The roof above us and the floor below were gradually converging, and the sides seemed to be closing in as well. We were definitely entering some kind of cul-de-sac, albeit a large one.

"We're still under the Atlantic Ocean," Pietro said, "but we should reach New Jersey soon."

"Home sweet home. I never thought I would say that about New Jersey."

"As you can see, the terrain out this way is rocky and uneven, so it's not going to be easy to find a place to land. Keep your eyes peeled for anything that looks flat."

"At Tanya's meeting, Abdul said these exits are going to be entrances someday."

"Don't hold your breath. That's not going to happen anytime soon."

I pointed. "Look over there. It looks sort of flat."

"It's not flat enough. But we are on target, which means we're getting close to the opening. As a matter of fact, that looks like it might be it." He was pointing up ahead at a rock wall with a large crack in it, but it was hard to tell from that distance how wide the crack was or if it went anywhere.

"Thomas, there's not a good place to land around here, so I'm going to have to lower you down by rope. There's a rope behind your seat. Are you game?"

"Do I have a choice?"

"You'll be fine. Even if you fall, it will only be a short drop. The most that can happen is you'll sprain an ankle."

Oh great. I didn't like the thought of having to hobble back with a sprained ankle.

Pietro put the beetle on automatic and reached back and got the rope. He tied one end to the seat and helped me tie the other end around my waist and under my shoulders.

"I'll keep the beetle steady and lower you down slowly. Once you're on the ground, go to the opening, and hopefully you'll be on your way."

"Are you going to stay around to make sure this is the right opening?"

"It's the right opening. The coordinates are perfect."

"Still, I would feel better if you waited. What happens if I go in and it doesn't go anywhere, and then when I come out, you're gone?"

"I'll wait long enough to make sure you're on your way. Promise."

He checked the rope to make sure it was firmly tied, then pushed a button that slid the door open on my side. It was scary looking down at the rocky terrain. It felt like I was on the ledge of a building seven or eight floors above the ground.

"I don't like this at all."

"You'll be fine. Just remember, we have you tracked, so if anything goes wrong, they'll send a rescue team. Time to go, my friend."

I hesitated, but I knew if I waited too long Pietro might be tempted to push me out the door the way they push out reluctant parachutists.

"Good-bye, Pietro. Thank you for all the chauffeuring you did."

"My pleasure, Thomas. I enjoyed it. Have a good rest of your life. See you again." He smiled. "But hopefully not too soon. Ciao."

I dropped down faster than I thought I would, but the rope held firm. When I landed, I glanced off the side of a boulder and fell down, but I got up with only a bruised knee, not a sprained ankle. I looked back up at the beetle and waved, but I don't know if Pietro saw me. I went over to the crack in the wall and waved one last time before I went in.

I was relieved to see that the crack widened out into what looked like a tunnel. Definitely a promising start. What little light there was seemed mostly to be coming from rocks that gave off their own glow. When it soon became apparent that the tunnel was actually going somewhere, I agreed with Pietro about Abdul. Controversial yes, but very competent. Amazing really. Thank you, Abdul.

It was a long trek, but fortunately there was enough air to breathe. When the light up ahead began to look like real daylight, I thought back to my first Dante class with Edward when he explained the long detour Dante had to take through the Inferno and Purgatory to get to Paradise and his Beatrice. Now there I was coming to the end of my own *viaggio* and would soon be seeing *my* Beatrice. At least, I hoped so.

The air was getting more humid, and the smells were sharper too. For the first time all weekend, I felt hungry. When I coughed, I hoped I wasn't coming down with something. "Welcome home," I said to myself. Welcome back to the world of germs, allergies, sweat, sickness, humidity, and pollution. But it was good to be back. Very good. Home sweet home.

I heard a brook bubbling on the other side of the wall on my right. When moments later I heard the sound of a car honking in the distance, it was music to my ears. It got darker when I entered a narrow, enclosed walkway under a bridge with wooden planks that rattled every time a car went over it. When the light suddenly got brighter at the end of the underpass, I remembered the end of *Paradiso* where Dante wrote that the meaning of his journey came to him "in a great flash of light."

When I came out of the underpass, I had to squint to protect my eyes from the daylight. I climbed up the bank to the road, assuming I was in New Jersey, not Pennsylvania or Wyoming or Mongolia. But I didn't know for sure. My watch stopped, so I didn't know what time it was. However, there was still plenty of daylight,

so I figured it couldn't be too late. At least I hoped not. I

wondered how far it was to Dover.

71

As soon as I heard a car coming toward the bridge, I knew what I had to do. So when I saw a blue Honda come around the corner, I got out in the middle of the road and waved my arms. When the car stopped and I approached the driver's window, the young couple in front looked at me suspiciously. The driver had a pony-tail and sideburns, and the girl had short, curly blond hair and glasses. They were wearing matching T-shirts.

"Excuse me for stopping you like this," I said to them, "but I'm trying to get to Dover. Dover, New Jersey. I seem to have gotten off the beaten path. How far away is Dover?"

"It's just up the road," the driver said. He looked at the girl, then back at me. "Can we give you a lift?"

"Yes, please do. Thank you. That would be great."

"No car?"

"No. I was out this way and lost track of the time."

"Hop in," he said.

I got in back. "What good luck," I said to them as we drove off. "I can't thank you enough."

"No problem," said the girl.

"I'm supposed to be in Dover at seven. What time is it now? My watch stopped."

The girl pointed at the clock on the dashboard. "It's quarter to seven, so you'll make it in plenty of time."

When I took out my watch to set it, it said 6:45, and it was running! That's strange, I thought. Very strange.

"Where in Dover do you want to go?" asked the girl.

"Barnes and Noble."

She and the driver smiled at each other. "This really is your lucky day," she said. "That's where we're going."

"You sure knew the right car to flag down," the driver said smiling at me in the rearview mirror.

"Are you going to the reading?" the girl asked.

"Reading?"

"You said you wanted to be there at seven. That's when the reading starts."

"No, I'm supposed to meet a friend there. What's the reading?"

"Dante's *Inferno*. Robert Pinsky's going to read from his translation."

I couldn't believe the way everything was magically falling into place. Beatrice, my watch, and now a Dante reading.

The driver looked at me in the mirror. "Janet's into Dante, but I'm more into video games."

She laughed and gave him a mock-punch on the shoulder. She looked back at me. "I knew he was the one for me when he told me his name was Virgil. I don't know if you're familiar with Dante, but Virgil was Dante's guide."

He said, "Janet's writing her thesis at Rutgers on the *Inferno*."

"Really? What a coincidence. I did that when I was in school too."

"Well then," she said, "you and your friend should definitely go to the reading. It's a special event because they hardly ever schedule a reading on a holiday week-end. You didn't know about it?"

"No, I wasn't aware of it. I'm sure glad you picked me up. What good luck to be driven to a Dante reading by Virgil."

He laughed and smiled at me in the mirror.

At Barnes and Noble the desk clerk told us the reading was in back and pointed to rows of chairs facing a lectern. Some of the seats were filled, and others had jackets and book bags on them.

I told them I was going to wait for my friend in front. "I doubt she'll be able to stay, but I'll come back and let you know."

"OK," Janet said, "we'll save you two seats in case you decide to stay."

"Thanks."

I went to the front and planted myself at the magazine rack where I could keep an eye on the door. According to the store clock and my miraculously resurrected watch, it was almost seven o'clock.

As I flipped through *People Magazine*, I figured by now Rachel was probably on her way to California. I smiled when I remembered the horrified look on her face when Abdul told her the California exit was connected to the San Andreas Fault.

When the door opened and in came Beatrice, my eyes feasted on her silky black hair, almond eyes, and her "I am Beatrice and proud of it" look that attracted me the first time I saw her. She was wearing dark-gray slacks and a short-sleeved burgundy blouse. Her green handbag with "Vegan" printed on it was slung over her shoulder.

"Beatrice!" I called and waved.

When she looked at me, I felt a momentary swooning sensation that Dante described having when his Beatrice looked at him for the first time. I knew the lines from the beginning of *Paradiso* by heart because when I came across them in college, I printed them out and put them next to Beatrice's picture.

> *Beatrice looked at me with eyes so full*
> *of the radiance of love and so divine that,*
> *overcome, my power of sight faded and*
> *fled, and, eyes cast down, I almost lost my*
> *senses.*

She came over and gave me a hug and kiss. "Welcome back, world traveler. How was the trip?"

"Very interesting. I'll tell you about it later." As soon as I said it, I wondered if I really would. I didn't want to risk losing her again.

"I'm glad you made it back for tomorrow. The boys are really excited about their first trip to Washington."

"By the way, there's a reading about to start." I pointed to the back.

"Oh?"

"Dante's *Inferno*. The Pinsky translation."

"That's right up your alley. Do you want to go?"

"I'd rather talk to you."

"Good. I'm glad you said that because I want to be home when the boys get back."

"OK, let me go and say good-bye to the very nice couple I met. Come with me. I'll tell them we won't be staying."

"Are you sure you don't want to stay? I know how all those Dante papers you wrote helped get you through school."

When Janet saw us coming, she stood up and pointed at the seats they saved. Virgil stood up too.

"This is Beatrice," I told them and said to her, "And this is Janet and Virgil. Janet's writing her college thesis on the *Inferno*."

"Good for you," Beatrice said. "You certainly came to the right reading."

An older woman with glasses and a Barnes and Noble badge arrived up front with a man I assumed was Robert Pinsky.

"Sorry we can't stay," I told them. "We have to be on our way. It was great meeting you and thank you very, very much for the ride."

"You're more than welcome," said Virgil.

Janet shook our hands. "It was a pleasure meeting both of you."

"It was very nice meeting you," Beatrice said. "Good luck with your thesis."

We went to the front of the store where just before leaving I looked back and saw the woman introducing Pinsky.

72

On the way to her house, Beatrice asked me again about my trip. "When you left your message telling me you were going to Italy, I thought maybe you meant Little Italy."

"No, no, I really did go to Italy. Big Italy."

"And you just got back?"

"Yes."

"How did you get to Barnes and Noble?"

"Virgil and Janet drove me."

"They picked you up at Newark Airport?"

I knew I was about to enter a labyrinth of deception. I hated the feeling.

"What about your luggage? Or do you travel light?"

I guess I could have said I put my bag in an airport locker, but I didn't want to lie. Not to her.

"It's a long story that I can go into later if you want."

I didn't feel comfortable saying even that. I probably could make up a story about going to Rome to do research about something like a scandal in the Vatican or whatever, but I thought if I can't tell Beatrice the truth, who can I tell?

At supper with her sons, I made up my mind to tell her where I went later when we were alone, even though I was uneasy about what her reaction might be. But keeping secrets locked up inside was not the way I wanted to live. Not anymore. The white wine she served with the vegan lasagna and tofutti softened me up. *In vino veritas*.

After we did the dishes and her boys went up to their room, we sat on the couch in the living room and had decaf and her homemade vegan cookies.

"So are you going to tell me about your trip?"

"I would like to, but you're not going to believe it."

"Try me."

"OK, if that's what you want." I took a deep breath and hoped I wasn't making a terrible mistake. "I'll try not to be offended if you don't believe anything I say. You'll see why I had to be secretive. My apologies about that."

She was making scarves for her sons, so she went and got her knitting.

"All I ask is that you hear me out. It will be better if you save your questions for the end since there's a lot to cover."

"Fair enough," she said and began knitting.

"So much happened I'm just going to give you the highlights."

"I'm all ears."

I took another deep breath and started with Edward's visits, Monteveggio, and the basement under the cemetery. Then I went into the cast of characters: Guido, Umberto, Pietro, Tanya, Natasha, Rachel, Claudia, and, of course, Edward. It was hard to know how she was taking it because she kept knitting with her head down, only looking up from time to time to ask me if I wanted more decaf or another cookie. A couple of times I wondered if she thought I was making it all up the way I used to make things up in college when I took creative writing classes and entertained her with the crazy plots I dreamed up.

I was glad she didn't interrupt although she occasionally made brief comments like when I told her about Tanya and Natasha, she said, "Sounds like the ladies are in charge. Good for them."

When I told her about my father, she stopped knitting and wiped away a tear. But I didn't want to press my luck, so I didn't go into Hashem or Satan or the trial. They could wait for another time.

"There's more, but that's probably enough for now."

"No, no, tell me everything. It's fascinating."

"You're not going to believe it."

She smiled. "I believe everything you've told me so far?"

I didn't know how to take that, but by then I had the impression she really did think I was making it up to entertain her like I used to do in college. I decided that was not a good time to get into it with her.

"Well, if you're not sick and tired of my voice, I'll tell you more."

"Please do. I don't want the abridged version." She went back to her knitting.

"OK," I said. "You asked for it."

I told her about my visits to Hashem and Naomi, how Satan captured me, and also about the trial. She especially liked hearing about Joan of Arc and GETA. However, when I got to the part about the history greats cheering and chanting my name in the auditorium, she excused herself and went to the bathroom. I probably should have left that part out. When she came back, she sat down and resumed her knitting. "So who cheered and chanted your name?"

"They all did."

"Like who?"

"Socrates."

"Socrates chanted your name?"

"That's right."

"Who else besides Socrates?"

"Alexander the Great. Queen Elizabeth. Einstein. Dante."

She stopped knitting and stared at me. "Dante was down there, and he chanted your name?"

"That's right."

"Did you see him chanting your name?'

"I didn't see him. Guido told me."

"Your guide told you Dante chanted your name?"

"That's right."

"But you didn't actually see him yourself."

"No. I don't know what Dante looks like."

She went back to her knitting without saying anything more. Her long silence made me uncomfortable. I was relieved when she went out to the kitchen and stayed there.

When she came back, I asked her, "So what do you think?"

She began knitting again with her head down without answering my question. When she finally looked back up at me, she said, "Tom, you have a wonderful imagination. I always loved that about you."

That was the first time she ever said my name and the word "love" in the same sentence, so maybe, just maybe, Pietro was right when he said my luck was going to change. Dante had to go through the Inferno and Purgatory before his Beatrice took him to Paradise, so maybe my Beatrice was doing the same thing although this wasn't Paradise. It was New Jersey.

When she took the cups out to the kitchen without saying anything more and stayed there longer than I expected, I sensed something was wrong. Just as I started to get up and go out to find out what was going on, she came back with a smile on her face and kissed me on the forehead.

"Tom, you're a gifted storyteller and always have been. Nobody's going to believe what you just told me, but so what? You want to be writer. Why not write about this? It will make a wonderful novel." She tapped my head the way Wanda used to. "Write it up just the way you told it to me, and you'll be the new Dante."

I stood up and took her in my arms. "And you'll be the new Beatrice."

We kissed and laughed and kissed again.

ABOUT THE AUTHOR

Charles Patterson is an author, historian, therapist, editor, and teacher. He grew up in New Britain, Connecticut, and graduated from Kent School, Amherst College, the Episcopal Theological School in Cambridge, Massachusetts, Columbia University (MA in English Literature, PhD in Religion), and the Yad Vashem Institute for Holocaust Studies in Jerusalem.

He lives in New York City where he has taught courses in history, literature, and writing at The New School for Social Research (Ancient Israel and Classics of World Literature), Adelphi University (Advanced Writing), Hunter College (The Bible as Literature), and Metropolitan College (Adjunct Professor, Human Services).

Patterson's first book *Anti-Semitism: The Road to the Holocaust and Beyond* was called "important" by *Publishers Weekly*. *Judaica Book News* wrote, "It deserves a place in every home, school and public library . . . excellent background reading in Jewish history and the history of western civilization."

The National Council for the Social Studies in Washington, DC, presented him with its Carter G. Woodson Book Award for his Young Adult (YA) biography of Marian Anderson at a special luncheon at its annual convention in St. Louis, Missouri.

His other books include *The Oxford 50th Anniversary Book of the United Nations*, *The Civil Rights Movement*, *From Buchenwald to Carnegie Hall* (co-authored with a Holocaust survivor), and his internationally acclaimed *Eternal Treblinka: Our Treatment of Animals and the Holocaust*, now in 16 languages.

Patterson lives on the Upper West Side of Manhattan and is a member of PEN, The Authors Guild, and the National Writers Union.